Life Water

Ejaz Khan

Dedicated to my wife and my children, without whose support I wouldn't have accomplished this task of writing the books of this series.

A journey into the Magical Worlds!

LIFE WATER

1

Simon and David lived in a big city. Their mother worked all day long to earn them a living. To be a single working parent and raise them was not an easy task, and no one could know the fact better than Nora, the mother of these two kids. No one knew if her husband was dead or if he had abandoned his family.

Nora had a very hard life and there was never enough to fill all their bellies. The only comfort she had in her life was the little house her mother had left for her. This single story house was falling to pieces; nevertheless, it was a house that was providing shelter to her and her children.

Nora was not so old, but she looked worn out. Unlike other single mothers around, one never heard her shouting, screaming or swearing. She was a kind, soft-spoken woman. Her dark brown eyes were always reflecting her loneliness and sadness.

Nora was well aware of her poverty and misery and wished her children to be out of it, but to drag oneself out from this terrible state was not an easy task. She worked untiringly and for long hours in order to send both her kids to school, the only place capable of providing them the opportunity to have better lives, or at least so she believed. Her elder son Simon shared her optimism, enthusiasm, and determination of finding a better life than the one they lived. He was a loving, kind and sensitive boy, who felt sorry to see that life was not treating his mother well. He did whatever stood in his power to help and assist her whenever and wherever it was possible. She always admired his efforts to keep the home tidy and clean while she was out working. He loved going to school, as it provided him with an opportunity not only to meet other kids, but even gave him the possibility to learn and thereby achieve a better life. There wasn't anything in the world that could make him happier than the promising future he so dearly wanted. His wish for a bright future was not just for himself, but for the entire family. He was very fond of books, which were not easy to get hold of, but he always succeeded in borrowing them somehow from someone or the other. His passion for books was developing so rapidly that he hardly wanted to do anything else.

David, on the other hand, was the opposite. He was a careless, easygoing child, who wanted to be away from school, teachers and books, as all these deprived him of his favourite activities, friends and freedom. He was fond of eating and that he did without caring if there was anything left for others or not. He was insensitive to all and everything. Why worry about mother? David would get irritated, "All the grownups go out and work. She doesn't do any different." He was simply incapable of seeing the suffering of his mother; for him she was a natural source, from where he could get his provisions. As to her hard work, he cared less, as he didn't know what it entailed. All he could notice was her absence from home for most of the day, which he considered even a blessing. She was seldom home to see what he did with his time and even if she did occasionally come home early, she was too tired to interfere or notice his activities. His biggest interest was the other kids of the area, who were roaming around, fighting, screaming, and having fun. He was unable to understand the logic of going to school while all his friends could stay at home and have playtime. Despite all her convincing, Nora failed in making David realise the importance of education.

"No," was David's final word as he refused to go to school one day. There wasn't anything Simon could do to make him change his mind. All his persuasions, threats to inform mother when she came home, and other tactics were useless. He knew that there was no way he could make David go to school and left the stubborn boy alone. If he didn't want to go to school, it was all right for her, but then he was supposed to go to work instead, was Nora's last attempt to convince him. David started crying, reminding her that he was too young to work. She was right in her calculation, the bare threat of sending him to work had forced him to retreat from his uncompromising position and he promised to resume school the next day. One could see that he did that involuntarily and looked miserable, which made Simon and Nora smile discreetly.

Nora was suffering from some mysterious disease, but it didn't prevent her from going out and working, she simply couldn't afford to stay at home and rest. She was losing weight so rapidly that other people took notice and advised her to seek medical care. Nora always nodded in agreement, but never went to a physician. She was too proud to confess that she had no money to pay for the doctor's visit and for the medicines he would prescribe. Her condition was deteriorating so quickly that people were afraid to be around her. She lost her job. It didn't take long before the illness forced her to stay in bed, making her feel even more wretched. Her despondency was double edged. If on one hand, some unknown disease was tormenting and consuming her, on the other hand, she was worried to death for their subsistence and well-being of her children if she was to depart this life. Her unattended sickness coupled with her worries proved to be too much for her weaker body. "Promise to take good care of your brother," begged Nora on her deathbed.

"I will, mother," said Simon with tearful eyes.

"I know that he can be naughty and stubborn, but have patience with him, you are the only relative he has after I'm gone," she added.

He was uneasy when he realised that her end had come. His head was filled with worries and fears, and his heart sunk in grief. He panicked and held her shaky hand, trying to prevent her departure. It seemed that her time was up and nothing could hold her back. For so long she had been desperately struggling and striving to cling to life, but now she was ready to give up her attempts. She looked sad, but peaceful when she passed away.

Both the brothers cried at their great loss, looking for comfort and sympathy from others, but found none. Everyone had problems and tragedies of their own to deal with, so they couldn't offer more than shaking their heads in silent empathy before moving on to their own bitter realities. "The boys are big and strong. Surely they'll manage and survive," were the comments of a neighbor.

David seemed more shocked, as he was least aware of the gravity of his mother's sickness and condition. He not only suffered from the bad conscience of not having taken care of her, but was also confronted with the question of how they were to survive from that point on. David looked a transformed boy who had emerged with a new realization and understanding. He seemed ready to step forward and take his share of the burden.

"Look, brother! You know that school is not for me. I'll just waste my time if I were to continue," David said offering him a deal. "You go on with your studies; I'll take care of the household."

When Simon looked at him in disbelief, he smiled and added, "You're right to judge me from my past behavior. The loss of the mother has awakened me from the deep slumber. From now on, I'll be a different person and take my responsibilities more seriously. Right after the mourning period, I'll start looking for a job in order to provide for both of us."

Simon was touched by the sudden change in his younger brother and silently cried, hugging his kid brother. David looked at him with astonishment and wondered what made his brother so emotional. He had always believed Simon to be a weird person, and therefore he didn't care to ask anything.

"You are so young and inexperienced, what kind of job can you get?" Simon asked when he got out of his emotional state. David looked at him and smiled with incredible confidence.

"Yes, I'm young, but also strongly built; surely someone will give me employment." David was less worried. Just by looking at the self-assured face of David, all his worries were gone and he stepped forward to hug his younger brother once again, but David quickly moved away, signaling that he hated the hugs.

David got up early and left home, when Simon would leave for school, saying that he needed to look for a job. He came back late in the evening, looked exhausted and not at all in a mood to discuss what he did all day long. According to David, it wasn't fun to go from place to place and ask for a job. The failures made him upset, and for that reason it was best not to remind him of the hopeless situation. Simon could understand the frustration of David and therefore never pressed him for details. For him, it was enough that his brother was trying hard to get some employment in order to earn their daily bread. He kept going to school, but his head was full of worries, as he knew that there was no food left at home and there was no hope of David getting some job in the near future. The more he thought about the gravity of the situation, the more worried he got. How was he to keep going to the school if there was no money to pay the school fees and other expenditures linked to his education?

Simon looked pale and worried, when the teacher asked about the homework. He looked ashamed when he told the teacher that he had not been able to do it. How could he tell the teacher that he had not eaten anything for the last two days and studying on an empty stomach was not an easy task. The teacher looked angry by his answer, but didn't react hard as he used to do. He knew that Simon was a good student who was going through a tough time after the death of his mother.

"I expect you to bring your homework tomorrow, if you fail to do so, I'll not show you mercy." The teacher made it clear.

"Yes, sir," Simon said, relieved, but all his thoughts were revolving around his hunger.

When he came home from school, David was still out there, probably looking for a job. Simon felt weak and obsessed by the hunger, which was tormenting. He fell on the bed and tried hard to be brave. His empty stomach drew all his attention and he felt like howling the pain out, but he kept fighting the pressures. David used to come after sundown, but that day he lingered longer. Suddenly he became worried about his brother, fearing some terrible thing had happened to David. He even started worrying about how his brother would manage his hunger. He knew well that David used to turn the home upside down, when the food was occasionally not served in time. It was the knowledge that had forced him to give all the food to David during the last two days, instead of taking some for himself. What was he to give his brother to eat, when he came home, he thought and got worried, forgetting about his own tantalizing hunger. The situation was getting unbearable and he had to find some immediate solution if they were to survive, he realized.

It seemed that David wasn't hungry when he finally came home, as Simon didn't hear him going to the kitchen and looking into the pots. Simon felt miserable and cried silently. Until then, he had withstood the temptation to sell the things left by the mother, but now he realized that it was the only option if they wanted to survive the dire situation. All night he slept badly and had nightmares when he dozed from time to time. The first thing he did in the morning was to take a few things from home and sell them in the market. He was astonished to learn how little value these things held, but he was not in a position to find a better deal. He bought food with the money and became a bit relieved by the knowledge that the danger of starvation was averted, at least for the time being. Simon stopped going to school as he realized that by no means could he afford to pay for his schooling.

Simon also realized that overnight changes don't happen in real life. He discovered that the transformation of David was not real, but his wishful thinking. In truth as soon as the initial shock of losing the mother and the funeral ceremonies were over, David was the same old kid: careless, headstrong and self-centered, not ready to hear any advice, and not eager to be reminded of the word 'responsibility'. David's pretension to look for the job was nothing but an excuse to roam about with his friends. The death of Nora gave him that which he had always wanted and wished for: unlimited freedom, where he answered to no one. The knowledge that Simon had stopped going to school didn't affect David in any manner; he kept his routines and felt comfortable with those. He never bothered to ask from where Simon got the money to run the house. He wouldn't even notice that almost all of their valuables were now sold and they were quickly moving towards a disastrous situation where they both would starve.

David hardly spent any time at home, and was always seen in the company of the bad boys. Simon tried many times to discuss and explain the gravity of matters, but David refused to listen. "Don't mother me," he would shout, and then leave, stamping the ground. Simon was aware that his brother completely lacked respect for him, but there wasn't anything he could do to improve the matter, except to wish and pray. But that helped a little. Despite the knowledge, he believed that David would ultimately see the truth and thus better himself one day, but there occurred no such drastic change in his younger brother who became more and more headstrong.

One night, he politely explained the worsening situation. He was deeply hurt to see the careless expression on David's face. "Why do you tell me all these things?" David asked, surprised.

Simon reminded him of his promise to take care of their livelihood, but he cut him in the middle of the sentence. "Didn't you see I was sorrowed; I was shocked and above all too hasty? Isn't it a privilege and duty of the elder brother to take such responsibilities?" He continued, "Besides, the deal was with the presumption that you would keep going to school. I can see that you too have dropped out, right?" Simon could see a sarcastic smile on the face of his younger brother. He opened his mouth to explain the reasons that forced him to abandon his studies, but refrained from doing so, realizing that there wasn't any point in discussing the matter any further There wasn't a single soul in the whole world, with whom he could discuss his problems, share his pain and sorrow, and find some sympathy and understanding. He was all alone.

With great pain still bothering his heart and burdening his soul, he felt the need to search for employment. For weeks, he would leave home looking for a job, but couldn't find one. He was sixteen and had just finished his school, making it even more difficult to gain the trust of possible employers who were looking for some experienced person. Some people were kind and polite while rejecting his request for employment. Others were harsh and arrogant, making him feel bad. With each day passing, he felt more desperation and anxiety. There wasn't anything he could do to change his desperate situation.

One day, sitting all alone in his home, he cried bitterly, feeling a pressing need to share his appalling situation with someone. But there was no one around. So lonely and desperate was he that he looked to the ceiling and cried, "Why! What have I done to deserve these worries?"

Simon was walking, and he was so deeply burdened by his thoughts that he crashed into someone coming from the opposite direction. He apologised without even looking at the person he had collided with.

"How very rude! Not only that your attention is somewhere else, but you have a nerve not recognizing me," said someone in a polite, friendly manner. Simon looked up to find Mr. Harry, his old history teacher, smiling at him.

He looked really happy to see Simon. That it happened in that accidental way made it more amusing for him. He was curious to know all about his former pupil and therefore asked many questions.

They stood and talked for quite a while. Mr. Harry was sorry to learn about Simon's mother's death. He offered his sympathies, condolences, and concerns. Simon didn't want to burden his old teacher with his own difficulties, but the kind person was putting increasingly pointed questions as to how they were managing without any regular income. When he realised that he had a sympathetic ear, Simon couldn't hold himself back any longer. With bowed head, he confided his troubles to Mr. Harry, who looked worried himself.

"Don't worry too much! Troubles and worries are not forever. There is not a single problem which doesn't have a corresponding solution, so surely your troubles shall come to an end as well." His teacher was optimistic, but it wasn't what Simon was looking for. He wanted some concrete help or advice. After a while, Mr. Harry gave him a name and address, asking Simon to go and meet the person who might be able to help him.

"Come and visit me some time if you need my help or advice," he said, before moving forward, wishing Simon all the best.

The next day Simon went to the given address, which was a bookshop, and asked for the man. A young boy who was dusting and arranging the books took him to the far end of the shop, where an old man with glasses sat with bent head writing on a register. Simon introduced himself. The old man smiled, got up from his seat, and shook his hand warmly.

"Come sit here," the old man offered him a chair.

"Sir, I'm here…," Simon cleared his throat and spoke in a trembling voice.

"Excuse me for a moment," said the old man, going back to his writing in the register. "I want to complete the sentence I was writing, before I forget," he said seriously.

After closing his register, he looked at Simon, with critical eyes and told him that he was well aware of the reason Simon was there. After a short interview, Mr. Jacob said he was ready to employ Simon, if he was ready to accept a meagre salary. "I must confess that I'm not in a flourishing business," the shopkeeper said honestly. Simon was told that if it was acceptable, he could start work the next day.

"I'm an old man and need some fresh young blood to share my burden with," the old man joked. Simon was more than happy to get the job. There was no better job he could think of. To spend days and nights with books was a great pleasure. He was allowed to borrow whichever book he wanted, with one condition: he was to handle them delicately. He was using this privilege to the maximum. Mr. Jacob was a kind and humorous old man, with so much knowledge that Simon could stand there and listen to him for hours in awe.

Simon was happy and satisfied with his job, as it not only provided him with the needed money to run the household, but also offered an outstanding opportunity to learn without going to school. His thirst for knowledge was constantly taken care of by those wonderful books that surrounded him all the time. The only thing that bothered him was David and his out of control behaviour. He had tried all possible methods to convince his younger brother that the path he walked would bring disaster one day, but his efforts were fruitless. Young David had learned new methods for dealing with him. He knew that Simon was away most of the time and when he did come home, he was immediately drowning himself in some book. David knew the best thing to do was to avoid his brother when he was without a book.

Simon noticed that David was not very interested in any communication between them, as it ultimately would have led to serious matters that he had no intention to discuss. The only times David approached Simon was when he needed some money, and that was happening more frequently. He was always in the middle of some emergency that required instant action on the part of Simon. He had tried many times to tell David that the little salary he got was just sufficient for their bare needs and that there wasn't any room for extravagance, but each time he failed to make an impression.

He was at his work, busy writing down on the register, when he heard David's voice. He was surprised to find him there. "Is everything all right? What are you doing here?" Simon asked. David looked at him and casually told him he needed some money. Simon looked upset, but remained polite. "You could have waited for me to come home. You know that I'm working now."

"I had no intention of coming and disturbing you, but the emergency couldn't wait." David was not apologetic.

"And what's the emergency this time?" Simon asked, a bit irritated.

David said one of his friends was in some serious trouble and needed the money immediately.

"But I don't have any money right now," Simon said, looking in his empty pockets. David would not leave empty-handed. He went on begging, pleading, and exploiting his brother's sympathy. He went on pressing until Simon agreed to give him the needed money. With a heavy heart, he went to the cash box, opened it and gave the money to David. He wrote a debt note with the hope that Mr. Jacob was never going to find out that he had used his money without any permission. His heart bled and he felt as if he had betrayed the trust of his very gentle and kind employer.

The whole night he could not sleep, tossing and turning, worrying about his brother, about his job, and the prospects of surviving if his employer found out that his money was gone and decided to throw him out of employment. He had not stolen the money, but it felt as if he had. That night, he promised to himself it was the last time he would indulge in such a stupid act. Never would he surrender to David's emotional blackmail again. The very first thing he intended to do in the morning was to put back the money in the cash register. He was early to his work in order to be there before Mr. Jacob. His heart came to his throat when he saw Mr. Jacob already sitting in his chair and working. Simon was all sweaty and shaky when he entered the shop, mentally preparing himself for the worst.

Mr. Jacob nodded to him before going back to the register. "You're early," he said without looking at him. Simon pretended he didn't know that he was early. "It'll just take a minute," said his employer. Simon was extremely nervous, while Mr. Jacob went on writing. "It's good that you are here early, as I wanted to inform you that I'd be away the whole day," He said. "It's a family emergency. I have to take my wife to the hospital for some checkups."

Mr. Jacob's apologetic way of expressing himself always made him feel uneasy and embarrassed, but Simon felt relieved by the fact that his breach of rule and trust had not been discovered by his kind employer. He assured Mr. Jacob that he would take care of all details in a responsible manner in his absence. Simon extended his best wishes. "I hope that all will be well with your Mrs."

As soon as Mr. Jacob was gone, Simon rushed to the money register, took the debt note, and replaced it with the missing money. There was a broad smile on his relieved face. Never ever would he break the rules set by his employer; never would he breach the trust Mr. Jacob had placed in him.

He could not have been more wrong in his judgement of himself. With great shame, he realised that he was too weak for his younger brother, who would repeatedly come and ask for money. He could never be prepared for David and his emergencies. The needed money always exceeded the amount he carried, compelling Simon to take the money from the cash register. He always wrote a note before taking the money, knowing well that it didn't make his action a rightful one. He hated himself for that, promising to himself that it was the last time he was doing the despicable deed. The more Simon resisted the necessity of unauthorised borrowing from the cash register, the more David, who had made it his routine to come with ever-newer demands, dragged him into it. How many times had he not begged his brother to stop bothering him at his work? But all his requests were unheard and unheeded.

2

Simon was in over his head. The money he had borrowed from his employer now exceeded his capacity to repay. Simon was tormented by his conscience day and night. He could not believe that, little by little, he had borrowed a huge amount without Mr. Jacob's permission. The question was not if, but when Mr. Jacob was to discover the missing money. The more Simon thought of the matter, the more depressed and pessimistic he became. Even if Mr. Jacob was to refrain from reporting him to the police for theft and fraud and thereby sending him to jail for years, without any doubt he would ask Simon to leave his job. If that happened, how were they to sustain themselves? Where was he to find other employment? Where could he find such a kind-hearted and trusting employer? Who would give a job to such an untrustworthy fellow like himself?   After long consideration, Simon realised that he must take the responsible way out.

Mr. Jacob listened to him with his usual patience and serenity, without looking angry, hurt or shocked. Simon was confessing all his wrongdoings with shame and regret. He was tearful and drenched in sweat. His tall but thin body was quite shaky as if being exposed to some powerful storm.

"Why did you do it?" Mr. Jacob asked at last, in a very cold manner.

"It's a bit complicated, sir," Simon tried to avoid the real reason of his unacceptable deed.

"I believe I'm capable of understanding the complications of life." Mr. Jacob was being sarcastic.

He cleared his throat and in a trembling voice, he spoke. "I don't intend to put the blame on anyone else. I take the full responsibility for what I have done."

Simon sounded sincere in his confession. With stammering voice, he confided in Mr. Jacob about his problems with his younger brother.

"Why do you allow him to drive you this way?" asked Mr. Jacob.

Simon said he was trying to play the big brother's role and keep the promise that he gave to his dying mother always to take care of David. He had felt that his sacrificial behaviour would make his brother realise the wrongness of his own attitude.

Mr. Jacob smiled at his words. Simon looked back in astonishment. He could not help feeling a great admiration for the man, who had the guts to smile in such a grave situation.

"Such a fool you are! What good has all that reading done for you? Why are you so ignorant of human beings and the way they behave?" Mr. Jacob was blunt and disrespectful, but nevertheless remained sympathetically inclined.

He shocked Simon by disclosing that he had been aware of the missing money since the beginning, but had decided to wait patiently for an explanation. "I trusted you. My heart refused to believe that I had put my trust in some unworthy person. Therefore, I waited and hoped that you would come up with some satisfactory explanations. I must confess that my disappointment in you is deep, but seeing your foolish love for your brother, I am ready to forgive your mistake, provided you promise not to indulge in such activity ever again."

Mr. Jacob was forgiving and understanding. He gave Simon a long lecture on what was good and what was wrong in a relationship. "Believe me; you are not doing him a favor by meeting all his unreasonable demands. Be firm and learn to say no, or you will suffer in your bones."

"How am I to resist his manipulative and blackmailing ways? The boy knows that I'm weak in his presence."

"You have to figure that out on your own. All I can help out with is to remind you of the consequences of not controlling your brother by deducting a substantial part of your salary as a payment on your debt."

Simon was thankful for not losing the job, for the continued trust of Mr. Jacob and most of all, for pointing out his handicap. No doubt, he loved his brother and wanted to do everything in his power to help and assist him, but he resolved to never compromise on principles again.

David continued with his visits to get money, but Simon made it clear that it was beyond his power to take a single dime from the cash register. David could stand for hours trying to manipulate his brother's feelings, but Simon would not waver in his determination. David was aware that Simon had changed his attitude and there was not much to gain from going on pressing him, but he would never give up, hoping that the sudden change in Simon's policy was temporary.

If Mr. Jacob was kind, wise and of an understanding heart, the same couldn't be said of other people. Simon's happiness that his brother had stopped bothering him about the money was short-lived. David had not mended his ways as he had hoped. The boy had simply changed his tactics. Simon learned about that fact when strangers started knocking at their door, demanding the money that David had borrowed from them. Simon wasn't ready for such an unexpected situation. He was a straightforward, honest young man, who neither indulged in such activities, nor knew how to handle such creditors. All his discussions with David came nowhere, as the boy refused to discuss that which, according to him, was none of his business.

"Tell them that you have nothing to do with me, they'll leave you in peace." David would shrug him off.

"But I do care about you and your well-being," Simon would try to argue.

"If you do, then why don't you pay them and save me from harm?" David would provoke, pushing Simon to become silent and gloomy.

Many times, Mr. Jacob asked Simon what bothered him as he worked. He was having difficulty in concentration, grasping the things most obvious and forgetting the instructions given to him earlier. He kept his problems to himself as he was convinced that no one could help or guide him in his plight. He was seeing less and less of David, partly because he himself had to work extra in order to pay back the debt to Mr. Jacob and partially due to the fact that David spent most of his time outside the home, coming back only to eat and sleep. He was worried for David's sake, anticipating some disaster to befall, but there was little he could do to prevent that from happening.

Mr. Jacob fell ill and stayed in bed for more than a week, obliging Simon to perform all the tasks on his own. Taking care of the business was not that difficult as he was used to working independently, but it was sucking the life out of him. After those long, hard days he would come home, completely exhausted. There was nothing in the world that could make him happier than the news that Mr. Jacob had recovered and was back to his ordinary duties, but instead his illness lingered, forcing Simon to work all alone. His heart pounded when he was called to come visit Mr. Jacob, suspecting that some bad news awaited him. His employer looked tired and more aged than he really was. Seeing Simon, he tried to get up, but was too tired to do so, on his own. Simon went forward and helped him sit erect in the bed, but he gave up his brave attempt and sat leaning on the pillow.

Once settled, he smiled and greeted Simon, asking how things were going. Simon reported the affairs briefly, realising that the man was not in the best of health to discuss the details and other trivialities.

"Look young man! My health is getting worse by the passing of each hour, I'm becoming more and more pessimistic. If this situation continues, I'm afraid that I have to close down the business." Mr. Jacob was talking without directly looking at Simon, who seemed to be taken aback by his words. "As you know, we are a couple without any offspring, who could take over the family business. My wife is also old and ailing, so I don't have much of a choice other than to sell the business or close it down."

Simon could see that Mr. Jacob was in pain when he talked about the probability of closing down. The old fellow had worked hard years and years to build his business and it must have been a painful decision to even consider the termination of lifelong activity. Without any shame, he confessed to himself that he was more worried about his own hopeless situation than the inner turmoil of Mr. Jacob. He felt sorry for him, but knew well that the man had spent all his fruitful years in a positive, rewarding, and stimulating atmosphere. Now at the end of the road, he was evaluating his obligations and ambitions of running a business. His choices were easier as he had nothing to fear about the daily bread; without any doubt he was a wealthy man. Mr. Jacob was watching Simon intensely, as if he was trying to know what reaction his words had evoked in the young man.

Simon was trying hard to not reflect his disappointment,

worries or fears regarding his own future. He didn't want to give his employer a harder time or bad conscience than he was already suffering from. "Sir, I fully understand your dilemma and agree that there are not many choices if your ill health continues to bother you. As you know, I love this job and working with you was a great pleasure, but if you find it necessary to sell or shut down the place, I'll remain understanding." Simon said with deep respect and empathy for the old man.

Before leaving Mr. Jacob's home, he embraced the old man, wishing him a quick recovery and a long, healthy life, trying hard to hide his own anxiety by smiling more broadly than usual. "I'm relieved that you didn't take things too hard. You are a young, energetic, and honest worker, who's surely going to find some good work very soon. I'll give you the best recommendations." Mr. Jacob said in a sad low tone as if he was not very convinced of his own words. Simon left without turning back to see the pale, tired face of his employer. The final word was not said yet, but he could say without any doubt that his days at the shop were numbered. He had put the money Mr. Jacob gave to him in his inner pocket. Simon wanted to make the payment before going back to the shop as it was a huge amount, and he couldn't afford to misplace it. That payment was a clear indication that the process of winding up the business had already started.

Simon was extremely disturbed. He was heading towards the address where he was supposed to leave the money. He would have moved on without noticing any detail of the dull surroundings, but he couldn't ignore the sight of a few people arguing loudly with each other. He was startled to see that David was one of those who were almost at each other's throats. He hated to come even near to such trouble, but found no choice than to go forward and see what was going on. The arguing gang noticed his presence and got silent for a while and looked in a confused manner at each other, as if they were assessing their next move. It seemed they had decided to ignore his presence. Despite his reluctance and inner voice warning him, he turned to David and asked what went on.

"It's nothing. We're just discussing some small matter," he said. David tried to get rid of Simon, but it didn't take long before he was engulfed by a storm of words. Once again, everyone was talking loudly, disrespectfully and in threatening tones, dragging him into their conflict, demanding his mediation. It was quite clear that the youngsters were divided into two groups and that the row was about money. Who owed who was neither obvious nor did he want to know.

"I believe you are all very clever, intelligent young people who are capable of solving the issues in a sensible and reasonable manner." Simon tried to calm them down.

"Don't try to patronise us! You need to control this monster!" some young fellow said aggressively, pointing at David. The noise of the quarrelling young fellows grew louder, making Simon shiver inside. The whole situation was getting out of hand and could easily turn ugly, panicking Simon, forcing him to defuse it somehow.

"Calm down!" He appealed to them, but no-one heeded and went on with their hot discussion. He knew that the money was the bone of contention. That knowledge and money in the pocket tempted him to jump in, pay the disputed amount and thus resolve the issue peacefully, but it was just in the last minutes of fury and chaotic pulling and pushing by youngsters that prevented him from committing the stupid mistake of breaching the trust of Mr. Jacob once again.

He was there the entire time watching the whole event,

but still he could swear that he didn't know how it happened and who did it. The only thing he could be sure of was that a young fellow lay in the middle of the street motionless, while all the rest ran away. There was no visible injury, so he presumed that the young fellow had just passed out and wasn't in any physical danger. He was absolutely wrong in his assessment and that realisation came a bit too late. The boy was dead. What had caused his death, he couldn't tell. Soon, other people were gathering around and looking at him with suspicion, making him realise that he had been involuntarily involved in some horrible happening. Panic got hold of him and he desperately tried to flee from the scene as well, but it was too late. He was chased and held against his will until he gave up and stopped struggling.

Strangely, there were no witnesses to the actual incident, but many had seen Simon standing among the group, so even if he was not the guilty one, he could lead the law to the culprits. He was taken and interrogated by the police. He was scared and nervous, but still wanted to protect his younger brother and therefore remained reluctant to reveal the identities of the youngsters who were involved in the wrangle. Of course, he didn't know most of them but certainly any hint from him could lead the authorities to the guilty ones. The finding of a huge amount of money in his pocket didn't make things any easier for him. He immediately became the main suspect. He was not so worried about that, as he was sure that Mr. Jacob would confirm his story and innocence. What he didn't know was that Mr. Jacob was no more in the world to witness his version. He had died a few hours after his visit.

Police had gathered some information and were now quite certain that Simon was not a party in the arguing group, but a passer-by who had tried to avert the fight. That softened their attitude a bit, but they were still not ready to release him. Simon had to hold on to his story and wait patiently. After a few days in custody, he was released when it became clear that the money Simon carried with him really was to be paid to the businessman he had named.

His experience at the detention was the most terrible thing that had happened to him. He had spent that time in soul-searching, trying to find the reasons for all that had happened in his life, pondering on the meaning of life, and most of all struggling to find some miraculous means by which he could reform his little brother. David had to understand the dangers lying ahead in the path he was treading. With a heavy heart, he realised that David had gone beyond his power and influence. There was nothing he could do or say that could alter his course. Nevertheless, David was his beloved brother and it was no secret that his heart ached from the realisation.

David pretended to be completely ignorant as to the actual happening of that day. He had a theory that the young chap was some weakling who had failed to handle the stress caused by the tumult and consequently had died. Simon looked into his younger brother's smiling eyes and knew that he was fooling him, but didn't pursue the discussion any further.

"I must confess though that you are tougher than I thought," David said with a wicked smile, pointing at his not disclosing their names to the police.

"You and your friends should be happy for that." Simon was annoyed. Simon had hoped that his announcement about losing his job would be a wake-up call for his brother, but he took the news with a broad smile and in a relaxed manner.

"That job was not good anyway. What did it provide you? A meagre salary? An unending slavery? I believe you should be happy instead of being depressed." David was hard in his words, making Simon upset, but he didn't protest as he used to do at such insensitive statements of his brother. There was no point in reminding David that that little salary of his had been the entire source of their economic survival. Simon's silence was translated as recognition that David was right in his presumption, making him smile triumphantly. "By the way, I need some money, can you arrange it?" David asked.

Simon looked staggered and kept silent. David repeated his request and sounded rude and irritated this time. "You know very well that I don't have any money to give and I still owe quite a substantial amount to Mr. Jacob." Simon was hurt by his thoughtless demand, but sounded more apologetic than angry. "But I need the money in order to pay off my creditors; they wouldn't leave me alone if I don't." David was as unreasonable as ever, closing his ears to all logic, explanations and voice.

"But how am I to arrange the money?" Simon demanded in a shaky voice.

"Perhaps we should sell the house; half of it is mine anyway."

Simon was stunned to listen to the awful proposition, but remained appealing to David's heart and intellect. "Look brother, I'm not denying your equal right to the inheritance, but where are we supposed to live if we are to sell the house? That is the only guarantee we have right now of not becoming homeless."

"That's for you to figure out. As far as I'm concerned, I have many places to choose from, if I was to move away from this rat hole." David was determined, making Simon explode of anger and disappointment.

"All right, if that's the only language you understand, then listen. There is no way I'll agree to your stupid proposition of selling the house. I really don't care what your creditors will do with you, as you are yourself responsible for getting into the situation." Simon left the house in anger, realising that things were not to remain controllable if they both went on with that angry exchange of words.

A few hours later when Simon came back home, he was still disheartened. He was even sorry for losing his characteristic serenity and resolved to himself to be more patient in the future. David wasn't home, which was not very surprising, as the boy used to come and go at his will. Unlike other times, David didn't come home that night and that was alarming. Simon knew that his brother must be cross at him for not agreeing to his unreasonable suggestion, but he was confident that soon David would understand and perhaps even appreciate the decision to not sell the house. He was wrong in his high hopes and calculations. David didn't return for two days, making Simon worry and feel terrible. He couldn't sleep even for a brief moment. He kept worrying about the well-being of his younger brother, wondering what made him take such a drastic step. Could he do anything to prevent such an occurrence?

The more he thought, the more he was convinced that he had not done anything wrong and that decision to resist the brainless proposition of selling the house was the most sane thing he had ever done. Nevertheless, he wanted David to come back and live there. He knew so little about David's friends and couldn't possibly know where he had moved to, but it was no longer possible to stay idle and worry about him. Therefore, he decided to go and search for him. The search for David proved to be easier than he had feared. The very first young boy he contacted and asked information about his brother's whereabouts could lead him directly to David's new address. "Why do you want to contact him?" The boy asked curiously. "I believe that he has sworn to never return to you." The boy said, looking at his face to trace the reaction.

"You know misunderstandings can happen between family members." Simon tried to ignore his comments.

As they walked, the boy told Simon about David's very real problems. He seemed to be worried about David and his incredibly huge debts, which he had collected rapidly. "He's just a fool, your brother, and everyone is exploiting this fact. He is part of the vagabonds who do nothing but roam about, but nevertheless need money to survive. David arranges that money. So you can see the problem."

Simon had been suspecting that for a long time, but he was still not convinced that it was the root of the problem. He kept asking questions of the boy and it didn't take long before the whole picture was clear. He was right to assume that his brother was in a deeper trouble than he could possibly have anticipated. Most of David's debts were collected in gambling, and that solved the mystery of how he could go on borrowing the money despite already having such huge debts.

David was not there when he knocked at the door. The decayed house seemed to be deserted and a dangerous place to live. Simon didn't like the neighbourhood, as it seemed to be even worse than his own. "Come later!" some little child suggested. "None shall be coming home until late in the evening."

He thanked the boy for his advice, but decided to wait for his brother right there, sitting outside and observing the semi-deserted street. The waiting wasn't an easy task as he was getting hungry and thirsty, but he endured with patience. When David finally approached the house, he looked a bit surprised to find Simon waiting for him. In a cold manner, he inquired the reason of his coming there.

"I had been worried for your sake, and have come to take you back home." Simon was embarrassed by his chilly behaviour, as David's friends were watching them curiously.

"You don't have to worry about me. I'm doing well," David said coldly. "I want to make it clear, I am not coming back. I have decided to live my own life." David was blunt and inconsiderate. Simon tried to convince him that it wasn't a very wise decision but failed to move him an inch from his position.

"I know that you are mad at me, but when you have cooled down, come home," were Simon's last words before he turned to go back.

3

A few days later, Simon was thinking about his unsustainable situation and getting frightened. He was lonely, without any money and without any job and worst of all; there wasn't the slightest hope for any betterment. Perhaps David was not wrong in his suggestion, and he reconsidered the whole idea. We could sell the house, move into some rented little place and use the money for survival, he was thinking. His mind was astray, he was still not convinced that that was the best solution. He had not visited and conveyed his condolences to Mr. Jacob's widow and felt bad for that. He was anxious for David and the possible dire consequences of the path he had chosen for himself.

His whole life was engulfed by darkness, without the tiniest stream of light. He felt miserable and wished some miraculous happening could lift him up from the pit. He needed some friend to share with; some sympathetic being to talk to and share his hopeless condition, but all he got was tormenting and threatening thoughts.

It was the middle of the night, but he was fully awake and struggling with his anxiety when he heard a knocking at the door. He wondered who could be there that late in the night. Thinking it might be David; he rushed to the door and opened it only to be taken aback by seeing two policemen standing there in the dark. They were looking for David. Simon told them that David wasn't living there anymore and inquired why they wanted to contact him that late. The policemen said they couldn't tell him the reason of their search, but requested him to inform them in case he knew where they could get hold of his brother. Anticipating some trouble, he pretended to be not aware of David's address. Once the policemen left, he had another worry added to his list. He was tempted to go straightaway to David and ask what kind of trouble he had fallen into or simply to warn him, but he was too scared to do so. His fears kept him paralysed, unable to act, and that was good in one way as he was ignorant of the fact that both policemen had been observing his house for the rest of the night, hoping that Simon would lead them to David.

Sadly, he discovered that David and his friends were drawn into some law-breaking activities. Whether his brother was directly involved or not was a controversial thing as his guilt had not been proven, as was the case for most of his friends, who were now in the custody of police and were asserting David's guilt. David had been quick to react and was on the run, far ahead of the law-enforcing agency. He was safe, but fugitive. Simon was devastated, losing his will to live. He felt like an absolute failure in all his tasks and duties. All day long, he would stay at home sitting and watching the ceiling, neither caring about hunger nor any other social needs. At times, he thought of his mother and cried.

He might have starved there, without caring to move and do anything to prevent such an ugly thing from happening, but something occurred that was to wake him up and renew his will to live. It was late in the night and he was sitting on the roof and staring at the stars, when he heard some strange flapping of wings. The sound was so incredibly strong that it forced him to look around and try to locate its source. The bird that made such flapping sounds must have been huge, more colossal than he had ever seen or heard of. He gave up trying as he was soon convinced that he had imagined the whole thing. He would have sunk into his gloom once again, had he not heard the same powerful flapping sound, entering into his ears. This time he even heard some melodious laughter, followed by a complete silence. He could swear that the laughter was female, which had vibrated in the cold atmosphere before dying out.

A strange feeling overtook his whole being and he couldn't help but be enthralled. He could feel his heartbeat and an indescribable sensation sweeping in his blood vessels. He waited and waited all night long, wishing to hear that magical sound and wonderful laughter once again, but the moment had passed and so had the marvellous being he had listened to. He was unable to determine the exact nature of the experience and could never tell what implications the enchanting sounds had held for him. One thing he knew for sure: his heart was alive once again. He felt forced to turn his attention to the pressing needs of his soul and bodily needs and sensed a need to take proper measures. He was quick to heed the call and ate whatever he could find in the house to appease his hunger and to get the renewed energies. Gone was the lethargy and once again he was full of the determination to change his prevailing condition. Perhaps, he himself was not aware of this tantalising transformation, which had occurred to him, and if he did understand that was only to a minor degree.

He visited the widow of Mr. Jacob, who was as kind as always. She accepted his excuses of not feeling well enough to visit her earlier. She was of a different view than Mr. Jacob and wanted to continue the business as long as her health allowed. "I need to be buried in work if I am to survive my late husband's death," said Margaret with a broad smile. Simon could not help looking at her with admiration. No doubt, she was a pleasant and intelligent lady.

"Do you have someone taking care of your business?" Simon asked.

"I'm taking care of the business myself," Margaret said proudly, making Simon more puzzled than before. She laughed, seeing him confused and explained that before Simon came into the picture, it was she who had been assisting and helping her late husband in his affairs. Very graciously, she offered Simon an opportunity to go on working with her, if he wished to do so. Simon was overwhelmed by that gesture and accepted it immediately. He was thankful and assured her that she would never regret her decision to employ him.

Once again, Simon had a job and activities to make him forget the unpleasant side of life. He could not take David off his mind, always wondering what had happened to him. What kind of life was he leading? Could it be possible that he had changed his manners, learned from his old mistakes and had some noble principles guiding him? He was unable to know what really became of him, but wished that his dear brother had changed into some better person. Now that neither David was there with his extravagant spending nor was Mr. Jacob deducting a substantial amount from his salary, he felt he was getting rich. All the money he earned was piled up, without any need to spend it. Margaret had even freed him of his only possibility to spend the money, by not only bringing his lunch, but even a meal to take home after work. When Simon told her about his debt to her late husband, she laughed, telling him that the debt was clear as far as she was concerned. "Your debt has died along with my husband. I had been begging him to let you off, but he told me that he was a man of principle. But I believe that he had difficulty in recognizing the truth. He was a stingy man," Mrs. Margaret said, amused by her own words.

Soon Simon noticed that Margaret was not only kind and helpful, but was even a shrewd business woman, who was making new strategies to run the business. She was charming, attentive, and innovative and that new approach of hers brought customers from far and wide. It was really fun to work with her and Simon didn't mind working long hours. She was a fair employer, compensating each and every minute he spent in his duty, almost to the extent that he felt embarrassed. The only irritating thing in her was her possessiveness. She demanded all the time on earth for herself, which was a very difficult thing for Simon, who absolutely needed a space and time for himself, if for no other reason than to ponder upon the things he cared about and to read the books that attracted him. He hated to lie, but had to do it every now and then in order to avoid her invitations to have dinner at her place or a request to accompany her to some important social meeting.

"You know Simon, I don't have any children, so it could be very well you, who may inherit everything I own," Margaret would say, giving him incentive to spend more of his leisure time with her. Simon used to just smile away, telling her that he didn't need any of her money or property.

He had developed a new habit of sitting on the roof until late in the night, hoping to hear the magical sound of flapping wings, and to perceive the sound of the melodious, soft laughter, but his ears only could imagine the sounds he so desperately wanted to hear. He was obsessed with the happening that could be nothing else than an imaginary one, but he had dismissed logic. He was bewitched.

"What's the matter with you?" Margaret asked one day. "You don't look well. Are you getting enough sleep?" She really looked concerned.

"I'm all right," Simon answered in a somewhat tired manner. Margaret was quick in lecturing him about the importance of proper rest.

Things were moving on in the ordinary manner without any major incident. There was still no news from David. He must have moved to some other city, but how he would have been managing was still bothering Simon. He was perfectly aware that his brother was not only lazy and inexperienced when it came to earning an honest living, but he had an attitude problem and this knowledge made him worried and troubled at times. He was sure that David would return one day as he was an animal of the herd and therefore could not live aloof for a very long time. But On the other hand, what made him believe that his brother had not already made new friends at the place of his new residence? Life without any friend or kin wasn't at all worth living he thought, and decided to go and search for his brother. Where was he to start looking he had no idea, but the best way to find the answer was to start asking those of David's friends who were still near the city. The tips he got from David's friends were many and contradictory to each other, leaving him almost no clue as to which direction he was supposed to proceed.

Informing Margaret about his decision to go and search for his brother was the most difficult thing to do. He was right in his presumption that she would dislike the idea and try to prevent him from seeking the impossible.

"Do you have the slightest idea how big the world is? And why do you want to destroy your own life for that headstrong, thankless man? He is grown up now and responsible for all his actions."

Simon was silent, as he knew she was reasonable and absolutely right in her judgement, but he wasn't thinking with his head, but with a passionate heart, where the measures were completely different. When Margaret saw that Simon had made up his mind, she smiled sadly, nodding with pitiful eyes.

"You are too stupid and naïve for this world of ours. Go and do what your heart desires of you to accomplish. You are most welcome to come and work with me, whenever you decide to come back." Margaret said with motherly affection. "Of course, this offer stands as long as I live."

After taking care of all the necessary preparations, he considered the most probable place his brother could have moved to. He had been considering all possibilities and therefore had left his will with Margaret, giving up his right on the inherited house in favour of David, in case he returned in his absence. He had even left a substantial amount of money for him, making Margaret protest, saying that he was nothing but a fool, and even they would not travel without enough money. He wanted to travel light and with the least money, convinced that it was the safest way not to endanger one's life.

4

He left the city early one morning and looked at its streets, buildings, and people. He had a strong feeling that he was doing it for the last time and never was to set his foot back on those pathways he had treaded millions of times. Everything appeared to be exactly as it always had been, but still there was a huge difference. He felt weak, distressed, and full of fear. This would be the very first time he was leaving the only reality he had known from the time of his birth. It was the most difficult thing that he had ever done in his life. There was no time to lose standing there being imprisoned by fear. He had to move on regardless of whether he was leaving the place for good or was to return after finding his brother. The best thing was not to look back because it anguished him to leave the security of known realities behind and to enter into something that he had never known. His mind was pulling his feet back to the world he had just left behind while his heart was dragging him to some unknown destination.

Where he was heading to, he did not know. He travelled from city to city, place to place, but nowhere had he found any trace of David. No one had heard of a young man of that description. Some people admired his courage to undertake such a tedious task while others laughed at his stupidity of doing the impossible.

"Didn't you say that your brother is a young fellow?" asked one stranger.

"Yes," answered Simon.

"You should give up your fruitless struggle of trying to find him. Go home and wait there, he'll come back when he's ready." Simon could almost feel his pity. "We beings have a tendency of worrying for our dear ones and especially our children. But we must not exaggerate and let things go when the purpose of such protecting is fulfilled."

The stranger was hinting that if David was not a minor, then he was responsible for his own actions. It was not the first time he was confronted with the argument, and he knew it was the most logical thing to do, but he was the prisoner of his own distorted feelings and there was little he could do to change the situation. From that point on, he stopped telling the relation and reason of his search of David, leaving it as an open question to be answered by the lively imagination of others.

His unstinted rummaging around was not bringing him any closer to the object of his search, but his unflinching resolve to proceed further and further away was remarkable. He loved his brother and was ready to sacrifice anything to get him back, or at least it was, so he thought. It was hard for him to determine if it was due to the promise given to the dying mother that he felt responsible for David's well-being or was it really his love for the younger brother. He was aware that love was a feeling beyond his control, and no logic functioned in that regard, and yet he kept thinking every now and then, questioning the rationality of his apparently impossible mission. He questioned himself about the real motives that kept driving him from place to place, giving him restlessness and discomfort. At times, he succeeded in convincing himself that his quest was genuine and that he did everything that was required of him, but at other moments he felt doubtful and lost, especially when his mind accused him of deception. According to that insignificant voice, Simon was using his brotherly love just as a pretext to keep moving. The real reasons for his unrest lay somewhere else, but he had refused to acknowledge the truth. What were these hidden motives, he tried to figure out, but failed to do so.

The trader listened to his description of David and believed that he knew where Simon could find him. Simon felt very excited and begged the trader to give him the whereabouts of his brother. The trader seemed to have regretted his spontaneous reaction and was careful to disclose anything further. He wanted to know why Simon looked for the man, and asked many such questions. Simon knew that the trader wouldn't tell him anything more till he told him the truth. He briefly explained that they were brothers and that he was worried about the well-being of his younger brother. The trader kept silent for a while, staring at Simon, till he smiled broadly.

"Of course you are brothers; I can clearly see the resemblance now," the trader said. "Why are you worried about him?"

Simon was reluctant to disclose more than was necessary and yet felt forced to say something. "Just before his leaving, we had an argument, and I feel very bad about it," Simon told the trader, who smiled and nodded as if he understood Simon's sentiments.

"How do you know my brother?" Simon was curious.

"I don't really know him, I met him just once. He came to our shop to sell some valuable thing. Just to be sure that it wasn't a stolen item, I was forced to enter into a dialogue with him. Your brother is indeed a charmer despite his odd looks." The trader said and laughed. Simon felt unhappy, but didn't react. The trader must have noticed the disturbed face of Simon, so getting serious; he tried to give an explanation.

"Even though you have a resemblance with your brother, you two give different impressions. Your brother looks crude and thus invokes some suspicion from others." The trader looked apologetic, but unafraid to tell it the way he believed.

"May I know, what was that valuable thing?"

"It was a diamond ring, not very expensive, but a ring with a diamond." The trader said with a smile and continued. "Your brother told me that it belonged to his deceased mother, and I believed that he was telling the truth and for that reason I paid him the price."

Simon tried hard to hide his emotions and disappointment; he remembered the ring, and the only valuable his mother ever had in her life. The ring had some kind of emotional value for his mother as she had refused to sell it even in the worst circumstances. When and how the diamond ring had come into her life was never discussed between the mother and her children, she was so secretive about that. Simon felt sad thinking that the ring could have saved her life if she had sold it at the right time and spent the money on medicines instead. The trader didn't know what went on in Simon's head, but was sure that he had touched upon some sensitive issue. Simon remembered the time when after the death of his mother they ran out of food, and he so desperately had tried to find the ring. He was astonished not to find it but had presumed that perhaps mother had finally sold it before her death. Even at that time, it had seemed improbable, but never in his wildest fantasies could he have imagined that David had stolen it. He was confused by the revelation of the trader. Why didn't David sell the ring right away, why did he save that for such a long time, especially when he needed the money all the time? He knew there were no answers to his question. Suddenly, he felt sad instead of getting happy to find out the whereabouts of David but tried hard to suppress his feelings of dismay.

The location was completely opposite in direction and hundreds of miles away from where he found himself. The news warmed his troubled heart, and he became pleased to hear that his brother was doing well, but strangely, he felt unwilling to move back, travel a long journey in order to visit David, who might not even be interested in seeing him. He felt confused by his reluctance to go and head towards the place where he could be finally be united with his beloved brother. The questions that followed were numerous, but the answers very few. His thoughts went on tormenting him, but he refused to confess that his real purpose of wandering around was more than his search for David. He felt furious about the insinuation and fought back by a resolve to go and find David in his new place of residence.

Coming back to the Inn, he was met by the owner, who informed him that someone had broken into his room earlier during the day, so it was best if he could go and see if all his belongings were still there. His heart came to the throat, and he rushed to his tiny room and met with a terrible scene. All his clothes and other things laid on the floor in a disarrayed manner. The owner stood right behind and watched carelessly. Simon scrutinized the place and fixed his gaze on the heap of dirty clothes. He went forward and started searching the pockets, but didn't find the money he had hidden there. He looked pale but didn't utter a single word.

"Is everything in order?" The owner asked.

"It's gone!" Said Simon in a sad tone.

"What's gone, all your stuff seems to be right here?"

"Someone has stolen my money." Simon could finally utter in a weak voice.

"What! Were you keeping your money here in the room?" The owner seemed to be taken aback.

"I thought it to be safer here, with so many people moving around; I thought none would dare to enter my room in the daylight." Simon tried to justify his thoughtless act. The owner shook his head in disbelief and kept looking at the sad face of Simon, without sympathizing with the young fool.

"Is all the money gone?"

"Almost, except the little money I have on me."

"Can you arrange some money to support your expenditure?" The owner asked in a matter of fact way. Simon's silence was a clear answer to his question. The thin man didn't say a word and turned to leave the room. He had decided not to take up the serious issue of Simon's continued residence in his Inn, but to leave the matter to be discussed some other time.

"What am I supposed to do, shall I contact police?" Simon asked, when the owner turned to leave.

"Do whatever pleases you, but the money is not coming back, write it down," the owner sounded realistic and detached. Simon watched the owner disappear and looked even sadder. Why the man couldn't show some sympathy and understanding, he wondered. He knew that placing his money in the room was a serious mistake, and he had even been warned against such practice by the owner, when he had moved into the Inn but wasn't it natural to make mistakes? He sat down on his bed and felt miserable. All of a sudden, he was worried about everything and no ray of hope was in sight. How was he to sustain himself from that moment on, how was he to travel in the absence of money and many more such like questions tormented him, and he had no answers.

All night he spent sitting in a distressed state, trying to find some way out of his dire situation, but it seemed the possibility of finding a solution was nil. He was certain that the heartless owner of the Inn wouldn't let him stay over there even a single night without getting the rent, especially when he knew that Simon was penniless. In his distressed state, he had completely forgotten about the diamond ring that David had stolen and sold. Just before entering his place of residence, he had thought that serious matter to be the most important issue in the world, and now something else had overwhelmed him to such a degree that the matter looked like something trivial he could simply ignore.

The first thing he did the next morning was to contact the owner and discuss his problem with him before he was to be homeless. The owner looked determined not to show any sympathy and insisted that Simon arrange the money somehow and pay as usual if he wished to stay on.

"Just give me some respite, I promise to start paying the moment, I find some job." Simon pleaded.

"Job!" The owner exclaimed, and laughed before saying, "Which world have you come from Mr. Who will give you a job? What are you good at?" The man was cruel; he wouldn't let him keep even some of his illusions.

"I'll at least try to get some job, if I succeed or not is a different matter. You can throw me out if I fail, but please give me a chance." Simon went on trying. The man was unmoved; he couldn't let Simon stay without the surety of getting paid for the room.

"You must have some friends in this town from which you can borrow some money, or have some valuable things that you can leave with me as security." The owner gave him alternatives to ponder upon. Simon stood there mute and sad, even unable to confess that he knew none that could help him out, and that he owned no valuable stuff.

"Sorry man, you have to find some other place to live, your rent is paid till the end of the week, and after that period, you have to leave." The words of the owner seemed to be final. Simon knew there was no point to keep discussing or begging for any favors.

With an anguished heart, he went out from the Inn and started walking down the road, without any destination or plan. He felt a sense of urgency, but didn't know how to address the problem. He had thought to start looking for some employment after having his breakfast, but all of sudden he felt hopeless, the laughter of the owner of the Inn still ringing in his ears. The man was right -- it was not easy for a stranger to find a job and especially not in the current situation when unemployment was widespread in the town. He was hungry, but didn't want to spend the last few coins he had in his pocket. All day long, he kept walking on the roads and felt exhausted and starving. Many times he tried to enter some shops and ask for a job, but refrained from doing so, fearful of being ridiculed and rejected.

He didn't notice the sundown as he was completely absorbed by his thoughts, walking in his miserable state of mind. The outer darkness had somehow matched the inner gloom, and he kept walking like a blind person. All of a sudden, he stumbled and fell down. Someone had thrown banana peel in the middle of the pavement. He didn't stand up immediately but looked intently at the banana skin. It reminded him that he was terribly hungry and didn't have the strength to keep walking aimlessly. He was tempted to inspect the banana skin closely to see if there was some eatable part left in it but withdrew his hand immediately. He was shocked at experiencing such a strong impulse. He was in no hurry to get up and resume his walk. He was busy arguing with himself, what few coins alone were to change in his dire situation? Why he went hungry while he still had time and the possibility to get a meal? He got up from the ground and looked a bit relaxed; he had made up his mind: he was having a proper dinner instead of going hungry.

Simon went to his favorite restaurant and ordered his meal and waited impatiently for it. When it finally came, he ate as if he had been starving for a long time. After filling his stomach, he felt a bit relaxed and less worried about the next meal or other worries. He was too tired to keep walking aimlessly and decided to head for the Inn, where he intended to go straight to bed as he was getting sleepy after the food. He saw the owner sitting at his desk, but had no intention of starting a new discussion with him. He still had three days to live in the Inn and what was to happen after that, was still in the stars, so why worry, he thought before going into his room.

It was the last day of his stay in the Inn, and still he had failed to acquire a job or find an alternative place to live. Simon and the owner had avoided each other, well aware that there was nothing further to discuss. It was when Simon took his few belongings out of his room and started walking to the entrance that his eyes met the face of the owner who pretended not to notice him. It seemed he had little interest in Simon or his hopeless situation. Simon silently sneaked out and started walking along the path, without having the slightest idea, where he was headed. He heard someone calling his name, and he turned to find the owner standing outside the Inn gesturing at him to come back.

"I'm just curious; did you find some place to live?" The owner asked in the same serious tone as he always had. Simon just shook his head, as he didn't find the strength to speak.

"That's a pity, you seem to be a fine person." The owner mumbled, but then asked where he was heading. Simon just shrugged his shoulders and looked miserable. For the first time, Simon could see that the owner wasn't as heartless as he had shown till then. The man regarded him for a while, looking worried. Simon was certain that it couldn't be more than a temporary change, where the man was struggling with his conscience, but was equally sure that ultimately pure reason and practical issues would get the upper hand. The owner was a tough person who had a business to run; therefore he couldn't afford to be humane, Simon reasoned to himself.

"I don't know why I care about you and want to help," the owner muttered again as if he talked to himself. "There are many homeless out there, and your joining them shouldn't be a concern for me and yet I can't help worrying about you." Simon looked astonished and wondered what possibly could have made the man change his attitude. He didn't know what to expect from the owner. He waited for a few moments, but the owner kept silent and just watched him with sad eyes. It was clear the man had given him his compassion, but more than that he wasn't ready to offer. Simon thanked the man for his concern and told him that he believed that one way or the other things would turn out better ultimately.

"Come in, we can have a little chat, but don't misunderstand me, I'm not offering you any help." He made it clear. Simon stood reluctantly, considering whether to follow the man or keep going his way. He was a polite fellow and besides had no hurry to leave from there, so he followed the owner into his office.

"Tell me, are you on the run?" The owner asked, looking straight into his eyes.

"Why? No, absolutely not."

"Then what are you doing here? Why didn't you stay in your home town and work there instead?" The owner was determined to know everything about Simon. Simon kept silent and just stared at the floor. He was reluctant to talk about his personal life and yet there was not a chance in a million that he would get any help from a stranger without telling the truth. After few moments' contemplation, he decided to confide in the owner and told him all about his reasons for being on the road. The man scrutinized him keenly while he spoke and could easily determine that the young man was not fabricating the story. He wore a sad, sarcastic smile on his face when Simon stopped talking.

"You're nothing but a fool; I would never have behaved like you. Look at you, you left everything behind to search for some stupid, careless idiot who even has some criminal inclinations."

"He is my brother, and as an elder brother, it's my duty to look after him." Simon felt forced to defend himself.

"Even if no one wants your help? Even if the person in question is an adult?" The owner looked amused. Simon knew that he couldn't justify his actions that were driven by his feelings, so he remained silent.

"Take my friendly advice and return to your home and live your life instead of roaming around the world searching for your brother. Believe me; he will come back one day, after learning that there is no place like home." The man advised him without putting any emphasis on his words. Simon told him that the search for his brother was soon coming to an end as he had learned about the whereabouts of David. The man didn't say anything about the matter and instead asked how Simon planned to survive in his hopeless circumstances. Simon's silence made him sigh, and he said. "I know, I'll hate myself for breaking the rule, not to get involved in others' problems, but here I am, offering you some help." He kept silent for a few moments before continuing. "You know I live off this business, so giving you back your room is out of the question, but I can give you a possibility to sleep during night time. I work till late, but if it's okay, you can use my office for sleeping purposes." The man was quite unsure. It seemed he was making the decision reluctantly. He made it clear that he hoped the arrangements were to be of a temporary nature, and Simon would move from there as quickly as possible for him.

"Now you've got a roof over your head, but you still have to sustain yourself by your own means. Keep looking for a job, you are young and strong, so I'm sure someone will give you work to do."

Simon looked in disbelief at the man who had just offered him such great help, and he grabbed the hand of the man and said that he would never forget his kind gesture. The man looked embarrassed and wanted the whole discussion to come to an end so that he could return to his business.

"You can place your belongings in the store and don't forget that this possibility to stay over here is not without a counter performance." The man added, making Simon worry. He didn't know if the man had consciously withheld some important information from him or he had just changed his mind.

"I'll happily do anything in return." Simon told him.

"No, I won't be charging you any money, but I would expect you to give me a helping hand, whenever I may need it. Are you good with that?"

"I will happily assist you, whenever you want me to."
Simon said and looked both happy and thankful.

"Go, and look for a job now," the man asked him in a
polite but firm way before he stood up from his chair.
"Don't forget to come before seven pm if you don't want
to miss your dinner," he said casually, without making it
sound like a formal invitation.

5

The owner of the Inn was much nicer and kinder than he was ready to show to others. Simon found him caring and generous in his own peculiar way. He insisted on Simon eating his dinner with him, thus saving him the hungering and suffering. Despite his vague suggestion, he never asked Simon to do anything in return for his favour; on the contrary, he had asked many of his acquaintances to think of the young man, if they needed a helping hand. The man spent most of his time at the Inn and didn't like to discuss his personal life with anyone. Simon was prudent enough not to ask many questions either. Now he had been sleeping in Richard's office for almost four weeks without finding any employment or a place of residence and felt ashamed. All his efforts to find work failed, and he knew that one day even Richard's patience would run out. He thought that it would be a good idea to discuss the hopeless situation with Richard rather than wait for the day when he would be forced to confront the issue in some unpleasant manner.

"Don't worry, keep trying, I promise not to throw you out on the street." Richard told him in his usual serious tone and went on, "I know now that you're a responsible person and not a parasite trying to live on others. I'm also aware of the job situation out there, but remain confident that sooner or later you will find some kind of work."

"I feel ashamed of being a burden on you," Simon spoke and looked ashamed.

"You aren't, this corner of the office you sleep over, can't provide me with any income anyway." Richard joked and smiled for the first time since Simon met him.

"I consume even your food." Simon tried to remind him.

"Do you think I give you some kind of courtesy, by offering you the food? Forget it; it's simply my trick to get some time to eat. Before you came, I used to eat half as much as I do nowadays." Richard was in a good mood and he wished Simon to feel comfortable, so he told him to relax and not worry about anything but to find out what he wanted from life. He asked Simon if he had contemplated lately on the matter of his brother and an eventual search for him. Simon told him that his determination to go and find his brother was unalterable. Richard smiled and agreed with him that one always needed to follow the heart, no matter how many hindrances lay in the way. He didn't question the sanity of his decision as he had suspected.

"It's your call and only you can determine what is right or wrong for you. I can just wish you well." Richard told him as he concluded the discussion but added in a warning. "Don't wait too long, if you intend to find your brother, things can change quickly."

"You're absolutely right, but I must earn some money before I can move in that direction." Simon tried to explain his position.

"I know that, but there is no job in sight, when and how will you be able to earn enough and save that kind of money?"

"Perhaps I should increase my efforts." Simon told him with determination in his eyes.

"You have even another possibility, get some money from me and start moving." Richard made an offer.

"How can I misuse your kindness, it's simply out of the question."

"Pay me back, if and when you have it." Richard provided him with another option.

"Imagine I never come this way again!" Simon looked skeptical about the idea.

"Then consider it as a gift from me." Richard seemed to have made up his mind.

"Why this kindness?" Simon asked, astonished.

"Don't think I make such offers to everyone? In some strange manner I consider you as my own and want to be helpful." Richard tried hard and seemed to have succeeded in convincing him that in the prevailing circumstances, it was the best option, but he was wrong. Richard smiled broadly when he looked in Simon's eyes that shone with joy.

"I am really touched by your kindness, but there is no chance that I accept your offer. I'm already deeply indebted," Simon said, and looked determined.

Simon was strolling when he saw the owner of the restaurant where he used to eat his meals before, standing outside his place. Their eyes met and Simon greeted him with a smile. The owner tried hard to recognize him.

"I believe I know you, are you one of my customers?" he asked.

"Yes, I used to come and eat here, but don't do it anymore."

"Have you gotten married and eat at home or have you found some better restaurant?" The owner asked frankly.

"No, I have stopped visiting the place because I simply don't have the money to spend." Simon told him with a smile and the owner looked impressed by his honest reply.

"I'll not ask why you don't have money to eat and how do you sustain yourself without money, but do come in and be my guest," the owner offered.

"That's very generous of you, but no thanks; I will eat later with someone who has been extremely kind to me for a long time," Simon told the amused man.

"I don't insist, do as it pleases you. It's really nice of you to think of the person who provides for you tonight, but promise to eat your dinner tomorrow at my place," the elderly man said.

"I'll try, but can't promise you."

"I hope you'll manage," the man said before entering his place to resume his work.

When Simon resumed his walk, he still had a smile on his face. He had the habit of appreciating the kind gestures of strangers. How little it required to make others happy, he thought. He had no intention of coming back for dinner the next day and yet he couldn't help feeling happy for the offer. Suddenly he was struck with the idea that he could return and ask the man if he could offer him a job. He wanted to retrace his steps, but refrained; it simply didn't feel the right thing to do.

The next day he told Richard that he wouldn't be eating his dinner with him before he left. Richard looked astonished, but didn't ask for details. Simon could imagine what he thought and explained about the invitation he had received. He smiled and said that it was a right decision to go out and eat for a change.

"Why don't you ask the man, he may be able to provide you some employment?" Richard asked.

"The idea struck me yesterday. I'll inquire if I get a chance to do so," Simon told him.

"You know, I would have given you the job immediately if I had such a possibility," Richard told him.

"I don't doubt it, but then you're already doing much for me and I'm thankful," Simon said with a smile.

When Simon came to the restaurant, he was told that the owner was not there for the moment and no one knew when he would come back either. Simon decided to wait for a few minutes, so he went out and stood few meters away from the restaurant. He was watching the crowd that passed towards all possible directions and felt amused to be a tiny part of that stream. At a distance he saw two policemen going with a handcuffed young man, his heart leapt to his throat, as from a distance the young fellow looked like David. He panicked and rushed towards the policemen and carefully looked at the face of the prisoner. It was not David, but someone not even remotely resembling his brother. Why he thought the person to have been David, he couldn't tell, but certainly he felt relieved. Slowly he returned to the place he had stood and waited for the restaurant owner. After one hour's waiting in vain he thought there wasn't any point in continuing standing there. Simon was about to leave when he saw the owner coming out of the restaurant He became astonished and wondered why he was told that the owner was out on some errand. He decided to go away from there instead of moving towards the owner. As he was about to turn, the owner caught sight of him and waved at him. Simon found no other option but to go and meet him. "So it was you who came looking for me. My employees told me that someone wanted to meet me. I'm happy that you could make it, come, we go in and sit down and talk." The man was speaking in a friendly manner. Simon watched him closely and couldn't find the slightest trace of falsehood in the person's behavior.

"When did you come back?" Simon asked.

"Can't be more than half an hour ago," the man replied briefly, and that was exactly the time that Simon had rushed to look at the prisoner walking along with the policemen.

"What would you like to order?" the man asked.

"To be honest, the reason for my coming is not to have a free dinner," Simon was straight.

"What brought you here then?" the owner asked, surprised.

"I know you have a business that goes well, I wonder if you could offer some kind of a job to me. You see, I'm in a kind of desperate need of it." The owner became silent and thought carefully before he opened his mouth.

"I'll be as honest as I can in giving you my response, but I insist that you eat first. We can have a chat afterwards," the man said in a serious tone, and Simon could guess that he couldn't expect a positive answer. The owner excused himself and went to the kitchen, promising to come back as soon as it was possible for him to do so.

The waiter brought some drink for him and then served him some delicious food. The heavenly food reminded him why he used to come and eat his meals over there. It was unusually many guests at the place that day, so the owner didn't come until it became a bit calmer with the new guests. He looked tired and yet smiled broadly when he came and sat beside him.

"It was delicious food, like it always is!" Simon gave him the compliments and added, "Thanks for the lovely dinner."

"It's my pleasure. I already feel rewarded," the man said with a smile.

"How?" Simon didn't understand.

"By the presence of these unusual crowds." The owner whispered and laughed softly. Simon smiled as well. They sat and chatted for a while until the man came to Simon's request.

"You can see that my business goes well and for that reason I have employed many people. Like all other businesses, even this business of mine has its ups and downs. Sometimes, it's a rush like today, while at other times; I'm forced to struggle hard to break even." The man looked apologetic and Simon knew what to expect.

The man was talking about his difficulties in calculating his labor needs and for that reason sometimes he had a shortage of workers, while at other times there was an excess. He wished to know some magic way of knowing it all beforehand. He talked about his carefulness in employing new people, as it was always extra hard for him to lay off the excess labour. He spoke as if all his employees were like part of his large family and he felt personally responsible for them. The man said that he would have loved to help Simon but couldn't do that at the moment because there was no vacant job. Simon could see that the man was not just presenting some lame excuses, but was telling the truth.

"I understand your position, don't worry about me, I'll find some job sooner or later." Simon felt sorry for burdening his host with personal problems.

"I really want to help you, but don't know how," the man said and looked worried.

"I got an idea, and only you can tell if it is feasible or not."

"Tell me, I'm attentive." The man became eager.

When Simon gave him his proposition, the man pondered in complete silence and looked at his guest at the same time.

"You don't mind taking the trouble?" the man finally inquired.

"No, I'll be happy to give it a try," Simon assured his host.

"Alright, we have a deal then." The owner smiled and shook hands with Simon.

Simon had listened to the owner's difficulties and presented a solution he couldn't refuse. For him, it was a wonderful option to offer Simon a job when the circumstances demanded so. Simon was willing to come each day and check if his services were required or not. He was to be a standby worker, available when the need arose. The owner knew that extra help was always difficult to arrange on short notices, simply because of practical reasons, so an intermittent like Simon could save him much trouble.

Simon was happy to find the possibility to work, but didn't know that he lacked the experience of physical work. What looked like an easy task proved to be effort consuming and much more tiring than he could have anticipated. He could see the co-workers smiling covertly when he made mistakes, but he was determined not to give up his brave struggle to overcome his shortcomings and inexperience. He noticed that he couldn't lift heavy weights, became easily tired even after performing some small task, and therefore exerted more effort than his colleagues. He had been working there for two weeks, and still found it difficult to get used to his new routine. The situation made him depressed, and he started thinking about quitting the job that seemed to be beyond his capacities, but dared not talk to Michael about his brooding. Strangely, he was able to work every day, as the business went as never before. Simon felt crushed by the work burden, but kept struggling. He was dead tired when he came to the Inn to sleep, and didn't know a thing till he woke up in the morning. He had hardly spoken to Richard since he started the work, but Richard seemed not to mind Simon's getting busy. On the contrary, he was happy that Simon was fighting bravely to achieve his set goals.

One day Simon was busy helping the chef in the kitchen and worked as effectively as it was possible for him. The chef was busy putting food on plates, when he remembered that the food on the fire was done and needed to be removed. He asked Simon to remove the large kettle away from the fire. Simon looked nervously at the kettle and didn't know if he could manage such a task, as he knew that the food pot was heavy.

"Remove it quickly!" The chef shouted, making Simon more nervous than he already was. Simon finally moved in a quick manner and tried to lift the kettle. He got a few splashes of hot sauce on his hand and almost dropped the container. He immediately placed it on the nearest counter, but spilt quite a bit of the sauce. The chef looked angry, but didn't shout as he used to do otherwise.

"I'm sorry, the pot was too heavy and then it splashed." Simon tried to excuse his clumsiness.

"Get lost, you are good for nothing, I don't know what an incompetent person like you is doing here in the first place." The chef was poisonous in his words. Simon looked hurt, but knew that the man was not completely wrong.

"Clean the mess and go do something else. I'll be fine without you." The chef was not forgiving.

As Simon cleaned the bench and floor, he saw Michael coming to the kitchen, but avoided looking at the owner. Michael pretended he didn't know what was going on there and left the kitchen after a few moments.

At night before going home, Simon told Michael that he wouldn't be coming in the next day. He was asked if he had some important matter to take care of. He was blunt and honest and replied that he was quitting the job, as he didn't want to be a burden.

"We all are tired after a hectic day, why don't you come

tomorrow, so we can take the matter up then," Michael suggested, and Simon agreed to be there the next day.

"Try to come a few minutes earlier if it's possible, I want to have this meeting without others around." Michael told him before he left the restaurant.

When Simon came to the restaurant no one was there, he waited until Michael came at his usual time. He looked surprised to find Simon sitting and waiting for him, it seemed he had completely forgotten that he was supposed to meet him there.

"Now you can tell me what this is about you quitting your job."

"I know you all are kind people and are doing everything to help me and even accommodate me, but I've realized that I'm good for nothing and for that reason I don't want to go on exploiting your kindness."

"Are you referring to the incident that took place in the kitchen yesterday?" Michael asked calmly.

"Yes, but that's just the tip of the iceberg. I am clumsy." Simon was hard on himself.

"Yeah, you are certainly not a physical person and make many mistakes, but aren't we all prone to mistakes? How can we learn if we don't make mistakes?" Michael spoke without trying to sound wise and went on. "You must remember that accidents do happen, even for the most experienced people, so stop being hard on yourself."

"I understand the chef's anger..."

"Forget about the arrogant fool, I surely would have kicked him out if he was not as good as he is." The man is blessed and therefore can cook delicious food, but as a human being he is rotten," Michael said patting his shoulders and smiled.

"Be honest and tell me, do you think I am hopeless?"

Simon asked.

"Would I be sitting here and convincing you to stay, if I thought so?" Michael said and made a point.

"I see that you are struggling hard to learn, and that's a guarantee that you will succeed. Now get back to your work and conquer it. Be merciless!" Michael said with a laugh, he was trying to uplift Simon's spirit.

Simon worked wholeheartedly and tried his best to avoid repeating past mistakes. He was aware of his physical weakness, but soon learned to overcome that handicap by using better techniques His meeting with Michael had given him some new incentive, some deeper insight and most of all, much needed confidence. He was ever ready to step in wherever he found it was required; it could be the kitchen, the store or the eating place. He was there long before others came and always found something important to perform. Michael was very impressed by Simon's work and never told him that his services were not required. He had developed a liking for Simon both as a being and a hard worker. He was generous enough to confess that Simon's arrival at his place had been beneficial for his business. There was almost no wastage anymore, the place always looked tidy and inviting and most of all Simon could replace every single person working in the restaurant, which was indeed the greatest blessing of all. Simon's hard work soon earned him the respect of his fellow workers. Even those of the workers who saw his presence as a threat realised soon that the young man was not there to harm anybody's interests but only tried to make things easier for them all. Michael understood soon that Simon was an asset he needed to use cleverly, so he offered him a manager's post. Simon felt honored, but reluctant to take the job.

"Why not?" Michael was astonished by the young man's

reluctance.

"You see, I'm quite new over here, many of my colleagues regard me as pushy, an intruder, so making me the manager is not a good idea. They all would hate me." Simon tried to explain his fears.

"I like the way you function, and it's exactly for that reason I believe you to be best suited for the job. You are considerate; you're structural, and most of all a good-tempered person, showing respect to all but firm in your decisions." Michael was not impressed by his arguments, he continued. "In the beginning, I too thought you to be cunning, who tried his best to create a job here, but now I know better that you did all that without expecting any reward and that knowledge has enhanced my evaluation of you as a person."

Simon listened to him, but remained pondering; he still didn't want the job.

"There's another thing, which stops me from taking the job."

"What's that?" Michael asked.

"It would be dishonest of me to take a responsibility and then not fulfill it." Simon told him and then elaborated by telling his employer that he intended to work and save money, and then he planned to be on his way.

"I didn't know you had plans to move on, where do you intend to move towards and why?" Michael said and waited for his answer with interest.

When Simon told him about his quest, he listened keenly and smiled.

"I won't be happy to lose a worker like you, but I won't try to stop you either. The only thing I can say is that with the salary of a manager, you will get closer to your quest."

"So you don't mind that I'll just be releasing you from your responsibilities only for a brief period of time?"

"No, not at all, every single day you are here you make things easier for us all and I just hope that by the time it's the moment for you to move on, the place will be more structured and manageable."

Simon worked there till he had saved enough money to move on. Michael thought that Simon could keep working there and save even more money, but he politely declined the offer, well aware that Michael would keep increasing his salary and thus make it more difficult for him to leave the life of certainty and security and enter into the unknown. He was fond of Michael, Richard and their families and therefore found it hard to take leave, but his mission to bring back his brother was stronger than anything else. Richard, Michael and all his colleagues wished him the best of luck when he finally took their leave.

6

After a long and tedious travel, he finally reached his destination and felt excited by the perspective of seeing David. He was aware that finding the whereabouts of his brother in the city wasn't going to be an easy task, but as long as he remained convinced that David was there, he wouldn't care about the difficulties. People of that town were quite rude and unhelpful, and that was indeed a discouraging discovery. Simon didn't mind their rudeness, thinking that his stay there was not going to be a long one. He intended to search for David as quickly as possible and then to convince him to come back home.

It was getting dark, and he still had not found any reasonable place to check in. It was quite warm, and he easily could sleep outdoors, but the warning words of Richard reverberated in his ears. He had cautioned Simon always to stay indoors during the nights as one never knew what could happen in the dark of the night. Simon knew that his little money wouldn't last long in that town, which was quite expensive as compared to the places he had recently been to. After sometimes indecision, he decided to stay at an Inn. After making a check in, he ate a meal and realized that he was terribly tired, so he went to his bed and slept. When he woke up, he was fresh and rested. Before leaving the Inn, he asked the manager how he could find a person he didn't have any address of. The manager laughed and told him that no such service was available in the town. Simon didn't like the way the manager tried to ridicule him, but kept silent and left without asking any further questions.

Just after one day's experience, he had learned that he

was just ridiculing himself by asking people about David and his whereabouts. He found it difficult to describe his brother to strangers as the portrayal was too vague and could fit any young man. He just shrugged his shoulders when people asked him if his brother had a beard, mustaches or was a clean shave, and many such like details, about which he had no idea. He had not seen David for a long while and didn't know how he looked these days, and by which name he had settled down in that town.

"How do you know the person you seek lives in this town?" someone asked him.

"Some trader from this town told me that."

"Why didn't that trader provide you with an address?" the same man asked.

Simon knew that there was no point elaborating and telling the story again and again to every single person he inquired about David. He felt quite disheartened and decided to search more discretely from that point on. He roamed around the town, vigilantly watching all the young people he came across, visited the kind of places David was fond of and was especially observant to the gangs, he was sure that David only could be found among some group as he was of a herd mentality. He was on the trudge all day long and came back to the Inn, just to have a night's sleep.

It had been raining the whole day, so Simon was forced to stay indoors. To stay in his windowless room was not something he would have preferred but there wasn't any choice. He stayed in x bed and thought about his life and felt miserable. He was young and energetic, and what he did with all his energies was not something he could be proud of. For a long time, he had kept searching for his brother and doing that he had gained nothing but miseries and sufferings. What bothered him most was the fact that David was neither aware nor cared about his wretched situation. The initial joy to get closer to his brother was replaced with the awareness that he was as far from his brother as he had been for a long time. "What! I can't give up like that, especially when I may be just few steps away from David," he tried to get out of the gloom and succeeded by remembering his promise given to his dying mother.

It kept raining the whole night and even the next day, forcing Simon to stay there, where he was. He couldn't afford to go out in the rain, get wet and become sick. Even his old shoes had big holes in the soles, and he knew that the wet shoes and clothes were a bad combination if he wished to remain healthy. The rain offered him a respite, and the opportunity to ponder, even if he didn't want it.

"Go, get a life." He was advised by some insignificant inner voice, but he instantly rejected it. "That's the only right thing for me to do," he insisted.

Why do you blame yourself for the actions of David? What makes you believe that David will voluntarily follow you back to your hometown? Even if he did, don't you think he will be become more headstrong after getting the knowledge that you are weak for him? What would you do if he returns on the condition that you give him the house? He kept thinking, and it became clearer and clearer that his entire search was futile and non-realistic, and yet he remained determined to seek David. "Come what may, I'll not abandon you, my brother," Simon said loudly.

In the evening when it finally stopped raining, Simon looked out at the muddy pathways and became reluctant to go and walk, but the mud covered roads and puddles here and there couldn't stop him from venturing out. It was encouraging to know that he wasn't the only one who walked down the pathway; there were quite a lot of other people around, as well. He walked aimlessly without caring about his wet feet as the mud had easily entered his shoes. From afar, he noticed a few young people standing in one spot, busy discussing something. When he got closer, he could hear their loud voices and laughter. It reminded him of David and his friends. For a brief second, he halted and wanted to inquire about his brother from those young men, but then he remembered his decision to stop indulging in such fruitless activities. The group must have noticed his indecision as one of them signed him to come towards the group. Without thinking twice, he went towards the young people, who looked at him a bit surprised.

Simon had hardly opened his mouth to ask about his brother, when two strong hands grabbed him by the arms and wouldn't let go. The strong and tall boy was shouting at him, and he didn't understand anything. Simon realized that the situation was threatening, and regretted his stupidity to seek contact with the group.

"You are hurting me, what I have done to provoke you?" Simon asked sheepishly.

"What have you done!" The strong boy asked in a sarcastic manner, and the entire company laughed.

"I have been looking for you for some time now. Do you think that by removing your beard, you will fool us? Give me my money or I'll break your neck." The tall guy was aggressive. Simon tried to convince him that there was some kind of misunderstanding, but no one seemed to be convinced. Simon went on pleading until one of the boys came forward and turned sleeve of his shirt from the right arm. They all looked surprised.

"What did you do with the tattoo?" Asked one of the

young men.

"I told you, you are mistaken, I'm not the one you are looking for." He said and felt the grip of the strong hands loosening. He should have kept silent and just walked away, but instead he stood there and asked many questions about the person they thought him to be.

"Why are you so interested in the scum?" One of them asked suspiciously.

"I'm curious." Simon lied. No one believed him, but kept scrutinizing him.

"You must be the brother of David, right?" said one of them finally with a derisive smile. Simon had no other choice but to confess the truth.

"That explains everything, so you are the softy brother," said someone and they all laughed.

"I'll be very much obliged if you can help me find my brother, I'll be extremely thankful," Simon pleaded.

"If we only could get hold of him, he would regret the day he was born," the tall young man said in an equal aggressive manner.

"If you help me to find my brother, I promise to make him pay your debts back." Simon tried to make a deal." The group laughed with amusement.

"You don't need to convince us that you have great influence over your brother, we already know. On the other hand, it's not a bad idea that you pay the debts of your brother, we know you owe him his inheritance."

"Which inheritance?" Simon looked shocked. "Didn't David tell you that we were raised by a poor, single parent?"

"Very good, you are a softy, but very cunning. Stop playing games and give us what you owe to your brother or we will beat you black and blue," said someone before encircling him.

Simon felt very nervous seeing all the ways to escape closing on him. He had stopped placing his money in the room after the last experience and always carried his money on him and therefore, was afraid of losing it at the hands of these young people.

"I don't have any money, but promise to pay you back when I get it from somewhere." He tried once again to get out of the situation.

"We don't have time for trickeries, search him properly and confiscate whatever he carries with him," the tall man said. Two of the young men started searching him and soon all his money was in their hands. The tall man wasn't impressed with Simon's a small amount of money.

"It's not even half of the amount your brother owes me, but it's better than nothing."

"Please don't rob me, I need this money in order to move on and search for my brother," Simon pleaded, well convinced that his begging was not going to touch the hearts of those young people.

"Go home, forget about David, he is not like you; you will never be able to win his respect. He is wild like us, a beast, a predator and not a wimp like you," one of them said, feeling pity for him before they all quickly dispersed and went their way.

"Don't try to be funny, we aren't robbing you but are just taking that what David owes to us. If you go to the police, we will not be as nice as we are right now." Simon stood there shocked and devastated, without any clue as to what to do next. He felt angry with himself for coming out of the Inn, for carrying the entire money on him and most of all for lingering there instead of immediately going his way, when he got released by the tall, strong man. He had no strength to keep walking. With tearful eyes, he stood and wondered if it was his own stupidity or was it destiny that kept dragging him deeper and deeper into some marshland. It was the second time he had lost his money, and therewith stood without any chance of bringing his stay in this city to a successful conclusion. Simon knew that he couldn't just stand there for all eternity, but needed to think clearly and find some way out this impossible situation. He had no desire to keep walking, so he turned and started going towards the Inn, convinced that the sole purpose of his coming out was to get robbed. He wouldn't have minded losing all the money again, only if the robbers had provided him with the whereabouts of David. What he did realize was that David no longer lived in that city, but had moved to some unknown quarters, but before doing that he had made fools of quite a few people and collected some debts. He had always wondered how David could manage to borrow money even from those who knew that he lacked the possibility to give the money back.

All night Simon couldn't sleep. He was devastated and broke, knowing that he couldn't afford to live in the inn. There was no motivation left as he was perfectly aware that David no longer lived over there. He could make a guess as to which direction his brother may have taken flight, but there was no point, he had decided to head in a direction at random and live his life wherever it was meant to be. Two incidents in a row where he was robbed of all his savings were an omen that he needed to abandon his search for David. Going back to his native country was not an option, as he was a stranger there as he could be anywhere else in the world.

The first thing in the morning he did was to talk to the manager of the Inn and tell him that he was moving away. The manager refused to refund the rent, insisting that it was against their policy.

"What happened? Why you are leaving in such a hurry, have you encountered some kind of trouble?" the young man asked, trying to understand Simon's hasty decision.

Simon didn't feel like narrating his story to anyone, but the manager could see that he was confounded.

"I have good connections with the authorities, just tell me what bothers you, I may be able to solve your problems," he offered. "With the right kind of money, one can always open even the closed doors."

His last words dissipated the confusion of Simon and a sad smile became visible on his worried face. He thanked the manager and set off on his journey towards his new unknown destination. As he was leaving the town, he could hear his conscience taunting him, but he tried to ignore it, well aware that no one could blame him for giving up the quest. Fate couldn't expect him to be robbed again and again, and yet keep doing the same thing until he dropped dead.

He felt a great unrest entering into his whole being, and functioning as a driving force. Simon sought after clarity, but instead, unknown forces kept dragging him further and further away from the city he had lived and loved once. He met thousands of people and learned new things, gained new experiences and felt richer in knowledge, but nothing could satisfy his yearning soul for very long. He had not completely rid himself of his thoughts about David but somehow he had accepted the possibility of never seeing him again. Traveling without money had made him tougher and now he could sleep in the wilderness, could live without food and water for days and survive in tougher climates. He was simply a person born anew.

Despite all his difficulties, he had remained positively

inclined and learned that sufferings were not there to break one apart but to make one strong and resilient. He realized that the bookish world was far behind him, and yet his compelling thirst for knowledge was very much there. He was still very keen to learn about the tangible world, but the thirst to know about the subtle and unknown was some new development. He realised that there were very few people who could satisfy such a need in him. He was no longer able to get access to the world of books, which he occasionally missed, but on the other hand, he was reading the living books around him, which were more interesting as it involved his participation. He realised that the world was full of kind, good hearted and generous people. His fellow beings were fantastic, cared for him. They attended to his needs and wished him well. Those beings loved him, though he was just a stranger among them. He was amazed to realise, how most of his fears before setting off on his journey, where he was robbed twice, were baseless. Not for a single day, had he suffered hunger or thirst. If he was out of money, then work awaited him. Perhaps the bad luck had finally left him in peace, he would think with a smile.

7

Months passed, and his moving ahead continued. He would stay in one place just as long as his heart was at rest, and then it was time to move on to some unknown, undiscovered place ahead. He had turned into a man without belongings, a man who was without any home to go to, a person without any long-lasting friends and relatives to care and worry about. He was a man without any responsibilities, a man without any bonds. At times, this realisation made him relaxed and happy, but at other times it was a killer, a reminder of his loneliness and state of non-belonging.

One day he came across a group of people who were travelling in the same direction he intended to pursue. When he asked for permission to join them, they happily agreed. All day long, they travelled and spoke little with each other. At dusk, they reached a village, where the very hospitable and kind people offered them food and space to spend the night. They thankfully accepted the hospitality that they were offered. The villagers were interested in learning where they were coming from and where they intended to continue from there. They had much news to exchange before they were left in peace to rest and sleep. After dinner, they all sat down and started talking about different things. It seemed that they all had much to impart. When someone spoke, the others listened with great care and attention as if not to miss any detail. Simon was listening to them with awe and respect, silently admiring their knowledge and experience as he always did on such occasions. He became more attentive when one man started telling them about a legendary kingdom. He was describing the wonders and the beauties of this strange place. Whether it was the charming style of the man or whether it was the enthralling story, or both of these factors, he could not say. The only thing he could tell with certainty was that they were all listening to the man with great interest. The man was a master storyteller. Simon was picturing the place as if he could see it with his own eyes.

"According to the legend, that place has sky-high mountains around it. These mountains are of pure gold so when the sun rises and its rays strike these golden rocks, there is a blinding illumination, with so much power and energy that it can burn all life which tries to enter this wonderful place. In this incredible valley there are trees and flowers of indescribable beauty and variety. Those birds and animals, which have long been extinct from our world and are no more in our memories, can still be found there. In this valley, there is never any scorching heat, nor is there any cold. There are neither any predators nor any prey in that fantastic place. Everywhere there are springs from which sweet water splashes and one can see beautiful crystals, rubies, diamonds, pearls and many other valuable jewels lying about everywhere. This valley is a kind of its own. But all ways leading to it are well guarded, and no being can enter it."

"Why is it guarded so vigilantly?" asked one voice.

"Because this valley is pure, containing in it not only many treasures, but also secrets of life. It's a sanctuary for those shapes of life, which have been and there are the seeds of new shapes that are going to be. There is no death in this valley, so it has to be guarded against the impure and evil."

"What do you mean by no death?" Simon asked.

"In this valley, there is even a "spring of life" which contains qualities and energies that award the drinker eternal health and immortality. "So you can understand where there is a spring of "life- giving water" how could there be any death?" said the man smiling. The company was tired and sleepy and had a long journey ahead, so they decided to go to sleep.

Simon couldn't sleep all night. He kept thinking about the valley of the legend with all the qualities, beauties, and wonders attributed to it. "Legends are just legends," some fabulous stories. He tried many times to overcome his stormy thoughts, but couldn't. Just imagine if such a valley really exists, he thought with excitement. "What a pleasure it would be to view all the marvels of that place." Has there ever been any human being who has set foot in this valley and come back? Had anyone ever drunk its living water? If yes, would they still be living among other beings? How were they disguising their eternal lives from people living around them? He kept thinking deeper and deeper. How would it feel to be eternal and immortal, while living with people and other life forms that decayed and perished? There were no answers to his questions, he knew that perfectly well, but went on with his thoughts.

From that moment on, he was a changed man. Gone was the gloom and purposelessness that had been burdening him. Instead, he felt new energies creeping in his whole being. The restlessness and attraction of the roads had gotten a name, and for the first time he was convinced of his purpose and quest. Now he knew what he searched for and asked everyone he met if they had heard anything of the legend. Most of the people who knew the legend couldn't add anything new, but he never gave up. The search for this legendary valley dragged him from place to place, away from the familiar tracts to people of strange customs and languages. It was not an easy task, but nothing could halt his march. His determination could move mountains. Neither hunger nor thirst prevented him from his quest. He searched in the old books for any clues, and searched in the human habitations for those who could provide him with any information he lacked, and he looked for secluded places for those who might have special knowledge. But despite his entire search, he didn't have a breakthrough. No one could say for sure which direction he was supposed to move in. The information he had collected from the ancient books was confusing and contradictory. Some placed this valley in the direction of the North Pole and others just north of the equator. The location of the valley was the question with no apparent answer.

He sat hungry and completely exhausted under a tree. He felt sad, broken, and desperate, without the least hint what to do next. All his efforts were futile. His entire search was in vain. Am I a fool, searching for something, which does not exist? Trying to find something which is just an illusion. Chasing confused and unreal dreams. His doubts were not baseless. His doubts were disturbing, but quite logical as until then, he hadn't met a single soul who could claim to having been to that valley, or who could swear that it was really there.

The more he thought about the matter the more foolish and ridiculous it appeared, but his heart refused to give way. Right or wrong, sane or insane, Simon decided to go on with his research. "So, what if the valley never existed? What does it matter if I don't ever find that valley. At least I'll have the fun of an adventure." Somewhere between belief and disbelief, he continued his pledge. He had nothing to lose and everything to win if he succeeded.

One night he was looking for some suitable place to spend the night, Simon saw a light at a distance he knew there was a human presence there. He approached the place and found out that they were gypsies. When they came to know that he was looking for a place to spend the night, they offered him a bed, which he accepted with thanks. They gave him some food and water and started questioning him about where he was from and to which destination he was heading.

"I'm also a wanderer, never staying in one place for very long. And I don't know where my destination is," was his honest answer.

"Come and join us!" offered one young gypsy in a happy tone.

Simon just smiled. These gypsies were very lively and friendly people. They seemed to be in no hurry to move on and so was the case with Simon. He was tired and wished to rest and collect new energies before resuming his dubious search of the valley. The head of the family insisted on his being their guest as long as he wished to do so.

"The guest is a blessing in disguise, an omen of good tidings and a guarantee of enhanced possessions," they said.

It was not very difficult to convince Simon that by staying with them, he wasn't burdening them at all; on the contrary he was extending them a favour, a golden opportunity to better their economic well-being. Simon smiled at their insistence and agreed to stay with them for some time. They were happy with his decision and expressed their joy by singing and dancing, making him feel loved and desired.

The experience of living with the gypsies was unlike any he had ever had in his life. He could feel the love and warmth flowing freely between the members of that big family who spent all the long day in idleness, moving only when the need compelled them. He could see that they were not a lazy bunch who hated to work. They simply had different priorities and acted accordingly. Simon was soon an integral part of that big household, without even striving for it. He helped them in small matters and was fed in a simple manner. There was a natural division, a hierarchical order existing, where the senior member had the best rights and privileges and the young children had the least. It was the experience of life that mattered the most. What really touched his heart was the sense of belonging, a thing he had ever longed for and which had never existed in his life before.

Simon was the most popular person with the small children because he not only treated them in a gentle and respectful manner but also even gave them assistance in their tasks. He was allowed to break the order of things as long as it didn't disrupt the general structure of their household. He was admired for his bedtime story telling. The kids loved him and enjoyed his interesting way of narrating those tales. He noticed that his stories were not only well liked by the younger children, but even younger, and the older members of the family were equally enchanted by them. They all would sit beside the campfire and silently await his breathtaking stories.

"Where have you learned all these splendid stories?" the head of the family asked.

Simon got red in his face, seeing that everyone was staring at him, expecting an answer. "I have been always interested in reading." He gave them the honest reply.

He was talking about different stories, legends, and myths, arousing their interest, when suddenly it struck him to ask if the gypsies had heard of the legend of the valley. They shrugged their shoulders and shook their heads in negation. They could not answer for sure until he explained a little more closely.

"Please tell us about the legend," requested a child.

"It's late, perhaps some other time," Simon said. They all insisted on listening to it, leaving no choice for him, but to narrate his favourite story.

When he finished his story, they looked with puzzled eyes at him. One gypsy child said, "Yes, we have heard of it before, but isn't it just a story, like many others?"

"No, it's more than a story. It's a legend with some sort of truth in it," Simon tried to explain.

They all laughed heartily, and he felt embarrassed. One elderly became angry, shouted at them, and ordered them to shut up. They went on giggling every now and then. The elderly gypsy signed for him to come out of the tent and into the open.

They came out and started strolling near their camp. He apologised for the stupid behaviour of the young. "You know we live in a world where truth and falsehood are intermingled, so it's not easy to separate one from another. This legend, which you spoke of, is as old as humanity. The valley has as many names as the legends themselves. Maybe it's just a fabrication of the human mind, or perhaps it's very much there. Who am I to say anything for sure?" The old man halted.

"Now tell me honestly, are you looking for this legendary valley? Is that the cause of your wandering around?" He asked abruptly, and Simon could say nothing but "yes."

"Why?" the elderly man asked, very astonished. Simon couldn't find the proper words, which could explain his quest and motives behind it. "Look! If it's the riches and treasures of that place that attract you, I guarantee that if ever you even succeed in arriving, you'll not find them worth the trouble," the elder paused for a while, perhaps to look at Simon's face. Despite the dim light, he felt the penetrating eyes of the old man.

"If you seek the water of the spring of life to attain the eternal youth and immortality, I beg you to think twice, aren't our short miserable lives long enough for us to bear?"

Simon explained to the elderly that he did not seek the precious jewels or birds and animals of unknown kinds and shapes, but did want to come to the spring of life's water. He wanted to drink it and live forever. He told him that he hated death and wanted to become untouchable, unattainable, and invincible. The elder shook his head, shrugged his shoulders as if he was at a loss to understand his logic. He tried to convince Simon to abandon his meaningless search, offering him a calm and harmonious life with them, but Simon remained as unbendable as ever. The elderly gypsy smiled in a tired way, giving up on him, he had done his duty by giving warning and advice. They went inside the tent to sleep as most of the other members were already either sleeping or pretended to be.

He couldn't say how long he had been with the gypsies, was it weeks or perhaps even months; he was unable to provide the correct answer, simply because he had not kept the record of time. The separation proved to be a more emotional and painful task than he could have anticipated. Everyone was tearful and sad when he was to leave his new friends and family. They tried to persuade him to stay with them, if not forever, then at least for a short period more. However, he knew that staying any longer would just make the separation process more painful, so he told them politely that he was unable to fulfil their wish.

He wanted to go forward and take leave of all the members of that great family, but knew that it would take an eternity to do so, making the whole procedure a painful event. Instead, he spoke aloud, thanking them for all the love, care, warmth, and hospitality they had been offering to him during his remarkable time with them.

"Each and every one of you has given me a wonderful time, unforgettable memories of great magnitude and most of all you have taught me the real meaning of the word family and bonds between different members of it. I thank you all from the depths of my heart." Simon was not shy to open his heart and showing his host family the gratitude he felt. He avoided looking at their sad faces as it would make his leaving them harder. "Goodbye my friends I'll always keep you in mind." Simon said in a shaky voice and turned to go. Before Simon left the camp to go on his way, the elder came to his side and offered him company for a distance.

"I'm not sure of your motives for looking for the valley. I even doubt your wisdom, as it is not a sane activity. But I want to be of some service to you," the elderly gypsy told Simon with piteous eyes. "I have been in this world for many seasons, so believe me; it's not a blessing to live forever. However, you are young and see the world with different eyes than me, so I don't blame you for anything. I'm giving you an address of a man that you should meet. If there is anyone in this whole world that can help you, it is this man, and if he doesn't know about the valley then no one does. If he can't help you find it, then no one can." The elder explained how and where Simon could look for this person.

"Reaching this man won't be easy, but don't give up. Try to remember that all hardships and hurdles train you for your impossible task," the gypsy said with a broad smile, patting his back and wishing him good luck.

8

The recommended person lived in a faraway country that wasn't easy to reach. Simon decided to leave for that country immediately. Simon knew that without money and a quick mode of transportation it would take years before he could reach his destination. But what choices did he have? His movement was slow, meticulous, and dependent on multiple factors, such as weather conditions and availability of opportunities. The only thing that kept him moving or rather crawling was his unwavering willpower. Most of the time, he was lucky enough to meet kind and compassionate people. Sometimes, he came across some mean and unsympathetic people as well, who made his painstaking journey even harder than it already was.

One day, Simon was sleeping under a tree when he was awakened by a loud noise. It was early morning and he still felt sleepy. Before his eyes stood at least a dozen soldiers; some of them were mounted. They seemed to be discussing him. Their conversation was loud and harsh and so was their laughter. Simon could see that their intentions were not good. He smiled in a sheepish way, greeted them in his usual soft manner and tried to move.

"Where do you think you are going?" asked one soldier, making the others laugh.

"I'm a stranger heading for a distant land," Simon tried to sneak out of the situation.

"From now on you are no stranger to us and you have come home, to your destination," another soldier pushed him to other soldiers. They all laughed, looking at the frightened face of Simon. They were enjoying the frightened state of the new involuntary recruit. It didn't take long for Simon to understand that the soldiers were out in search of young and able men to enlist them in the army. There was war preparation and they needed as many soldiers as possible and it was even better if they were to be strangers or the ones taken into service by force, as it could be all free of charge.

Simon tried his best to get out of the terrible situation, giving all types of arguments, sometimes telling the soldiers that he was needed by his sick mother, who depended on him for her survival, and other times saying that he was not good at handling the weapons. Nothing stopped those soldiers from taking him. They seemed to be used to all of those petitions and begging as it was their daily routine, and some even were enjoying the whole situation. They didn't go to their quarters but were out on a hunt for other young persons they could kidnap. His hands were tied and he walked behind, forcing his tired body to keep up with the moving band. He was hungry, tired, and most of all humiliated by these degrading circumstances but had no choice but to drag his body forward.

The soldiers were only stopping when they pinpointed a new victim. Simon saw no point in his continued begging or argumentation with these heartless soldiers and was seriously worried about his difficult situation. By noon, the soldiers had captured more than twenty young men and seemed content. "I believe it's enough for today," said the one who appeared to be their leader.

"Unless we find more of such animals on the way back," added another soldier and they all burst into laughter. The joke was not without some truth in it, as they really added a few more people who were not even young.

"What would we do with these good-for-nothing creatures?" demanded the officer angrily.

"We need people to take care of other duties besides going out and fighting on the battlefield," he was told, and he liked the thoughtfulness of the soldier and praised him for that, in a grudging manner.

It was almost sunset when they came back to the army quarters, where the dinner was being prepared and served, making him realise that he hadn't eaten anything for a long time. He impatiently waited for the food, which was never served. Strangely, the captives of the day were completely ignored, if it was just a coincidence or done deliberately, he was unable to determine. They were all pushed into a small room and were locked in for the rest of the night, where they cried and groaned, tormented by hunger, sores, and fatigue. Every one of them was completely absorbed by his own suffering and misfortune and had little thought to spare for his fellow captives. Simon didn't sleep for a second, as it was impossible to do so with all his body aching and the distressed sounds of his fellow prisoners. All they had gotten on their arrival was water, which was now vaporising in sweat.

In the morning, they were attended to and treated little differently. A young officer greeted them and asked if they were well taken care of. There was a complete silence before an angry outcry of indignation replaced the stillness of the place. The officer smiled at the reaction of his audience, as if he had anticipated it. He ignored their protest and told them that the treatment they could expect from that point on depended on their acceptance or rejection of the situation they were in.

"We'll treat you well if you cooperate and adjust to your new realities, but if you chose to resist or try to escape,

the doors of hell shall be opened to you." He sounded clear in his message, making no secret of his intentions of turning them into an effective fighting force. "Many of you might not be good at the use of weapons, but don't worry. We shall make you all into strong men and capable soldiers. If we are wrong in our assumption that we have selected the right people and fail to materialise our goals concerning you, then we shall not waste a single loaf of bread on you." He smiled maliciously and added, "Those of you who are of no use to us can't hope and expect to go alive from here, we'll swiftly free them from their misery."
The young officer's cold, calculated words were entering their ears like a sharpened sword that cut to the bone. They were getting the message loud and clear; they had to adjust to their new life or they were to perish.

Simon was caught between two alternatives: he could accept his fate by becoming a soldier and die in fighting some ruler's ambitious war or he could die resisting his captors. Both of these choices were nothing more than choosing between cholera and a noose. Suddenly, a third option struck his mind, making him a bit hopeful. He could consider the possibility of escaping that well-guarded place, but in order to do so he needed some time and observations on how the camp was run. He decided to cooperate and give the impression that he was willing to learn the new trade and eagerly wanted to pursue a career in the army. His strategy worked and, little by little, he began to gain the trust of his trainers and captors, who were impressed by his interest and zeal.

He was learning with a remarkable speed the tools of the battlefield; he was presenting to his tutors intelligent solutions to theoretical problems and, to everyone's surprise, he could come up with hypothetical war strategies no one had ever thought of before. So much did he startle his superiors, that soon he had their full trust. They were even considering his unprecedented promotion to the full officer status. They were extremely happy about making a perfect catch, and wanted to exploit it to the fullest.

He was already allowed to make short distance movements in the company of other trusted soldiers who were impressed with him, but kept him under strict observation. Simon was careful not to raise their suspicion and acted normal. He needed all the caution on earth if he was to succeed in escaping from that place. The army headquarters were in the vicinity of the city, but still quite far from the royal palace, requiring them to commute between the two places, and Simon was doing it frequently without showing the slightest signs of any intentions of running away. He was patiently waiting for the right moment, which seemed far away.

The city was quite large and protected by a strong stone wall, making it impossible for any invader to break or penetrate. There were four large gates, which remained closed, but one, for much of the time. The only gate, which was opened during the daytime, was guarded very robustly by alert soldiers, who would not allow anybody in or out without a special permission from the city authorities, making it practically impossible for anyone to leave the city without the consent and knowledge of the administrators. There was hardly any point in hoping for a miraculous chance to escape, but Simon was almost certain of getting a fair chance of doing so, and therefore patiently waited for it.

"Tell me, are you really bad with weapons, or did you just pretend?" One of his fellow soldiers asked one day.

"Why should I pretend?" Simon sounded surprised.

"Don't try to be overly clever, no one wishes to be dragged

into a war machine without trying to safeguard oneself," said the same soldier in a suspicious tone. Simon just shrugged his shoulders, indicating that he did not care if his fellow soldier believed him or not.

"I must confess that you progressed remarkably, if you are telling the truth. I have never seen any person who could learn the use of weapons in this short time. Believe me, you are a natural talent." The soldier told him.

"How long have you served as a soldier?" Simon inquired.

"Oh, it seems I was born with a sharp sword in my hand," the soldier said with a laugh.

"How come that you are not sent with any fighting bands to go and fight for the glory of the land?" Simon jested.

"You really want to know?" asked the soldier, and looked at Simon with a broad smile. He waited for a few moments before he lifted his shirt and showed him his body that was still full of unhealed wounds.

"Don't you need to rest properly until you recover completely?" Simon asked, not believing his eyes.

"These wounds will surely heal, so why care?" he answered nonchalantly.

Simon couldn't help admiring the tough soldier in his heart, though he didn't say anything aloud.

Paul must have been a few years older than him, and yet looked very much older and more experienced. A stern face with smiling eyes left the others quite unsure, and this was where his strength lay. He was content being a simple soldier as he believed himself unable to command and control others, simply because he preferred to be without assuming the responsibility for others.

"I was once an officer, but realized that it wasn't for me to lead; I'm too dull for such things." Paul whispered and looked embarrassed.

"What happened?" Simon asked.

"Stupid me, I led my men in some hopeless battle and saw them all perish one after the other, a very cruel way of learning that I was not a good officer." Paul looked remorseful.

"We all make mistakes, so you shouldn't be so hard on yourself," Simon said and smiled, realizing that he tried to imitate old Michael. He could see that his words didn't have a soothing effect on Paul, as he looked as serious as before.

"I would do nothing but better my skills in weaponry, if I were you," Paul suddenly changed the topic.

"Why would that be?"

"Don't you want to go to the battles and return back alive?" Paul taunted.

"Yes, but who is going to some battle, we are both placed as city guards," Simon looked astonished by his words.

"You believe that's your permanent place of duty?" Simon could notice that it was less of a question than a taunt; he looked at Paul who burst into laughter.

After having a hearty laugh, Paul got serious again and explained to Simon what awaited him in coming times. He was being prepared to become an effective part of some combating band, which was supposed to fight for the motherland and the king.

"Why, it's not even my motherland, and he is not my king either." Simon felt anger. Paul looked up in surprise, but then relaxed and laughed.

"You're right; you aren't even a citizen of this land. Okay, then go and fight for the glory of your master, little slave."

"Am I a slave?" Simon felt degraded.

"What else? Did you join the army voluntarily? Do you get any wages? Can you act according to your own will? Of course you are a slave." Paul sounded cruel, but at least he was honest, Simon concluded and kept pondering for a while in a wretched state of mind.

"When do you think I'll be sent to war?" Simon asked, still a bit depressed.

"I don't know, but the king does like adventures, so it could be any time soon. Right now our prince is engaged in some expedition, when he comes back there would be a preparation for the next one, I presume."

"You believe I will be part of that mission?" asked Simon.

"What else, why do you think they feed you and train you?"

"I don't want to go and fight; I'm a peace loving person who could never kill anyone, not even my worst enemy." Simon said in a trembling voice, and looked terrified by the mere thoughts of some battle.

"You are in deep trouble then, my friend," Paul laughed, showing no respect for Simon's feelings. "On the other hand, we all learn the art of survival, there is no exception. On the battlefield you will encounter the god of death and war who will present you with the options and I'm sure you too will choose prudently."

"What choices does he present?" Simon asked, anguished.

"These options are simple, and all soldiers are aware of them. Kill or be killed, is the eternal code of the warriors confronting each other."

"I'd rather prefer to die than to kill someone who never did any wrong to me." Simon told him in a determined tone.

"Then why go all the way to some far away land, tell your captors and they can free you of the anguish." Paul teased him, well aware that Simon's principles were merely empty threats.

"No, my friend, it's far easier to die defending one's precious life than to surrender without offering any resistance."

"How will I be able to confront my conscience if I ever killed some innocent person?" Simon said in a weak voice.

"Let it be, you'll be surprised to learn how painlessly it all goes." Paul tried to calm down Simon who looked aghast.

That night Simon lay in his bed and couldn't fall asleep; he was terrified by the prospect of going out and waging some war. He had believed that the worst was over and that he could stay in the city till the opportunity to escape presented itself, but now his heart was filled with all kinds of fears and anxieties. He stayed awake all night and dreaded the day when he was to encounter death and make his final choice of killing someone or dying himself. Why did it have to be that way? Why couldn't they all live and die a natural death? He couldn't ignore the irony that he sought eternal life and instead was getting closer to death than ever. He must have fallen asleep as he saw himself engaged in a fierce fight with someone, where he tried his best to kill his counterpart, and there was no remorse or regard for one another's lives. He was steered by some natural instinct to survive at all costs. He turned and twisted, trying to safeguard, to assault and inflict wounds on his counterparts without even thinking about the pain he inflicted on others. He was a savage, a brute and a ruthless person defending his right to be. The entire scene was too brutal, too bloody and horrifying, and he woke up all drenched in sweat. He sat upright and trembled with fear, he felt so lonely and worried, but there wasn't anyone to comfort his troubled heart. His dream just proved what Paul had told him earlier on, so there was an apparent risk of his growing insensitive to the lives of others. He dreaded the need to kill in the process of defending one's own.

The next morning when Simon went on duty, he saw Paul coming with a broad smile on his face. Looking at

Simon he became serious and asked if all was well with him. Simon told him that he just had a bad night.

"You are too sensitive. Stop worrying about things; they can be taken care of by the hands of destiny." Paul tried to cheer him up without knowing what bothered him. He had completely forgotten about his last discussion with Simon, and could never believe that it could cause a lingering anxiety to his comrade.

Simon was told by Paul that Prince Edward was on his way to the capital after a long expedition in some faraway land. The news arrived by messenger that the prince had been successful in his undertaking, but unluckily had lost most of his men while trying to accomplish his mission. No one but the king knew about the exact number of the men who had perished, and no one dared to guess. Such matters were not considered to be of public interest. Paul interpreted the news in his own peculiar way. He believed that the new expeditions were to stay on hold till the new bands were prepared to launch some fresh attacks in future.

"You're a lucky bastard; I bet you will not be thrown into some battle for some time. Who knows, we may even become comrades in a battlefield, as I'm sure to have recovered completely by then." Paul teased Simon who suddenly felt a bit relieved by the news.

"Are you sure that it'll take some time before the king ventures out again?"

"How would I know for sure, but isn't it more logical that he builds another combatant force before he attacked some new countries?" Paul said, and shrugged his shoulders as if it was not an important issue with him.

The argument held some weight in it and made Simon ease up and soon he was his old self, relaxed, confident of future and hopeful. Paul watched his face and laughed, as he could easily understand what bothered Simon before he broke the news to him.

The king was told by his wise and cunning advisors that victory and defeat were not the only parameters to measure the inner state of mind of the warriors. They warned the king about the dangers involved with his returning prince and tried to make him aware of the possible disastrous effects of such a devastating experience as his son had recently lived through, and which must have affected the psyche of him as a commander. No victory could take away the wounds inflicted on one's soul and mind. Nothing could wash away the guilt feelings of losing most of one's loyal and trusted warriors, he was told and agreed that the words contained much truth.

"What could I do to alleviate the possible effects on the psyche of the prince?" The king sought advice.

Shift all the emphasis on the victory and black out the tragic happenings in the war. Let no one mourn the dead, but celebrate the victory as you never have done before. Such were the words of wisdom given to the king

"How am I to do that without angering the families that have lost their loved ones'?"

"Let the chief priest take care of such things, he certainly knows how to satisfy sorrowful hearts. He can surely make even the families of the fallen soldiers partake in celebrations with joy," one of his advisers said, and the king smiled in agreement.

9

The king had arranged the best of feasts for his victorious but burdened prince. Decorating the whole kingdom like a bride, he waited for his son to arrive and forget the tragedy of losing his best men. He was prepared to talk to his inexperienced and sentimental son. He intended to have a very serious talk with him and impart the innermost secrets of the art of ruling. He was to tell the Prince that those soldiers and armies were nothing but the tools, a replaceable force, which was to be used to reign, to control and to conquer and expand. The king was aware that his heir needed much training before he could be safely trusted with the affairs of the state. But these were his long-term undertakings, what he needed to do immediately was to make him forget the sorrow of losing thousands of his soldiers, and the best way of doing that was to demonstrate before his eyes the magnificent and awe-inspiring force that the king still had at his royal disposal. He wanted to give the returning prince a welcome he never could have expected even in his wildest fantasies. He would show him the splendor that didn't disappear with the destruction of some army units. His message was supposed to be simple: the glory of the king remained even when the armies had perished. The royal guards, the army units, and all citizens were ordered to gather and give their returning crown prince an astounding welcome that he would not soon forget. The ordinary soldiers were to join the welcoming parade, which was being arranged in the vicinity of the city while the more trained and well-disciplined troops were being sent to meet the prince and extend their welcome miles away from the city wall. The meaning was to give the returning prince a proud entrance into the city.

In the middle of these feverish activities, Simon saw his opportunity knocking at his door, and he was ready to avail himself of it. He wasn't sure if he was to succeed or fail, but found it the only possibility to escape from a well-guarded city where he was kept as a slave. He needed to regain his freedom if he was to resume his quest. He had hoped to be entrusted with the task of welcoming the prince, along with all the other soldiers, who were to remain within the city. It was his plan to get over the wall in the chaos, which would ensue at the exact moment of the prince's arrival. However, he was astonished to hear that he had not only been selected to join the troops, which were to welcome the prince miles away from the city, but was even to be given a powerful horse to ride during the ceremony. The news made him jump with happiness. It surely would enhance his chance to succeed.

Paul saw no reason to be excited by the opportunity of welcoming the returning prince but looked astonished to notice the enthusiasm of Simon. He just watched without asking any questions. By now, he knew that Simon wasn't truly happy to be a soldier, but just did his duty without being involved, so Simon's excitement couldn't be less than a mystery for him.

"What makes you that excited? You aren't even a royalist."

"I'm happy to be given a horse to ride." Simon didn't want to raise the suspicion of his comrade.

"I can see that you're a good rider, so it can't be that it's something new and exciting." Paul wouldn't let him off the hook. Simon tried to avoid the subject and Paul let the topic go, but nevertheless he kept observing Simon more closely, giving Simon some bad notions. He knew that Paul's attentive attitude could create problems for him, but there was little he could do to get rid of him.

Finally, the day of Prince Edward's arrival came, providing him with the rare opportunity to escape from the city he had been taken to, where he was nothing more than a prisoner. He had endured the whole period of captivity with patience, prudence and cunning. Now that all soldiers were rushing in madness to be the first ones to be spotted by the prince, all Simon had to do was to remain at the tail end, waiting for the moment of action. That precious second of time was provided to him by luck, when the advancing front units saw the prince and his small band only a distance away. There were loud shouts, an unending clamor touching the morale of every soldier, giving them the sense that they were returning from the battlefield as a victorious force. They all halted and looked at their commander as if waiting for his sign to advance once again, and when he did give the sign, they madly rushed to join their prince as they had been ordered to do. They were so absorbed in the activity that they hardly noticed that they were moving like a storm while Simon stayed where he was smiling at his luck and opportunity to be free once again. His smile was frozen when he noticed that he was not the only one who lingered; Paul sat and watched him vigilantly just few steps behind. The expressions on his face betrayed that he was not happy. Simon got panicked, knowing that not only his only chance to escape was slipping out of his hands, but he had to quickly find out some viable excuse for his weird actions of not obeying the orders of the officer and the reason of his staying behind. Paul rode his horse in a lazy manner and came closer to him.

"What's going on here?" Paul asked in the stern and unfriendly tone. Simon looked back in anguish, but didn't say anything. His heart pounded hard as he knew that it was all over for him, but he didn't want to give up his plans just like that. He was busy considering his chances of making it through while Paul stood and watched his moves. He glanced at Paul's horse and realized that the beast was much stronger than his own, and there were not even the slightest chances of his escape.

"You thought to escape, right?" Paul asked with a sarcastic smile on his face. Simon looked defeated and didn't deny.

"What hinders you now from trying your luck?" Paul was provocative. Simon didn't answer his question, but remained as if frozen, well aware that Paul would effectively hinder all his attempts to run away.

"How very foolish of you to believe that you can cheat me, I could read in your eyes that you were busy weaving dreams of escape. Don't you think it's a good place, where you are fed properly and taken care of?" Paul spoke while staring in his eyes.

"Are you going to report the incident to the officer?" Simon asked anguished.

"I'm not an informer, but it would have been different if you had tried to escape." Paul said still looking somber. "Nevertheless, we do need some valid reason for not following the orders of the officer, when he sees that we never drove forward as we were ordered to."

Simon glanced back at his companion and looked terribly sad, seeing the golden opportunity to regain his freedom disappear like a mirage. He was less worried about the officer as he had already decided to confess his intention of running away.

Paul smiled for the first time, but it was a strange smile. He drove closer and said in a whisper, "Don't even dream of doing that. You'll regret the mistake as long as you live. In this country, a fallen soldier is raised to the status of a hero, a martyr, but a deserter is merely a criminal of the worst kind. The choice remains with you, so choose wisely."

"What can they do to me, hang me for the crime?" Simon tried to be tough.

"You're not as wise as you give the impression of being, there are worse things than death in this world and such truths are even known to a simple soldier like me," Paul said while looking at the troops that slowly approached towards the city.

"We still have the time to join these troops and thus skip the interrogations." Paul suggested.

"How can we do that without being noticed by others?" Simon asked, still feeling hopeless.

"Just follow me; I think we can make it. They are all absorbed in what's happening and move in a very slow manner, and that is our opportunity to join them without being noticed.

Paul signaled and galloped his horse towards the East, and Simon followed him. They made a wide semi-circle before they came to the rear of the troops and rode behind them in a slow manner. Simon could see the soldiers belonging to their band at the rear.

"What are these doing in the rear?" Simon asked a bit astonished.

"What do you mean? Had you expected them to ride in front of the prince and his returning troops?" Paul said and looked amused. He had already shaken off the stress and strain that engulfed him a few minutes ago.

"What if they notice us and ask why we lag behind?" Simon asked anguished.

"We do that to watch the rear and warn if some strange things happen, don't you know that?" Paul said with a dampened laugh.

They rode without speaking any further. Simon was absorbed by his thoughts and regretted his failure. He was well aware that the rare opportunity was not to come soon or perhaps he was doomed forever.

"You owe me an explanation, but I can wait for that," Paul said. Looking at him, Simon remained silent.

When the marching troops neared the city wall, the entire atmosphere changed; there was much fervor both among the returning soldiers and the welcoming masses. They all sang patriotic songs, played rhythmic music and shouted slogans for the victors and their king, showing their joy and pride. The pompous entrance into the city was indeed the climax of the euphoria. Simon had never witnessed anything like it before in his life. Despite all the colorful activities, his thoughts were somewhere else, and he felt devastated and defeated. The citizens stood on the sides of the pavements and waved at the returning heroes, making them forget about the grim realities of their recent endeavors. The songs, the music, and dancing youth made the atmosphere appeasing and uplifting both for the body and the spirit. The procession moved in a very slow and rhythmic manner as if it was deliberately stretched out to the maximum. It finally stopped at the large boulevard outside the royal palace, where the troops were re-arraying themselves all according to their ranks and the units to which they belonged. They knew that no one was allowed to move away until the king came out and made his welcome speech. They all stood and patiently waited for the event while Prince Edward went into the palace to meet his father, the king.

The king and his most trusted advisors didn't rush to come and greet the victorious troops; they were busy attending the prince and listening to his preliminary account of the war. They were involved in listening, appreciating and congratulating the Prince. The king asked the prince to take some rest before he went out to his men, but he declined the offer by saying that he couldn't rest while his soldiers stood outside tired and devastated.

"Don't you think he is the best commander?" the king asked his attendants in a proud tone, they all agreed without any hesitation or exception.

"Okay, then. Let's go out and greet the troops," the king said.

Prince Edward, the king, the Chief Minister, the Chief Priest and all other important functionaries emerged from the palace and sat on the temporary stage built for that purpose. One after the other they all spoke and gave their praise to the returning troops. They were called heroes, men of great strength and shining stars of the nation. The king said that he was proud of his soldiers, both those who fell for the motherland and those that stood in front of him. He promised the families of dead soldiers that they would get great rewards as an appreciation for the deeds of their loved ones. He told the survivors that they too would be rewarded generously. The king had saved the details for the time he was to speak before the families of the fallen soldiers. Prince Edward praised his men more than any other speaker and declared them to be living heroes, they all could see the tearful eyes of the soldiers who loved their commander and were ready to sacrifice their lives for him. Paul looked stealthily at Simon and smiled as if he too was taken in by the words of prince and wanted to show that he shared the pride of his superiors. The ceremony was far shorter than Simon had anticipated. Most probably, the king wanted the prince to go and rest while the kingdom could indulge in the festivities and make merry.

"Come, we go and drink, it's all free today," Paul said when they were off duty. Simon replied that he felt tired and wanted to rest instead.

"You would be the only person doing that on a day like this. Enjoy life while you can. Who knows what will happen tomorrow." Paul tried again, but realized that Simon was too down to participate in the ongoing feast.

"The Feast lasts for three days, I'm sure soon you will change your mind," Paul jested before he went along with his other friends.

Simon was sure that most of the soldiers had remained out and drinking and now would be sleeping like dead stones. He was still disturbed by the last minute surprise of Paul and yet didn't hate him for that. He was thankful that Paul had refrained from reporting his failed attempt to escape. He went to the officer to report for duty, but was met some half sleeping, drunkard soldier.

"Go and enjoy the feast. You all are released from your duties for another two days, but don't forget that it can be terminated without any forewarning." The soldier said waving his hand in the air.

"Why aren't you allowed to be off duty?" Simon asked.

"It's a long story, go and stop worrying about me." The soldier didn't look sad; it was obvious that his duty didn't hinder him from enjoying himself like his fellow soldiers.

How wonderful the timing could have been, if Paul hadn't come and spoiled it all, he thought and became even sadder.

Simon walked around in the city, which looked quite stale at the moment. Simon knew that many of the inhabitants still lay in their beds after the festivities of the night before, but he didn't mind walking through the half empty streets. He went towards the city gate that used to remain open during the daytime, and found it open even for the day. He saw three soldiers guarding the entrance. Seeing him coming, they greeted him in a soldier-like manner. Simon stood and talked with them briefly and asked if everything was in order. They said that it was, as far as they could tell. Where was their officer in charge, Simon asked. They looked at each other before they broadly smiled, indicating that the officer had been also out during the night and now rested in his quarters.

Simon waved and went on strolling; just by giving a visit to the place had filled him with renewed hope. In some bizarre manner, he saw some secret doors opening for him and felt some excitement. He couldn't figure out how he was to cross that magical point to become a free man once again, but indeed was trying hard to find out. In the evening, he saw Paul going out from his barracks. He waved at Simon and came closer.

"You missed a lot of fun yesterday; we all had a wonderful time, Paul told him. According to him, he had had only a few hours' sleep, and yet he looked as fresh as ever.

"Where have you been? I was looking for you," he continued.

"Why, don't you have some better activities?" Simon tried to joke but still looked serious.

"I knew you were down yesterday and wanted to see if you had succeeded in coming out of the gloom."

"Don't worry about me, I'm just fine." Simon assured him, but he still didn't look convinced.

"Let's go get something to eat," Paul said and started walking in the opposite direction to the mess.

"Are you still toxic? The mess lies in this direction," Simon said with a smile.

"I have no desire to eat the same boring food; today we can eat at some ordinary restaurant," Paul said making grimaces at the thought of the mess food. He looked more like some spoiled child than a soldier.

"You go ahead; I can't afford such a luxury." Simon reminded him that he was penniless.

"Don't worry about the bill, it's cheaper today, and besides you'll be my guest," Paul insisted, leaving no choice for Simon but to accompany him.

They sat in a restaurant that was full of people and noise. They had to wait long for their meal, but when it was finally served, Simon thought it was worth waiting for. He remembered his days at Michael's and felt a bit sad but recovered quickly.

"What were you thinking? Does the food remind you of your mother's lovely food? To me it always does."

Simon kept silent, remembering the days when his mother was alive. He couldn't forget those miserable days when his mother struggled hard to feed her two young children. She was never a fantastic cook, but nevertheless she did her best to provide them with nutritious food. He remembered how David used to make a fuss, each time they sat down to eat. He always wanted more and was never satisfied with whatever mother made. Simon just stared at his meal while he drifted far away in the murky days of his past. He had lost all appetite and was in the iron grip of gloom.

Paul didn't ask anything, but watched him carefully while he enjoyed his own meal.

"I can see something is burdening you. Confide in me, I assure you that you'll feel better after doing so," Paul offered, making Simon smile.

"You are dying of curiosity, aren't you?

"To be honest, yes I am but also I want to understand my comrade-in- arms," Paul said looking into his eyes.

"You have many comrades, why you are just interested in me?" Simon asked.

"Because none of them wishes to run away from here. Not one of them is even half as mysterious as you are; in some strange manner I want to know more about you."

"There must be many here who may be dying to get a chance to flee this damned place as not all came here searching for employment." Paul smiled and agreed that one could force individuals to perform any task but couldn't take away their dreams to be free. He kept pushing Simon to narrate his story until he sighed and started telling it. He listened with great care and didn't interrupt even a single time. When Simon finally fell silent, Paul sighed and said, "What a story!"

"So your mother did succeed, leaving some inheritance anyway." Paul spoke after a few moments' pause, making Simon look up in surprise.

"Yes, she left a house for us to live in as I told you earlier on."

"You did, but I am referring to your monstrous brother David, how he keeps tormenting you, making your life hell." Paul said with a smile and then went on. "David reminds of a character, I knew long ago."

"Did you also have a brother like him?" Simon asked.

"No," Paul laughed. "That stupid fellow was none other than myself. I made everyone around me unhappy and saw nothing but me and my needs."

"At least you are remorseful about that period," Simon said.

"Remorseful! Heavens no, on the contrary, I am happy that I lived through those times."

"Why?"

"Because they did help me gain insight and develop. I'm sure that even David may have grown out of his stupidity. He might be a completely different person now." Paul went on, "Time is the best teacher. We grow and realize that there are not many people in the world that care and, therefore, we need to hold onto those few who do care."

"So, why didn't you return home, when you gave up your search for David?"

"The place doesn't attract me any longer. What awaits me over there, except bad memories?" Simon was honest, and yet he didn't tell Paul that his quest was on, but had just changed its focus and its name.

"You said that you were on the way to meet some mysterious person, who is he and why did you look for him?" Paul asked, and Simon felt uneasy, not knowing how to reply to that uncomfortable question. He had tried hard not to reveal anything about his real quest, and yet he had left enough clues in his narration. He felt forced to confide even the rest of the story to Paul.

"Do you really believe that such a valley exists in the world?" Paul asked, trying hard to stop his laughter.

"There is a fair chance," Simon tried to defend himself.

"You are a dreamer. No wonder you hate the profession of soldiering, it doesn't suit you at all," Paul said, still amused. "Nevertheless, what a great blessing it would have been if a soldier could fight with a conviction of immortality in hand." He didn't expand the idea, but looked deeply at Simon and shook his head.

"Don't you forget to bring some water for me too, if you ever reach the valley with a life spring," he jested. Simon didn't like his making fun of him but refrained from making an issue of it.

"Now I understand why you wanted to run away from this town. The secrets of eternal life keep calling you to discover them." Paul found it so funny an idea that he wouldn't stop joking. He noticed that Simon wasn't happy about his jokes and tried to get serious.

"I think that I would do likewise if I were you as well." Paul spoke seriously, but Simon could see his hidden giggle.

They sat there and talked for some time. Paul made it clear that he was a simple soldier who didn't like mysteries and was happy to live a carefree short life rather than to expect a long boring life. He was not interested in starting a family. His present status provided him with the possibility of living his life without worrying about those who might come to depend on him. He wished to live and die in accordance with his fate and didn't want anyone to mourn him the day he left the world behind.

"Do you mean that soldiers should refrain from marrying?" Simon asked.

"I don't speak for others, but for myself. I know I have chosen a dangerous profession, and therefore, can die young, so why should I need to worry about any offspring?" Paul explained.

"What about your family?" Simon tried to steer the discussion and wanted Paul to open himself.

"What about them? I hardly visit them, I presume they fare well." Paul shrugged his shoulders as if he couldn't care less.

"Do they live around here?" Simon asked.

"No, they live in a village that lies far away from here, so far away that it takes months to reach there," Paul explained casually.

"They still live in the same kingdom?"

"You really don't know much about our country, do you?" Paul asked with a broad smile and then continued. "This kingdom is widespread, and yet the king wants more of it. Personally the king has not been away from his capital for years, but his armies keep expanding in all directions. Most of his subjects haven't even seen their king, but administered by some local rulers who represent the king."

"Is life better, out there?" Simon inquired.

"Are you kidding? These local lords are many times worse than the administration in the center. The slow communication and remoteness from the center make these rulers fearless and headstrong," Paul told him.

"Why don't you bring your family to the capital, where they can have a somewhat comfortable life?" Simon asked, and Paul looked at him in disbelief. "Comfortable life!" he exclaimed.

"Do you know what it entails to live in the capital? Are you aware of the high cost of living here? Do you know the difficulties of finding a place to stay and the almost non-existent job opportunities? You don't have a clue, do you?" Paul seemed to be shocked at his ignorance.

"Even if I could afford to provide them with a residence and very expensive food, I wouldn't recommend them to come and live over here. This city is not for them; they will simply get depressed and die of deep depression. They are better off there where they live in some insignificant village, where at least they have plenty to eat and no worries of surviving the day." Paul talked about his family without showing much affection for them.

"How many siblings do you have out there?" Simon asked.

"Maybe ten, maybe twelve, who cares?" Paul laughed,

"Come on, how is it possible that you don't know exactly?" Simon pushed him.

"To tell exactly, I need to concentrate and count, and I don't have time for that." Paul answered with laughter, making it clear to Simon that he had a large number of siblings and cared less for the exact numbers.

"I think we have had enough talk, let's now move to some bar and have some fun." Paul said after paying the bill and getting up from his seat. Simon thanked him for the dinner when they came to the street but excused himself from joining him in drinking. Paul looked a bit disappointed but didn't insist on his company. He was sure of finding some company, once he started drinking.

Simon didn't go to his barracks as he had told Paul that he intended to do. He went strolling in the streets that were oozing with people, men, women, young soldiers and the other youth. He felt at home with the crowd and watched them curiously. He was a big city dweller and always felt comfortable in the bustle of the towns. The well-dressed people moving around had intentions of enjoying every single moment of that magic night, where they were given the opportunity to sing, dance and drink as much as they wanted for almost no cost at all. Simon noticed that some youths were already drunk and were noisy and yet no one showed them any irritation. The level of tolerance was higher, and things remained functioning despite the fact that there were so few guards out in the streets. Many glanced at him and waved, believing that Simon belonged to those few unlucky ones, who were not given time off to celebrate, how otherwise could he walk as straight as he did. He kept walking and observing the unending crowds and smiled back when anyone waved at him.

He was busy thinking out the details of the plan that had struck him earlier that day. He was sure that if he kept his head cool and his nerves in control, he could succeed in accomplishing some remarkable deed in the morning. The night was still young, and the feverish activities were in full swing when he finally decided to get back and try to sleep for a few hours before he tried his luck. He knew that his plan had equal chances of failing or succeeding, but saw no consequences of a failure, and that calmed his waning nerves. Falling asleep was much harder than he had anticipated. His mind was fully awake, and he just lay there struggling to get some rest and sleep.

Simon must have slept at last; the sun was high in the sky when he woke up. He quickly changed his clothes and started walking through the almost empty streets. His brisk walk and the sound of his heavy shoes betrayed the fact that he was perfectly sober and alert. He had chosen the perfect time to visit the gate, which opened at sunrise. He saw two soldiers sitting there and dozing as there was no traffic of incoming or outgoing people. These were not the same soldiers he had met the day before. The soldiers greeted him and looked curious.

"Where is the officer in charge?" Simon asked in a loud voice, trying hard to dampen his nervousness.

"Why?" One of the soldiers countered.

"Go and fetch him instead of asking questions," Simon tried to be tough and noticed that the young soldier was nervous.

"He is out and won't be back before a few hours," the soldier that had remained silent until then spoke.

"Was he out having fun last night?" Simon asked with a smile.

"I guess he did have fun! Aren't these hilarious days of festivities!" the soldier said, relaxing a bit. Simon told a few jokes before he said to the soldier that he would come back later if it was required.

"Do you have any message for the officer?" asked one of the soldiers.

"No, I just wanted to check that everything is in control, have you guys made the routine check-ups around the city wall?" Simon asked, well aware that a drunken officer couldn't have accomplished such a duty. No one said anything and that gave Simon the opportunity he had been waiting for ever since he had come there last; his heart pounded with nervousness.

"It seems that you have neglected the most important task. I don't want to report the incident to my superiors, but…." Simon was making them nervous, as well.

"We can do it now," one of the soldiers said.

"No, you all are needed at the entrance, you're already undermanned, and that's in breach of the regulations. Do you have horses around?" he asked in a commanding tone. Yes, they had fresh horses, he was told.

"Fetch one horse for me; I'll make the inspection myself." Simon said confidently and saw the reluctant faces of the soldiers and knew that he had to be more firm and commanding if he was to get his chance.

"I don't have all day. Think about the consequences if there is some danger lurking out there and we didn't do anything about it." His words had a magical effect; he had succeeded in scaring his fellow soldiers. He knew the truism that soldiers without the capacity to think, knowing only how to obey commands blindly, were easy to manipulate and was making the best use of that knowledge. One soldier brought a beautiful horse for him, and he smiled, knowing that the beast was powerful and swift and could carry him far away from this place of his captivity.

Simon was aware that in the chaos of the city, no one was going to notice his disappearance, except the guards at the entrance who would be scared to death to confess their mistake of not only letting him pass through, but even deadly mistake of providing him with a swift horse. He was certain that when his disappearance was finally discovered, he would be far, far away from their reach. The possession of a swift horse had given him the opportunity of moving ahead with great speed. The recent dreadful experiences had taught him to be careful in his behavior. He had always known that not all people were kind, but now he knew that one needed to protect oneself from the evils of others. Despite his difficulties in the last few months, he remained positively inclined to strangers and kept moving towards his goal, getting nearer to through a painful process of unremitting hardship and toil.

10

After many months' back-breaking travel, he finally reached the country he sought. It was a very strange town before his eyes. People were noisy, aggressive and hostile. They stared at him, laughed at his dress and said rude words. Simon ignored them, but the more he wanted to avoid trouble, the nastier these people got. He was terribly hungry, but dared not stay there and eat, for fear of getting into trouble. He felt insecure and threatened, and had a strong urge to leave the place as quickly as possible. Nevertheless, he found it hard just to turn and leave. He had spent months in hard conditions on the road to come over there looking for the person who could provide him with the answers he sought. He decided not to run, but to face the situation. His resolve to stay proved to be fragile as he watched the people around him and felt the approaching danger. At that point in time, he sensed the lurking risks and felt he was being treated like a prey. He quickly looked around to discover the possible retreat routes, but found none. Fleeing wasn't an option because he was too fatigued and there were no open roads to escape through. Simon realized that those strange looking people were chasing him wherever he went. They were giving him a scary feeling, but he pretended to ignore them. The only tool available was not to show them his fear, but even that seemed to be without any effect. These wicked people were getting closer and closer, soon they had him encircled. What had he done to provoke them? he wondered. Soon they were so close that he could smell the stench coming from their mouths. For a brief moment, he was paralyzed by an overwhelming fear, but the very next moment he remembered the words of Paul, who told him once that fear was not that bad as a human being perceived it to be. According to him fear could be turned into an effective weapon. It made one more alert, more charged with energy, and most importantly, it provided one with the will to fight back. He had no time to find out if these assertions were right or wrong. He looked at those people that chased him while his heart still pounded with fear. He tried to look right back into their eyes and stopped fleeing. He found it very difficult to get rid of his qualms as they were much stronger than he could possibly wrestle with. He remembered that he was a trained soldier and could withstand any attack, if only he had the guts. Simon was without any arms, but he believed that he could handle that cowardly gang with his bare hands. Though still unsure, he was ready and anticipated a sudden attack, but instead he saw the gang standing still, not daring to attack him anymore. They all looked perplexed and even scared of him; it must have been his resolve to face them that had made those people jittery. Just few moments ago, he had feared kicks and blows, but instead he saw the gang moving away from him until they came to some safe distance. Simon got confident and the clouds of fear started dissipating from his eyes. He stood there more and more convinced that no one would dare to attack him any longer, but was prepared in case he was wrong. As he expected, nothing happened. He was about to leave when he saw two soldiers approaching him. He felt relieved that now even the threatening people would disperse, but what really astonished him was the fact that all those threatening people stood there as well, standing and looking furiously at him. They said something to the soldiers, who drew their swords and drove him forward. They locked him up in a tiny room and disappeared. He fainted from thirst and hunger and lost all sense of time.

The next day, he was brought before the judge, who read the accusations against him, which said he had attacked innocent citizens, tried to rob them, and had resisted his arrest. He looked bewildered at the judge and denied all charges.

"There're enough witnesses, so there isn't much I can do for you other than to pass my judgement," said the middle-aged man behind the desk. The judge ordered the soldiers who had brought him to leave the courtroom. He looked at Simon with pity and said in a low tone, "I know your innocence because it's not the first time a stranger is brought to me with such accusations, but my hands are tied. I must follow the law and sentence you," said the judge, who seemed to be different from his fellow countrymen.

Simon collapsed. The judge clapped, signing his clerks and soldiers to come in. They attended to Simon, who was too weak to talk and signaled for some water. The judge gave him food and water and felt so sorry that he refrained from sentencing him. But more than that he could not do, as the law didn't allow him to release the accused without punishing him for the crime committed. The only thing he could do was to refer the case to the king, by implying that according to his own judgement the stranger was not guilty of any of those charges brought against him. Simon could see that the judge was still anguished and avoided looking into his eyes, and soon he was to find out why.

With great disappointment, Simon noticed that the king and his court members didn't look different in their behaviour from the people he had earlier met on the streets. Everyone looked at him and whispered and laughed openly.

"What a repulsive people," Simon thought, his hope for justice quickly fading. He stood passively and awaited the sentence.

The king asked in a harsh, unfriendly tone who he was, where he came from, and which errand brought him there. Simon didn't want to raise the ridicule of these people, so he spoke with measured words and told the king all he wanted to know. He said he intended to stay for a short while in his kingdom and by doing so, meant no harm to anyone. The king and his courtiers laughed.

"You know that you've committed a very serious crime," the king spoke angrily and loudly.

"So you've already harmed, yourself." They all laughed again. "I sentence you to five years imprisonment," the king decreed and dismissed him.

The soldiers came forward to carry him to prison. Simon was so horror-struck, he couldn't believe his ears.

"It's not justice! It's horrendous! How can you sentence me for the crimes I never committed?" Simon was protesting without making any impression on the wicked court attendants and the king. "I came here only to meet a friend, and that can't be a crime," Simon cried desperately.

"That's interesting," smiled the king, ordering the soldiers to bring him back. "Which friend have you come to meet?" They all laughed.

There fell a complete silence, when he mentioned the name. He could feel some kind of unease sweeping through the courtroom and nervous, pale faces staring at him in confusion. Gone was the arrogance and ridicule from their tone, replaced with fear and worry in their eyes. It didn't take long for him to understand they were scared to death of the name. Was that fearfulness beneficial or harmful, he could not say. The king seemed reluctant to decide as if he was perplexed at the choices before him. At last, he laughed and laughed timidly. Everyone else joined him. "Why didn't you say this before that you're a friend of our friend!" the king smiled as if making a great effort. He ordered his soldiers to not only release Simon but to lead him to the abode of his friend.

They rode all day in the carriage until they came near a forest. The soldiers were still unfriendly,and ignored him completely. He was asked to leave the carriage and go his way. He looked around and saw no signs of any habitation. He wanted to ask a few questions, but the rude soldiers weren't interested in entering into any discussion with him. They seemed scared and wanted to leave the haunted place as quickly as possible. They told him they were unable to accompany him any further, before turning their carriage and riding away in a great hurry. It was surprising to watch their panic-stricken faces.

He walked for the rest of the day without knowing if he was heading towards the right direction. The forest was getting thicker, and daylight was fading rapidly. He could not say if it was already dusk or that the rays of the sun had stopped penetrating the thick treetops. He thought it best to find some place to rest because it was impossible to move any further.

He couldn't sleep a second all night. The soil was damp and full of thorny bushes. Millions of mosquitoes kept tormenting him, buzzing, threatening, and biting him all the time. He could hear terrible sounds of wild beasts, though he was sure that no large and dangerous animal would come to that part of the forest where he was. The only thing that was making him worried was the fear of creeping creatures such as snakes; he was utterly exposed to their malicious attacks.

It was still very dark, but he could sense the day above and beyond the high treetops. After many hours of struggle, he succeeded in coming out of that thick forest and felt relieved. He filled his stomach with wild berries and continued walking. This great forest seemed to have no end, and that realisation made him terrified. How could anyone live in a place like this, he thought? Maybe the soldiers had made some sort of joke, he thought with unease.

For four nights and three days, he was in that forest, painfully toiling forward. On the fourth day, he had almost given up hope of ever coming out of that damned forest alive. Then something happened. He heard laughter. He looked around in astonishment, was he losing his mind or did he really hear the laughter? He couldn't decide. Then he heard it again, and rushed in the direction from where the sound came from.

They were a few young kids who were busy playing some game and laughing from time to time. They looked equally surprised when they noticed Simon coming towards them. They stopped playing their game and came to meet him. Not one of them spoke. They just watched him curiously.

"Good morning stranger, where are you heading to?" asked one youth at last, smiling at Simon, who stood speechless, as if in a dream.

Simon told them that he was looking for a certain person who was supposed to live in those tracts.

They told him that they could help him come to the address as they were so very close to that place. His happiness knew no bounds at the great news.

"There it is," said the same boy, who had been communicating with him all the way. He looked and saw one little wooden cottage hiding behind large trees. It was almost inconspicuous. He felt disappointed because he had not been expecting that the man he had travelled almost a year to meet would be living in such a little cottage. On second thought, he felt ashamed.

"How could I judge the man on such grounds?" He turned to thank the young kid, but he found no one there.

An old man opened the small wooden door when he knocked. He looked at him with deep eyes as if he was trying to recognise him. After the exchange of greetings, the old man invited him in. The interior of the house was very simple. No doubt it was all neat and clean, giving it a very homey and harmonic atmosphere. He was given some delicious juice to drink, which made him feel strong in his exhausted soul. He was happy to notice that the man, despite his hard features, was a kind and gentle person, who was not asking him millions of questions regarding his arrival.

"I can see that you are exhausted. Why don't you have a proper rest before we take up our conversation," the old man suggested. Simon nodded in agreement, but dared not speak out that he was terribly hungry. "Before you go to sleep, you should eat a little," said the old man going out of the room to fetch the food. Simon was amazed at his words and wondered if the man could read his mind, or had it been just a coincidence that he had taken notice of his intolerable hunger?

He was given a light, delicious meal to eat and then a warm comfortable bed to sleep in, where he fell into a deep sleep as soon as he lay down. He went on doing so for a very long time. His host smiled when he finally woke up from his deep slumber.

"I hope you had a peaceful, pleasant sleep!"

"No doubt I did. I slept like a dead stone," Simon responded getting up from the bed. "It seems I needed a nap."

"A nap?" His host busted into laughter. "Do you have any idea how long you have been sleeping?" He said, quite amused. Simon shrugged his shoulders and just smiled back, anticipating that it had been some unusual happening, which had cheered up his host. Seeing that Simon curiously waited for him to reveal the time he had been sleeping, he didn't find it the right moment to let go of his amusement. "What a nap! If one can call non-stop sleep of forty-eight hours a nap!" Simon joined him in his laughter.

"We have had enough of the fun of your sleep," said the old man, getting serious. "Your body probably needed the rest in order to recover from the fatigue you suffered in the forest. These are not the friendliest woods, I must confess." He had quickly grown sober as not to embarrass his guest any further." You can freshen yourself up while I bring something for you to eat. You must be starving by now."

Simon had not noticed his hunger by then, but mention of it had made him aware that he was very hungry.

His host, Bahor, was curious to know about the purpose of his unexpected visit, but showed patience and restraint from asking him any direct questions. Perhaps he wanted Simon to take up the matter by himself, but when he continued talking about everything else but the real purpose of his coming, Bahor could not remain silent for any longer.

"All right young man, I must admit that I'm curiously waiting to know what brought you to these unattractive parts of the world?" he said politely.

Simon explained about his meeting and staying with the gypsy family, and how he had been given his address by the elderly gypsy, but Bahor still looked a little confused.

"Yes, I know the man, but in no way could he provide you with my address," said Bahor a bit puzzled. Simon smiled and assured him that the answer to his question was to come to him if he gave him a chance to narrate his story. Bahor admitted his impatience and promised to be more patient from that time on.

Simon began describing his interesting story from the time he had left the gypsy family. He recounted the difficulties he had faced and the time consumed in the dreary task of reaching his destination. Bahor listened with care and interest, smiling from time to time. He told his host that the worst part of his journey started after he believed that he had reached his goal.

The old man laughed, "isn't that always so?"

He was a bit careful in the use of his words and sounded apologetic, when he said that he had had a very bad experience in Bahor's country and with his countrymen. "I must regretfully confess that I have never come across any people, who could match the wickedness prevalent in this country."

Simon was perhaps too hard in passing his judgement. He looked at Bahor to see his reaction to the statement, but he looked untouched by any of his remarks, giving him courage to go on with speaking his mind. "I'm sorry to say, but your countrymen are not only rude, hostile, deprived of any human touch, but also unaware of the word justice." Simon's description of the country made Bahor smile sadly.

"I agree with you in every detail," he said.

"How did you get rid of those evildoers and how could you find me?" asked the old man inquisitively. When Simon told him the details, he laughed and laughed, then serious he said, "Have you heard the old maxim, 'like subjects, like king'?

"I'm sorry for whatever you had to go through. But that place, which I loved once, has turned so evil that it's wise to be a hundred miles away from it," Bahor said getting serious. He was ashamed of the unacceptable and rude attitude of his people and wished he had the power to improve the prevailing conditions. He was quick to underline that not always were the people like that. With the passage of time, the people had abandoned their good nature and turned into some kind of evil, which in turn was dragging them further and further away from qualities like sympathy, compassion and understanding. "Unfortunately they have gone beyond any hope, or possible betterment," Bahor concluded.

When Simon had narrated his entire story, Bahor smiled and said, "I can say that I now know the difficulties you faced in reaching my place. But I'm still unable to figure out, what's required of your hard journey?"

Simon was quiet for a while as if he was weighing his words before speaking them. He was selective and careful about his choice of words and watched the face of his host carefully while telling him the real purpose of his coming. A strange smile spread on Bahor's lips as Simon mentioned the legendary valley with all its wonders. For a few minutes, his host kept silent and just watched him with deep, critical eyes.

Yes, he had heard of the myth of the valley and about the water of the spring of life. But he never cared if it was true or just a fable, was his answer. Simon waited for some elaboration on the subject, but the silence of the old man indicated that he had spoken his final words about the subject.

"Was that all?" he thought. The disappointment was so acute that it almost killed him. All those hardships he had faced, all the toiling, all the wounds inflicted by the thorny paths, were they all in vain? Simon bowed his head in grief and acceptance of his defeat. He uttered not a single word because he knew his emotions were out of control and didn't want to break down before some stranger. He was a proud young man, who could not bear to expose his despair to his host, so he didn't touch the subject again, assuming that Bahor had nothing to add to the information he had already imparted.

Simon did like his host, the kind old Bahor, who kept asking new questions, each time he paused in his detailed descriptions. Simon's inquisitive mind wanted to ask questions of his own, but never got the chance to do so. It was his third day at that cottage since he woke up from his 48 hour sleep. He had hardly seen his host leave the house, and yet he went on bringing fresh fruits, sweet drinking water, and even hot meals. He never had the chance to ask, but assumed that there were other people living around. How was this colony able to sustain itself? How many people lived there? What did they live on? How well connected or isolated were they? He kept thinking of questions.

11

At dinnertime, he got the chance to ask all those questions he had been so patiently waiting for. His host informed him that he lived all alone in that secluded place, and had no knowledge if there were other humans around. About the question, how he got food and drink, he had a simple answer. "I'm provided by my suppliers."

Simon was not satisfied with the answer, but would not anger his host by putting further questions. "Dear sir, forgive me for asking, but something is puzzling me very much," he said apologetically. His host smiled, as though permitting him to ask.

"The king called you his friend, and yet I haven't seen more terror in any eyes than his, and I can say the same about his soldiers. Just the mention of your name has saved my life; I don't understand. Why are they so afraid of you?"

"That old rascal!" laughed his host. "He is not a friend even to those, who are of his own blood. No, he is not afraid of me, and he has tried so many years to destroy me, but surely, he's scared to death. He has agreed to a truce, by which he has sworn to leave my friends and me in peace, and in return, my friends shall not punish him for his evil doings." The old host was hesitant to speak of his friends, but after pondering over the matter, he decided to open up.

"I've some very powerful genii friends, who have been protecting me from the king and his cruel soldiers, the same, take care of my needs in my old age."

"Did genii, lead me to your house?" Simon asked.

"Yes," said the old host.

"Say honestly, is this forest really that big, or was I just going in circles?"

"Both," replied the host and smiled. "I'm sorry for the suffering you were being exposed to, but that was a necessary step. I had to be sure whether you were a friend or a foe." Bahor looked truly sorry. "I had no previous knowledge of your intentions and found it necessary to delude your senses by the help of genii friends."

"Just one more question, if you don't mind," Simon waited for permission to proceed further.

When Bahor signed him to ask whatever he wished to.

"That day when I talked about the legendary valley, why did you pause at the subject?" Simon asked.

"I did?" his host looked surprised. "Perhaps I did so, without even noticing, but the most natural reason could be that I knew less of the subject than you did." Bahor was generous to confess.

"Then what was that strange smile on your face?" Simon dared to ask.

"I don't know which particular smile you are referring to, but I did find your whole narration very interesting. I saw your eyes glowing with excitement, I noticed the fullness of life enthusiasm overwhelming your entire being, and I witnessed the innocence of a child flowing through your words. Maybe that made me smile." His host was poetic in his expression, making Simon feel bashful. Seeing him go red in the face made Bahor laugh heartily.

"And did you know that you suffer from somniloquence?" he asked Simon and laughed when the young man looked back with a question mark on his face. "I had known the purpose of your coming, long before you verbalised it. You talk in your sleep, a habit which you should change if you are to hold your secrets to yourself." His host was in a joking mood, so there was not much point in discussing any serious matter that day.

Simon tried to take up the subject of the legendary valley and each time his host avoided the matter by talking about something else, convincing Simon there was no point in discussing it any further. They talked about everything as the old man had a keen interest in all the fields of life, and was full of knowledge about things and places so remote. He was well aware of the human psyche and its vulnerability in relation to loved ones, accidents, and incidents. He knew perfectly well what types of questions to ask that would cause him to lower his guard and talk openly about his family, circumstances and life in general, etc. It didn't take long before Simon was telling him the tragic loss of his mother, the unfortunate developments that seduced his beloved brother David, and many other things, which had left permanent marks and prints on his soul and character. Simon was hardly aware that Bahor had him in a position where he had no other choice but to open himself completely. Bahor disagreed that Simon had failed in his task of giving a better life to his younger brother.

"You did whatever stood in your power, and beyond that you could not tread. Your brother was not a bad person either; he was simply chasing his own destiny as you were supposed to follow yours." His host was comforting him without feeling pity for him. "Tell me, why do you want to chase eternity?" Bahor's question was direct and without the taint of mockery or any prior judgement.

Simon remained silent for a while as if he wasn't prepared for the question, but then he smiled in a shy manner, asking whether not everyone was interested in living indefinitely?

No, was the answer of his host, who believed that most of the shapes and forms in the world were not seeking any means to live forever.

"To tell you the truth, the idea hadn't struck me either before learning that such a prospect could be possible. But ever since knowledge of the valley has entered my consciousness, I burned with the desire of achieving that immortality, which the legend promises." Simon was not hiding the fact that he was getting obsessed by the mere thought of that wonderful place, where existed the possibility to defeat the inevitability of death.

"It's not for me to tell you if it is a good choice or a stupid option, to seek that which is unnatural, but I'll do my best to gather as much information about the subject as is possible. I have already requested my learned friends to inquire and check if the place really exists in reality or is just a myth," Bahor said in a careless style.

"Do your friends look like humans?" Simon asked.

"I don't think so, though to me they always appear in human form," said his host with a smile.

They sat and discussed the world of Ginni, the way they behaved, the means they used in communicating with each other and modes of transportation used. Simon was listening to all of Bahor's narrations in a baffled state. He could not believe that all those wonders could be possible. He wished to see and meet those supernatural friends of his, but his host was reluctant to make any promise. "I've to get their consent, maybe they'd agree, or perhaps they would reject your request to meet them. They are not very fond of human beings, and usually avoid any direct contact with them," was his straightforward and honest answer.

In the middle of the night, he was awakened by Bahor, who told him that his friends were there with some information regarding the valley.

"What did they tell you?" asked Simon with excitement.

"I have presented your request of meeting them, and they

seem to have nothing against you. Therefore, I thought it wise that you listened to the news they have brought directly. Come and join us," the host said, going to the other room.

Simon was full of excitement when he walked into the room, finding two young men sitting along with Bahor. There was nothing in their appearance or behaviour that could differentiate them from other human beings. Watching him enter the room, they greeted him with a smile. Bahor introduced him to his genii friends and invited him to sit beside them. The guests started their conversation by mentioning the request they had received regarding some mythical valley.

"The information we're to impart is neither authentic nor reliable," one of the young men said without looking at anyone. The very start did not look promising, requiring Simon to readjust his expectations. The myth was equally known in the jinni world, of course with a different name and slightly different characteristics. Nobody knew the exact place or the location of it, but it was generally believed to be north of "Fairyland". A place in itself almost impossible to find and reach. From one side, mighty giants protected it. No one dared to come that way, and the giants themselves were too clumsy and big to cross these high mountains. To the other side of the fairyland were the thick forests, where the elves dwelled, which were cunning and awake. They had strong historical ties with the fairyland and had taken the task of guarding it against all types of intruders. The other two sides nobody knew anything about, and therefore, none could say if anyone lived there or they were just wastelands.

"My kind host has been telling me a great deal about you and the incredible powers you have at your disposal, when it comes to travel from one part of the world to the other.

How come you are not aware if some place exists or not?" Simon asked politely but distrustfully.

The host and the young men couldn't help in noticing his suspicious tone. The host opened his mouth to say something, but the same genie who had been talking for most of the time spoke, looking directly at Simon.

"I really don't know what you have been told about us, but I want to assure you that despite our enormous powers and capacities, we are equally tied down by the laws of nature and don't have access to all corners of the world." His words were still polite, and his attitude was forgiving, making Simon regret his earlier remarks. He avoided looking at his host; he felt as if he had let him down.

"Even if this valley does exist, it seems impossible to reach there," the same genie said with skepticism, shaking his head.

"What makes you that pessimistic?" Bahor inquired softly.

The genie looked confused as if he had not expected such a rhetorical question. The other genie smiled, getting the point that Bahor had placed the question on behalf of Simon, who was too conscious and scared to put more offending questions out there.

"You know very well why I doubt the capacity of any human to succeed in such an enterprise. If we genies dare not go to the Fairyland and beyond, how could this human possibly do it?"

"What prevents you genii from entering into fairyland and beyond?" asked Simon in a hesitant manner.

"It's a long story," the genie said with a sigh. "And we have to blame ourselves for the tragic outcome."

Before Simon could ask for further explanation, the genie started telling him the long history. He was telling him about the period when the genii world and fairyland lived in perfect harmony and were completely open to each other. The natural intermingling had been advantageous to both kingdoms, but the genii were the beneficiaries of that contact.

"That wonderful interaction might have been allowed to continue had there not been some malevolent elements from our side, which destroyed the relations between the two kingdoms for centuries or perhaps even for good," told the genie as if he was regretful of the history. "The law had endorsed the intermarriages among the members of these two kingdoms, but it was clearly stated that it required mutual consent, which was the most natural and obvious thing for anyone. But when some despicable genii began kidnapping fairies and marrying them by force it shocked fairyland and its citizens, which rightfully demanded the return of the fairies. Our king at that time, not only refused to heed the request, but even declared an open war on the fairies, who were not prepared for such a terrible thing. Many of them perished, many were imprisoned and enslaved, and most of all, fairyland became occupied for a long time to come. Those who had started that entire inexcusable nightmare perished with the passage of time, but the unhealed wounds were to torment Fairyland for all time to come. When they finally got rid of Genii slavery, they had vowed to never trust Genii again. They not only broke all types of contacts with them, but even prohibited them from visiting their world." The Genii were not very proud of their dark history.

"What happens to the Genii who head to Fairyland?" Simon asked.

"Not many genii would dare to venture in that direction to see what awaits them there, but we have been given clear warnings that despite their peaceful nature, they would punish intruders from our kingdom in a severe fashion. We have been told about bottomless pits, which they have prepared for the trespassers, from which there is no escape."

Simon could see the fearful expressions on the faces of the Genii. "But as we told you earlier, we are here without any claim of knowledge about the valley, all we have imparted is a mere possibility of its existence, and that's all," said the genie as if he was concluding the meeting.

Bahor thanked them for all the trouble he had caused them by putting out a request; the genii were equally well mannered and assured him that his requests were their commands. The only person, who felt bad in that whole courteous talk was Simon, and that was not surprising either, remembering his rash and offending participation in the discussion.

Before leaving, the genii were extra kind to Simon as they saw his remorseful face. "It was a pleasure meeting you. We wish to be of more help regarding your inquiry."

Simon thanked them for everything and asked for their forgiveness if he had been sounding thankless or rude.

"Don't worry! We are not easily hurt. You were just fabulous." After they had gone his host asked him to go back to sleep as they could discuss the subject in the morning, but he told him that he was awake and couldn't possibly sleep.

Bahor tried to persuade him to give up the risky and hazardous adventure, which he sought, but Simon was stubborn as ever, resolute to follow his vision, regardless of what it entailed.

"Look, I fully understand your determination, but what worries me most is your unpreparedness for your task," said Bahor in a troubled tone. "You are neither aware of the difficulties, which await you, nor are you equipped with the road map. Take my friendly advice and go back to your own world and live," Bahor told him honestly.

However, Simon had not travelled that far to listen to such advice. He just smiled and assured his host that there was no return for him as he had his eyes fixed on a destination. Bahor just sighed and remained silent.

Simon stayed there for more than two weeks, and then begged for permission to take leave of his kind host, who refrained from reminding him, once again, of the difficulties and dangers of his far-fetched destination. "How would you proceed from here?" Bahor asked.

Simon was speechless as he completely lacked the knowledge of the direction where Fairyland laid.

"Suppose you find the way leading to Fairyland. Which of the two possible entrances would you opt to enter from?" the host asked him.

"I don't know," was the answer he got from Simon.

The host looked at him with great surprise, "I must confess that your approach is worrying me more and more. Your zeal is one thing and your ignorance another. You have to decide your strategy, before you could set out on your journey."

How could he decide, which entrance to choose, when he knew so little about both the elves and the giants? he confessed helplessly.

"Then you simply have to stay here and try to learn the things you don't know," the old man advised.

Simon knew nothing or very little about the worlds he intended to confront. Most of his knowledge was based on the books he had read, which wasn't enough or even true. He needed a real schooling from a learned teacher and who could be a better fit for the task than his kind host, who willingly took the assignment of providing the required knowledge. A short and comprehensive schooling was started, because there was no time for intensive long-term studies. His host wasted no time.

"Our planet earth was not the only one, which was full of thriving life. There were many others, which hosted different forms of life. What made our planet interesting or rather unique was the fact that it housed numerous, enormous, and diverse kingdoms," Simon was told. "All these kingdoms were so different in their forms, appearances, and characteristics that there seemed to be no apparent connection between them. Without entering into the details and similarities existing between them, we can divide these kingdoms into two groups. One group consisted of visible ones, while the second group was composed of invisible ones. They all shared the same space and the planet, but had parallel worlds, to live in, flourish, and seek their set goals. The evolutions that they followed were completely dissimilar to each other and yet required some kind of cooperation and interaction between them. In simple words, one could say that these worlds were not completely in isolation and totally unaware of each other. Occasional contacts in certain circumstances and on certain levels were permitted, but that was more as an exception than a rule. Very, very long ago, before the division of the visible and invisible came about, entire kingdoms lived in close contact with each other, enjoying all the fruits of nature and each other's qualities. Then came evil and chaos, placing great disasters on everyone. Deceit and greed cultivated death and destruction in all kingdoms alike. At that point in history, it was decided to separate them into two groups, by placing a thin wall between them. Memories of those times were completely erased from the minds of the remnants of those kingdoms, but strangely, that memory still lingered on through legends, myths and fairy tales. The visible world could see, feel and touch all the solid things around them, but were blind to see those things and beings that belonged to the other world, with the exception of certain animals that continued feeling or even seeing those invisible beings when they moved in their physical world. On the other hand, the beings belonging to the invisible worlds could still appear or disappear at will in both worlds."

Simon listened carefully and was amazed to learn those new things. Whenever he got a chance, he asked questions.

"Why were these invisible beings granted more freedom? Are they better than us?" he asked.

"It's not for me to decide and know why greater freedoms were granted to the invisible ones, but it's obvious that they do carry certain advantages. As I told you earlier, this contact is neither permitted, nor sought by those kingdoms without a valid reason. However, their eyes are constructed to be able to see in both worlds. I can only say that all kingdoms in nature are still imperfect and walk on the path of their evolution," replied his host.

"Isn't that unfair that the invisible kingdoms can witness and learn from our evolutions while we are deterred from doing the same?" asked Simon.

"Perhaps it's so, or perhaps it is done for our benefit," Bahor said smiling, before coming to the subject.

The giants belonged to the solid physical world. Therefore, if he chose to approach Fairyland through that kingdom, he could watch each and every movement they made without any problem. They were very huge, clumsy and slow, but that was not a great advantage since they had such enormous leaps.

The giants were neither good observers, nor very smart and clever. What really distinguished them was their incredible power of smell. For miles, they could feel the presence of odours, both familiar and unfamiliar. They were especially sensitive to unknown smells because that meant danger. Once they detected the odors, it was impossible to hide from them. They would go on searching until they found the source. What they did to intruders wasn't a pleasant thing to listen to.

Their big size forced them to live quite aloof and afar from each other, so practically the radar range of their smell covered all the territory they occupied as their dwelling place. They were good hunters, a necessary quality because they needed to fill their large bellies. They had been running big animal farms, which was an important source of nutrition. In short, the kingdom of giants was bare and dangerous. It was not a recommendable entry. Just their walking made the earth shake, and the very sounds of them made many a heart tremble. Behor smiled when Simon asked difficult questions. He confessed that he knew little about the big-bodied species and their history. He had no idea about their exact numbers, habits, weaknesses and other such details.

"You say they are all physical and can easily be detected by the eye, so why has no human ever reported those?" Simon asked.

"Most probably, no human has ever survived the dangerous territory, so how would they have warned others?" Behor said with a smile. "You wouldn't be able to confirm their existence either, if you go that way."

"So you believe that I don't have a chance if I go that way."

"I never said that. You wouldn't come to tell us even if you were to succeed in fooling these creatures and did cross their territory safely." Behor tried to calm Simon down.

"What stops these giants from venturing into our part of the world?" Simon asked.

"That's a very good question!" Behor looked impressed,

but remained silent for a while before he sighed, signaling that Simon needed to be attentive.

Behor had been trying hard to avoid details about the giants, but finally was ready to let go.

Many years ago, the giants lived almost everywhere on the earth and thus could easily live on wild animals and humans that came their way, Behor started telling him. Physically, there was no comparison between them and even the strongest beasts which they could just grab and devour without finding any resistance. The only places these giants were unable to penetrate were the thick jungles and other such places where their movements were hindered by nature. Human beings were one of their favorite foods, and they were happy to live near human habitations which they visited quite frequently to find prey. Simon listened in terror, trying to imagine the fears of people coming under attacks during such hunts.

"What forced them to go and settle in some faraway land? Why did they stop hunting human beings?" Simon was curious.

"These brutes continued enjoying the power and size advantage for quite some time until they realized that their most delicious food was also the most dangerous thing for them. They had no idea that the weak humans were only easy to hunt when they were just individuals, when they formed a group then they turned very nasty and difficult to catch. The weak humans had developed weapons and could easily fight back and inflicted wounds on them, which at times were even deadly. The human beings had given them new worries and forced them to be careful. The giants had stopped attacking these humans in their natural habitats and instead started relying on chance. When they encountered a human being on his own, it was no difficult task to overcome him." Behor paused to see the reaction on Simon's face and smiled finding him a bit relaxed.

"The Giants realised that humans were very different from all other life forms and functioned intelligently and were even full of courage. To their horror, human beings had started wars against their species, attacking them when they didn't perceive the danger, killing them when they slept and ambushing them when they sat and relaxed. Their strong smelling power was deluded by different scents, which were even used to attract them into snares."

"So our attacks forced them to retreat and hide in some faraway land?" Simon looked proud.

"No, that didn't take place overnight, but was accomplished in the process of history," Behor replied and went on, " Over time the war between humans and the Giants went on, where sometimes the Giants had the upper hand, while at other times the humans were more successful. The Giants didn't increase as fast as humans, and yet they would have managed to live with the increases in the human population, but something happened that forced the Giants to be on defensive."

"What was that?"

"Some strange disease that killed many of these Giants and they retreated so they would not lose more of their kind at the hands of the human race. They never fully recovered from that loss. The disease disappeared after some time, but the Giants would never be able to prey on humans again. The human numbers kept increasing, forcing the Giants to move further and further away, till they decided to move that far where no humans could penetrate their refuge. They have stayed in their new territories for centuries and watched over their land very vigilantly. They still remember the good old days and blame humans for their restricted movements and happily consume any human that comes into their land, as a delicacy and as revenge for being forced to leave their former dwelling places in the world."

"They must have increased their numbers again. Why don't they try to reclaim the world?" Simon asked.

"No, they never recovered completely. Their numbers are mysteriously constant while the humans have increased their numbers many thousandfold. " Simon could see that Behor had summed up the situation, and there was nothing more he could expect from him.

"Ever since I came here and got to know about other worlds, I have been thinking, is there any world or species with which we humans have forged a better contact?" Simon said as if blaming himself for all the problems existing between his and other worlds.

"Yes, we made many mistakes, but it would be wrong to blame us for all the complications that arose between the many different worlds. What was wrong with fighting back and trying to protect human beings from the rapacious Giants?" Behor defended his race.

"You are right, I have no right to judge my race like that, I'm sorry, I don't know what I was thinking." Simon was apologetic and made Behor smile.

"Don't ever be sorry for the questions that arise in your mind. They always help you grow, regardless of how ridiculous they may sound."

Elvesland and Fairyland both belonged to the invisible world. The elves were the opposite of the giants in appearance at least. They were so tiny that one could place them on the palm of one's hand and not feel the weight. The tallest of them could hardly be taller than a hand. They lived in a territory, which had beautiful lakes, thick forests and a lot of greenery. Their kingdom was full of wonderful flowers and trees of delicious fruits. They were believed to be the custodians of rare herbs, which could cure all types of diseases. Rapidity of movement was their trademark. The speed with which they moved made it almost impossible to see them, even if they took on a visible form.

These elves were neither violent nor hostile, but they were very alert and watchful of their land, and didn't hesitate to trap and eliminate any dangers threatening them. They worked in a strange way, never opting for a direct confrontation. They worked in a team ensnaring their opponent with each other's help until they had it trapped in a web. They were all magicians, creators of illusion, an illusion, which blinded and killed, so opting for that kingdom could be equally dangerous and life-threatening.

"What about Fairyland?" Simon asked.

"That should be your least problem right now!" answered the host coldly.

"Please, give me at least some information," Simon pleaded.

"I'm not sure if all I tell you is true or just a myth but listen carefully."

According to Behor the world of Fairies was different from all the other worlds that existed in the universe. It was a magical place where the inhabitants lived in harmony and positive energy that gave all its creatures a heartfelt peace that went deep into the soul. "That is what makes this world so unique and beautiful. At dawn, all the flower buds are brought to life by the morning dew and transformed into the most beautiful works of art that will take your breath away. These flowers spread the most harmonious scents like a gentle wave over the countryside, the beautiful waterfalls and over high mountain peaks.. Fireflies act as the guide for the fairies at night," Behor painted the Fairyland in such a fabulous way that Simon couldn't help but long for it.

"WOW, it'll be really fun to visit that wonderful place. What do these fairies look like?"

"Some people describe them as tiny creatures, almost the size of Elves while the other believed them to be closer to human height." Behor was not sure which of these descriptions was more accurate.

"Fairies are warm creatures that can be described as mysterious as few have the opportunity to get to know them and their abilities. They are very intelligent, but their knowledge is mostly about nature, animals, plants, herbs and berries. Fairies live in small beautiful houses that are made of natural materials, like flowers, plants, wood and mushrooms.

"Girls are quite innocent and cute in appearance and have the most beautiful hair. They have big beautiful eyes that reflect the stars and beautiful, delicate wings in different shimmering colors. The girls have the most beautiful dresses that they make out of flowers and other materials that nature has to offer. The boys are handsome in appearance and have smaller wings than girls. Fairies can charm any being with their playful, light-hearted nature. They have the ability to talk to animals and help them.

"Are they hostile creatures?" Simon asked.

"No, I believe that they are peaceful, but safeguard their territory vigilantly."

Behor knew that there was no way Simon could learn every important detail regarding the worlds he so eagerly wanted to venture into, simply because no one had access to such knowledge. He firmly believed in the existence of such worlds, but hadn't visited them himself. He was still unable to understand Simon's wish to become immortal, but didn't want to discuss the matter any further. It was Simon's headache to find out why he needed an eternal life, he thought and yet he wished to have a serious chat with the young man before he took his journey towards the unknown.

"I believe I have told you all that I know about these subtle worlds and even warned you about the dangers that lie ahead. You must know that there is an overwhelming danger of failure. Do you feel prepared for such an eventuality?" Behor confronted him.

"I'm ready to take my chances," Simon said with determination.

"What about your brother, have you really decided to leave him behind and press ahead on your own?" Behor asked unexpectedly and saw Simon turning nervously.

"What else can I do? I have tried to find David for years now. If I succeed in finding the spring of life, I am confident that I will find him sooner." Simon made it sound as though he sought the eternal life even for the sake of David. Behor didn't say anything, but just smiled.

"Well, it seems you have only one brother who ties you to the human world, and even that bond is not so strong any longer, so there is little I can say to prevent you from seeking the spring of life. Don't be disappointed if there is no such spring, just try then to live an ordinary human life as well as you can." Behor was realistic till the end.

"How far is Elvesland from here?" Simon asked.

"Honestly, I wouldn't know, but I presume that it is far, far away. Have you already decided to go that way?" Behor asked curiously.

"I don't know as yet, but it seems to be the best choice," Simon told him.

Simon sat and pondered deeply about the two choices

he had. He considered all pros and cons in the light of all he knew about both giants and elves and finally he made his choice. Though the way of elves seemed most treacherous and dangerous, he decided to move in that direction. In the meanwhile his host had been calculating, he concluded that with the modes of communication available, it would take years for Simon to reach it, with a big IF. According to him the way to Elvesland was not only dangerous, but inhabited by even more dangerous animals and human beings than he had recently encountered.

"How am I to afford such a huge expense, even if I don't mind the hardships of the journey?"

"That's an important question, but remember you are about to undertake an impossible mission." Behor sounded serious, making Simon's heart sink.

"As a last favor, I can arrange your transportation to the Elvesland," said his host.

"But how do you intend to help me?" asked Simon.

"I'll find some way or another. Go sleep earlier tonight, so you've enough energy for your task," said the host smiling.

"As a last favor, I will arrange your transportation to the Elvesland," said the host.

"How can I ever pay you back?" Simon said in thankfulness.

"But how do you intend to help me?"

"I'll find some way or another. Go sleep earlier tonight. So you've enough energy for your task," said the host smiling.

After that, they talked for a while and walked as usual in the woods. When they returned, Simon got something pleasant to drink before going to bed. He lay down on his bed and fell asleep at once.

12

When he opened his eyes, he looked around in astonishment. He found himself in a large plain. It took some time to figure out what could have happened. It seemed he had already been transported to the place his host had promised him earlier on. He looked around and saw peaks of giant mountains in the far distance. In the other direction lay small hills full of greenery. He knew at once in which direction to move. Suddenly he looked at his clothes and was even more surprised. He was dressed in dark green clothes. In one pocket of his trousers, he found an envelope which contained a letter and some seeds. The letter was from his host who explained how it was thought best to transport him while asleep. There were some final warnings and cautions.

"Do not rush! Have patience," was the last minute advice given to him. His host wished him the best of luck, which he needed badly. He did not know what the seeds were for, but he kept them in his pocket. The small green hills were not as close as he had thought. He kept walking towards them, and never got any closer. He could swear that he was as far from the hills as he was at the time he had started walking towards them several hours ago.

He decided not to waste his time, and walked all day long. By the evening, he looked at the distant hills and decided to halt. If he was to survive, he had to pass his very first trial, to get out of the huge field, which seemed worse than a desert, without any signs of life, without any trace of water. The only thing that made it look different from a wasteland was the green grass all around. Grass indicated the presence of water, and for that reason, there was supposed to be life. But ever since he had come to that strange place he had not seen any. He had become worn-out and felt sleepy. The complete silence was nerve-wracking. He felt a great unease creeping into his body. His sixth sense started warning him about some affliction that was about to descend over him.

"It's nothing," he tried to calm himself. The very next second he began running like a scared animal of prey, running with all the energies left as if struggling for his very life. He kept running all night, only stopping from time to time to catch his breath. He felt tired, his legs refusing to carry him any further. He attempted desperately to go on running, but after stumbling a few feet like a drunkard, he collapsed and lost consciousness. When he woke up, the midday sun was looking down at him. With tired eyes, he looked around and uttered a surprised, happy sound. He was standing at the foot of some green hills. Forgetting about his tiredness, he leaped towards them but fell. The muscles of his legs had not recovered yet, and he needed to take it easy. He was very hungry and thirsty, but gone was the panic and fear of last night. Painfully but steadily he climbed the small hills and came to one valley, where he found water and berries.

He saw small animals running around, and heard the chattering of all kinds of birds, and felt pleased. It was such a great feeling to be in the midst of life once again. It was a perfect place to stay and plan his next movements. Which strategies could he adopt that the Elves would not consider him a threat? What could he do to make contact with them so that he could convince them to let him pass? He confessed there was not much he could undertake, other than to wait and hope for a stroke of luck. All day long, he would go around exploring different parts of the valley. The valley in itself was not large, but contained many different types of bushes and trees. Some had berries and fruits, and others had beautiful flowers. There were even small lakes.

He sensed that he was being watched by the animals and birds. Perhaps he was already in Elvesland if not, then surely he was on the outskirts of that kingdom. For a few days, he just relaxed and collected his energies, and moved further away after feeling strong enough. This range of small hills seemed endless, with small valleys lying here and there. Amazingly, they all looked identical, making it a hard task to separate one from another. Was that just a coincidence or on purpose, he could not say.

Nothing worth mentioning happened, and he started relaxing. The beauty of the place was soothing and the atmosphere so peaceful that he almost forgot why he was there. One day, he saw a rabbit that seemed slow in its movements. Simon felt a great urge to catch and eat him, forgetting that in the absence of a fire, a rabbit was useless to him. He ran after the rabbit and got closer. In his excitement, he jumped and leapt forward to catch the rabbit, when he realised with horror that he was falling. He desperately tried to catch something, but found nothing. Luckily, he landed on a strong branch of a tree. Down below was a bottomless ditch. He sat still, scared and shocked.

From that moment on, he was more careful. The elves had started attacking, and he needed to be on his guard day and night. He measured each step before moving further. He chose his fruits and berries with a great care, and avoided those which he knew nothing about. He was even watchful when he slept because he couldn't afford another blunder. All this carefulness resulted in no further attacks. After almost two weeks of moving forward, he came to the end of the hill range. He felt triumphant and happy, but only temporarily. He was exactly in the place he had started his journey. He sat down in despair and silently cursed the enchanted hills. Far away, he could see the mighty mountaintops.

He tried three times to cross those hilly tracts, but kept going round and round in circles. He started believing there was no way out of that labyrinth. After the third attempt, he felt drained of all energies and cried out of a sense of frustration. He lay on a hilltop and watched the sky apathetically until it became dark and the stars appeared in the sky. It was a moonless night, so the stars looked extra bright. Suddenly, an idea flashed into his brain, and he jumped to his feet. He quickly made a new strategy and set out on his journey, with new energies, this time taking the guidance of the north star. He kept walking at night and resting and sleeping during the daytime. After five nights of travel, he was able to cross the belt of green hills. He felt happy at his victory over his obstacle, but knew that by no means had he succeeded in achieving his goal. Downhill lay a big meadow, and beyond that he could see nothing but large trees. The plane itself was quite an ordinary one, with a lot of bush-like trees bearing strange fruits. He dared not try any of them and kept walking towards the forest, fearing the new tests and trials awaiting him.

Those were the most interesting and beautiful forests he had ever seen in his life. In the beginning, the trees were thickly grown, near to each other, and stopping the growth of younger trees. The deeper inside he went, the more orderly they appeared, with strong stems, neatly arranged as though they were well tended. There were even natural paths, making it easier for him to walk. The whole view was lovely. There were millions of colours spread all around him. Flowers of rare beauty kept attracting his eyes. He could feel spring in the air and felt happy, forgetting his exhaustion. All day long, he didn't rest and moved on looking, liking, and appreciating all that came into view.

He had been in this forest for the past three weeks or perhaps more than a month. It was not easy to keep a record. He had a constant feeling of being watched, but never felt threatened. Neither did he come under new attacks, nor did he find any unusual activity around. Were they planning some deadly scheme against him or had they come to terms with him, accepting the fact of his presence? He had no way of telling which of those probabilities were closer to reality. Sometime he felt more at home than before, while at other times he felt like an intruder, an open moving target, and a declared enemy. He wasn't bothered at all but wanted more than that. He wished contact with the elves, as he sought their help, and desperately wanted a breakthrough. The members of the invisible world remained absent from his sight. This impasse was not what he desired.

"Ok, if you don't want to be friendly come and show your enmity," he challenged the elves in extreme anxiety. He listened to his own angry words, which he had shouted, and became bewildered. "Am I losing my sanity?" he thought with horror. His own loneliness was shattering his nerves. He longed for some companion, with whom he could talk and share his feelings.

There seemed to be no end to that giant forest. All around him was the forest, without any beginning or an end. He had lost all sense of direction. No northern star could ever help him again, since he didn't know where his direction and destination lay. A strange depression took hold of him, and he kept sitting, staring in front of himself without making any movement. "What's the use?" he thought in a resigned manner.

He was under a new deadly attack, but was unaware of it, and for that reason he could not defend himself. His nervous system was slowly poisoned and weakened and could collapse with little effort. His strong will was now destroyed, and he was even losing the will to survive. Few days more of such a state, and he would be unable to provide food and drink for himself, and would die of starvation. He would either die of starvation or kill himself in some bizarre way.

Simon started hallucinating. Sometimes he saw old friends from school, sometimes he saw his mother calling his name. At other times, he saw strange forms and figures going around, playing, laughing, and inviting him to follow them. He sat bewitched and didn't move.

"Come, don't hesitate," one little girl invited him.

"We know a wonderful place to rest," she invited once again.

He got up from his place and started walking behind her. Some powerful music was hurting his eardrums. The music was rhythmic, strange but beautiful. The girl walking before him seemed to be dancing to the tune of that music. Gone was his weakness and depression: he felt filled with the power of the music. The girl turned and smiled at him, and he felt joyous. Suddenly, he stumbled and fell on the ground. He got up and looked around, searching for the girl, but the whole scene was gone. The girl had disappeared as if she was just a mirage. Pulsating, beautiful music kept streaming into his ears. It seemed to be coming from a distance.

He started walking in that direction. Hiding behind a big bush, he saw a giant grassy ground filled with thousands, perhaps millions of very tiny beings. They were drinking, singing, and dancing in the moonlight. He noticed that it was a full moon, the traditional festive day of Elves. All night long, they went on with their activities, unaware of being watched. Drinking some toxic drinks had put them off guard. All of a sudden, a siren shriek replaced the wonderful music. A wave of surprise swept through them, and elves disappeared from his sight as if they were never there.

Was that luck or a coincidence that had saved his life once again? It was less important to know the answer than the bitter reality that he was very vulnerable indeed and needed some miracle to happen if he was to leave the place alive.

"Go back, go back!" he could hear clearly, the wind whispering in his ears.

"That's out of the question," he shouted back, knowing his behaviour was irrational and absurd.

He had moved and found a small cave to live in near a beautiful lake. He had lost interest in deep forests and went there only to search for food. He loved sitting at the lake's bank, or swimming in its dark green, murky water. He watched the daffodils and praised their beauty. He watched all kinds of animals and birds gathered there which made the whole atmosphere wonderful. He had almost forgotten the seeds he was carrying in his pocket. He decided to sow them near the lake.

Very shortly afterwards, there appeared some tiny plants, which grew rapidly. It didn't take long before they were full-grown and gave flowers. These white flowers had a wonderful smell, which spread miles and miles away in all directions. He could feel the presence of unseen Elves around him. In the beginning, this feeling was infrequent but grew stronger. Simon knew in his heart that had been surrounded by his mysterious unseen companions all the time. He couldn't have cared less as he had given up all hopes of having any contact with elves.

One day something strange happened as he came out of the lake after a swim. He noticed an elf staring at him. The little elf stood firmly without any sign of fear. After some hesitation, he came forward and stood few feet away from Simon.

"Who are you and what do you want?" asked the elf, in a straightforward way.

"I'm a human," Simon tried to explain.

"We know that!" The elf interrupted his explanation.

Simon introduced himself in short words and told the elf that all he sought was the way and passage to the Fairyland.

"I love your country, and I am a friend. I would be very much gratified if you let me pass through."

"Why should we? Do you carry any invitation from the Fairyland? Do you have the free passage seal? What's the purpose of your visit?" The elf asked so many questions.

"No," was his answer to all the questions.

"Then, we can't let you pass. It's best for you to turn back. We offer a safe return."

"No, I won't go back. I'll not retreat. I've to accomplish my mission or perish," Simon told him coldly.

"And what was that mission?" demanded the elf in a rough tone.

Simon explained his quest and determination to pursue it. He said he had come from the other end of the earth, and had not gone through all his sufferings for nothing. "Life without goals is empty, and it is worthless if you don't pursue them."

The elf didn't move from his stance. "Our territory can't be used by any human in their attempt to reach Fairyland. That's been a rule for centuries, I can't change it," was his final answer.

"I understand your rules," stated Simon.

"Do you know how much trouble and pain your kingdom has inflicted on all other kingdoms?" The elf didn't seem angry.

"I'm really sorry if human beings have been the cause of your sufferings," he apologised. Not all humans were bad, not all of them meant to do harm. He tried to convince the elf, who agreed, but still refused him the free passage.

"What made you change your mind, to become visible?" inquired Simon. He found reluctance on the tiny face of the elf.

"From where did you get this plant?" asked the elf.

"You've millions of fruit bearing and flowering trees and plants of your own, so why this curiosity?" Simon counter-questioned.

"This plant," the elf said, pointing, "was once part and parcel of our kingdom. We loved these beautiful flowers and believed that they were the most fragrant flowers that existed in any kingdom. But there was a big problem — those seeds. They needed little care and grew fast into plants. We had to do something before they dominated our kingdom. We stopped the production of new seeds, and were happy to contain them," the elf became silent for a while, and then he continued. "But one day to our utter shock and surprise, we found the roots of these wonderful flowers destroyed, plucked from the roots and impossible to save. We were devastated, but could never find out, what really lay behind that insane act of ruining our national treasure, even until this day, we are unable to know who were guilty of such an unforgivable and deplorable crime. We did our best to find the seeds of that plant, but failed to do so," the elf continued.

"We know that these flowers are not found in your kingdom, so we want to know from where you brought the seeds?"

Simon was reluctant to mention from where he had gotten the seeds, though he was certain that they were given to him by the genii world. He did not intend to disclose that he had been helped by the genii. "How do you know for sure that these are the long lost flowers?" Simon asked.

"We know and have no doubt in our minds that you have brought back the flower, which we had been looking for in many kingdoms for centuries."

Simon shrugged his shoulders and honestly answered, "These were given to me as a gift by a friend, from where he got them, I really don't know." The little elf knew that Simon was telling the truth.

"I'll not appear to you again, so follow my advice and leave," said the little elf in a cool tone.

"You know better than that. You can't force me out of here. All your previous attacks have failed."

"What!" cried the elf. "Who attacked you? When and where?" He looked amazed.

When Simon told him about the incidents, the elf laughed. "All you told me is coincidence or a fabrication of your own mind and have nothing to do with us."

"Now do confess that you want to eliminate me?" Simon demanded.

"Why would we want to do that?" questioned the elf.

He told Simon that they were peaceful beings, with no grudge against anyone. The only object of their strife was to stop his march towards the Fairyland and to convince and persuade him to return to his own world.

"Why are you so interested in it?" Simon was mistrusting.

"It's for own good, we have nothing to win from your decision," the elf said frankly. Answering a question, he told Simon that they had no king. Their world was governed by a council, which took care of the affairs of the kingdom in consultancy with the others. Before leaving or rather disappearing, he promised to take his request to the other members of the council to see if they could make an exception to the centuries-old rule and let him pass to the Fairyland.

Many days passed without any incidents. Each day, Simon hoped and waited for the elf, but he didn't come back. One day as he was walking, he heard someone calling his name. He turned and saw the elf, who was waving.

"I've been talking to the council members, and they share my opinion that you seem to be a stubborn but a good-hearted person. Very soon it will be autumn, followed by a very hard winter, which you in no way can survive. So we are in a dilemma. If we let you pass through, we shall be breaking the rule. But if we don't, we shall be responsible for your death," in amazement, he looked at Simon and laughed. "Isn't it ironic?" He asked, "To die while you seek eternal life."

"So, have they agreed to my request?" Simon asked excitedly.

"Not at all. I'm telling you that your appeal has not been rejected right away. You can go on hoping, although I'll not hope too much if I were you." The elf was full of humour.

Simon disliked most of his jokes as they were hurting his ego. Sometimes the elf said something witty Simon forced himself into joining the little person in his laughter. The elf promised to come back as soon as there was a decision by the council.

"How long a time can it take?" Simon asked.

The elf just shrugged his shoulders. "Who can tell? Maybe, a month! Or perhaps even a year!" He laughed, seeing the miserable face of Simon. "I'm only joking. I believe the decision shall be taken very soon if you are to be given a fair chance to move out from our territory before the harsh winter sets in," the elf told him getting serious.

In gratitude for bringing back their long lost flower, the council had finally agreed to make an exception to their rule and decided to grant him a free passage through their territory. With one and only condition attached that he was never to set back his foot in their land. Without giving it a second thought, he agreed and started dancing with great joy.

13

As a gesture of friendliness, hospitality and good will, the Elves gave him a farewell feast. Very select members of their society were invited. Tables were full of foods and fruits of various kinds, the aroma of which made it hard for him to wait any longer. After one of his hosts made a short speech, wishing him luck, and signed them all to eat, he had to restrain himself from jumping on the food and from hastening from one dish to another. He was conscious that they all were watching him. They kept eating and drinking until each stomach was filled and they could hardly move. His tiny hosts were amazing, they were going on filling their plates with big portions of food, filling their large cups with toxic drinks, never getting their needs quenched, making him wonder, where they stored all that stuff?

The elves were tremendously funny and entertaining people. They told amusing stories and laughed heartily. The strangest thing was that they went on drinking alcoholic drinks without getting drunk.

"Why do you want to live forever?" asked one elf, who sat beside him.

"To live life fully," answered another elf, and they all laughed.

"Wouldn't you?" Simon asked.

"No, not at all, answered the elf. "Why bind myself to this miserable world forever?" They all laughed again.

Simon asked if they could provide him with some information about Fairyland. They all kept silent and avoided the subject.

"Historically, we always have had very good, and cordial relations with Qaf, said one of them.

"What's that?" Simon asked.

"Didn't you know that it's the name fairies used in their world?" the tiny creature asked before continuing. "However, we don't have very warm and friendly relations with them at the moment." There was no time to discuss the causes of that sad happening. So they requested him, not to ask many questions about the Qaf or Fairyland as he called it.

"What do you call your own world?" Simon was curious.

"Mysco, what else!" the elf said after a moment's hesitation and looked proud.

"That's indeed a beautiful name, much better than the one we humans have given it," Simon said to please the elf, who just smiled.

Suddenly, a hot debate started. They all spoke in a language that he could not understand. They were presenting their arguments with strong voices and made strange acrobatic movements. He was sure the debate involved him, but dared not ask any questions as he didn't want to offend his hosts. Slowly, they all calmed down and became normal as if they had not held any discussion at all. Holti, the elf he had first met, came and sat beside him. "You, my friend! Have brought some life into our otherwise very dull country," Holti smiled and patted his shoulder. He told Simon the argument was about him. They had just realized that granting you the safe passage was not a very clever idea. The matter had made them realize that the already constrained relationship between the two countries would suffer a further blow, when the ruler of Qaf saw Simon coming from Mysco. An act of ill will, an unfriendly gesture and most certainly a breakdown of all agreements made in the past.

"If there was any precedence, they would have reversed the decision," said Holti and smiled.

"So what've they agreed upon, then?" Simon asked.

"Our wise ancestors left the saying behind, where there is a man, there is a trouble."

Simon joined him in laughter. Somehow, it touched his heart. Getting serious, he said, "I don't want to cause any trouble, I would be really sorry if the relations between the two lands got worse because of me."

"Maybe you should withdraw your request, saving us the embarrassment," suggested Holti.

"Yes, maybe I should," said Simon in a gloomy voice.

"Or maybe, we should just be clever and improvise!" Holti said, and laughed and laughed.

Holti's plan was no doubt a cunning one and was immediately accepted by council members. Though morally wrong, it seemed quite harmless. They had decided to transport him near the border of Devia, a name given to the Giantland in their own language. When the inhabitants of Qaf would notice Simon's presence, they would take it for granted that he had approached their country through Devia.

"Have you been to Devia?" Simon asked Holti, who affirmed it without saying the words.

"Aren't you afraid to visit that dangerous land?" Simon asked.

"Why dangerous, they are too enormous to even feel our presence there, they are too dull to catch us, even if they could see us. Besides, we are furnished with magical powers and therefore, never fear anything in that land."

"I would have been terribly afraid to go that way," Simon confessed.

"It's exactly there you would be taken to, but luckily it is on the other side of the border. Be joyous!" Holti said with a tiny laughter.

"How much time will it take to reach that border?" he asked.

"Sooner than you can anticipate," was the answer.

"Close your eyes and count ten," he was told. He did as he was told and waited for further instructions.

"When shall I open my eyes?" he asked, but got no response. After some waiting, he opened his eyes, and was surprised to find himself on the top of a hill, looking at vast fields. At his back were great black mountains. They were full of precipices and looked impossible to climb. He thanked his choice of coming through Mysco, instead of choosing Davia. Easily he came down to the fields and started guessing, which direction to follow, but he had no clue.

He felt weird in his stomach, remembering the warning of Holti that since the Fairyland was an invisible kingdom and he lacked the eyes capable of seeing the invisible, there was a great possibility that he would just pass by their dwelling places, without even noticing them. There was hardly any point, sitting and thinking about the direction. He had to make a blind choice, and that he did, by choosing to head straight to the west.

For miles and miles there was nothing except some fruit trees, and some thorny bushes scattered all over the fields. His intuition told him that he was heading in the right direction. The only thing worrying him was the fear of not noticing the habitations of the fairies as he went, therefore overlooking them.

For days, he kept walking and came nowhere. The boring, dull surroundings made him remember and miss the wonderful Mysco. "What a contrast exists between the two places," he thought. He didn't feel lonely because he saw small animals and singing birds on the way. The only thing he needed was a guide, who could lead him straight into the heart of Qaf, their dwelling places, and their capital city, the place he had been feverishly seeking since he came to know that clues to his search could only be found there. Yet he was never that frightened as he was at that moment. It was the fear of missing the final opportunity.

The only thing that remained clear in his mind was the simple fact that if the journey was his, then the ordeal was his too. His whole body ached, and he felt sick. He saw a beautiful lake and became happy because it was the first good-looking thing he had seen in a long time. He felt weak and lay down to rest on the bank and started watching the flying birds. He felt dizzy and closed his eyes and fell asleep. He had a high fever and had no strength to go on. He kept dozing all day. He was forced to stay there for more than three days. The fourth day the fever left him, but he was still weak and exhausted. He had consumed all the fruits he was carrying with him. Despite his poor condition, he decided to continue his journey the next morning.

The next morning, he woke up at dawn. He was still very sleepy, but some strange flapping sounds prevented him from falling asleep again. He was convinced that his fever had not left him completely and that he still suffered from hallucinations. He tried hard to push the memories back in order to sleep, when he heard the sound of wings flapping once again, making it clear to him that he was not imagining the things but that there was really a powerful sound in the air.

It was dawn, but still very dark. He sat down and looked towards the lake. With great difficulty, he pinpointed a dark silhouette and saw someone taking a bath and singing in a melodious voice. Slowly he came closer to the bank to watch and saw some clothes lying there. There was not enough light yet, so he could not see the bathing person, but knew for sure that it was a fairy.

Simon stood there perplexed, his heart pounding with excitement, and his whole body shaking from the thrill of the experience. He waved at the fairy without making a sound.

Suddenly, the fairy caught sight of him, looked in disbelief, and disappeared. He sank down in disappointment; his golden opportunity to meet a fairy had gone with the wind.

"Please, please don't disappear," he shouted at the calm lake, but he knew that his pleading was useless. He looked for the clothes, but they had disappeared, as well. He waited and waited for the fairy to become visible again and finally gave up when the sun rose. With a heavy heart and weak body, he resumed his journey. The landscape changed drastically, and now he was walking through a desert, without signs of any vegetation or water. He realised his mistake of entering into that wilderness and decided to turn back, but it was too late.

All around him were the sand dunes, and he lost the direction he came from. If he had any doubts before, they were gone now. Without food, water and a sense of direction, he was already a dead man. He looked at the sky and saw some vultures hovering at great heights, and knew that they too were sure of their coming meal. The scorching heat of the sun and the shortage of liquids in his body made him more vulnerable. He felt the effects of dehydration becoming more evident. He was losing his strength very quickly. His feet were sore, his legs heavy and weakened, and his whole body swayed back and forth until he could go no further and collapsed. He was still conscious, or rather semiconscious, knowing perfectly that his time was up.

He heard a flapping of the wings and knew that the vultures had started gathering around him. Those vultures could patiently wait for hours or even days for their feast to begin. He was scared, but too helpless to move. He tried to open his eyes to look at the vultures. His vision was unclear and shaky. He couldn't see any vultures. With great effort, he turned to the other side and saw a beautiful fairy looking down at him. Her long golden hair shone and her beautiful blue eyes looked down at him with sadness and pity. He tried to smile back at her. His heart was filled with joy. He was going to die happy, looking into the eyes of a beautiful creature. He could have done much worse. Simon fainted.

He woke up and found himself in a cozy bed. Was he dreaming? He was in that large room, lying on a comfortable bed. He jumped from his bed and looked around at the strange but beautiful objects in the room. He could just remember up to the time he got sick, and all the other memories had faded away. How did he come there? Where was the bedroom located? Who were his hosts? He kept thinking. The best way to find the answer was to find the people that lived there.

When he was leaving the room, he heard someone approaching. A radiant fairy entered. She smiled when she saw him standing in the middle of the room. Simon looked at her and kept staring without speaking. Smiling, she introduced herself. She explained to him how he ended up in her bedroom.

"When I was taking my early morning bath in the lake, I had not the slightest idea of being watched, and therefore, was stunned to see you standing on the bank. My only and natural reaction was to become invisible," she told him. "I was curious to find out what a human was doing in our land? How did he enter it? What were his intentions? To know more, I decided to stay and watch. But then you took the path to the desert, I knew you were lost and would surely perish."

The fairy told him that the law, neither allowed nor accepted her pity for him. By saving his life, she had committed a crime and was going to bear the consequences.

"What consequences?" he asked.

"I don't know; it's the first time in centuries that a human has come to Fairyland. And perhaps I'm the only one who has ever broken the law," she answered in a light way.

He felt sorry and ashamed for putting her in trouble. "But you don't have to report it," said Simon.

"Yes, we have to. I've already informed the queen," answered the fairy.

"That was not very clever," Simon said in disbelief.

"What makes you believe that I did something wrong?" asked the fairy, a bit surprised.

"Isn't it obvious that you try not to disclose a secret if it is going to harm and hurt you?" Simon looked equally surprised by her irrational way of thinking.

The fairy smiled, understanding that he was a stranger who did not know their way of thinking and living. She could easily ignore his logic and discuss something else, but her sense of responsibility compelled her to explain the matters that were important to her, as an individual and a member of society. Smilingly, she told him that his awakening from a long sleep had delighted her, and his conversation was a further indication that he was functioning to his full mental capacity.

The fairy was more interested and curious to know what brought him to her land, and how he managed to penetrate her otherwise isolated country. Simon noticed that she was not very argumentative and didn't fuss around about things she didn't agree with, but simply went on with her unending questions. Simon briefly told her about himself, his quest and the tiresome journey. While speaking, he could not help looking at her beautiful face. He couldn't get enough of that incredibly good-looking person, who felt embarrassed by his daring stare.

She was patiently listening to his remarkable and baffling story and didn't interrupt him during his narration. "Not that I doubt your account of the things or challenge your wisdom, but is it not that you have taken all the risks and the hardships for such a diffuse and vague story?" the fairy asked, perplexed. Simon didn't mind her questions; by now he had gotten used to the doubts people had about his sanity.

He was not reluctant to confess that he was a weird person, making the fairy smile; she seemed to be sympathetic. Simon wanted to ask many questions, but found her distant.

"I'll leave you to rest and recover. Feel free to move around in the house, but don't try to leave it, as it may cause some problems." What problems she was referring to, he felt like asking but dared not. The fairy left, promising to come back later, when her other activities permitted her.

Simon was half-asleep, when he heard her coming into the room. She was almost on her way back, when Simon made a sound to get her attention. She turned and smiled apologising for disturbing his rest and sleep. "Don't worry about my sleep. That's what I have been doing all day long," said Simon. She could see from his face that he was happy to have her company.

"How was your day?" the fairy asked in a friendly tone.

"I am in heaven. I couldn't have dreamt of a better bed, and such a cozy room I have never set my foot in." Simon appeared to mean each word. "I'm thankful for your kindness. There is no way I can ever repay your generous gesture to a stranger." The fairy looked at him and smiled, trying to figure out whether the man was trying to flatter or was just being gifted with eloquence.

She apologized for not coming back earlier. "I had to meet the queen in order to clarify certain details about you," the fairy explained. The word queen reminded Simon of his particularly uncomfortable position in that country, and he felt jumpy. She was aware of his anxiety, but there was little she could do to make him relax. The only thing she could really offer was a discussion so that he may not only understand the gravity of the matter but even mentally get prepared for the possible outcome. Despite Simon's reluctance, she started talking about the subject. With patience, she had listened to his story and the purpose of his coming into their world, now it was his turn to listen to what she had to say. She tried to be explicit, full of sympathy and tact, avoiding the serious matters, if for no other reasons than only to spare him the anguish and unease. She was talking about her own society, the rules that governed it, the way it functioned and reasons of their isolation from most of other kingdoms. She was plain and honest, telling him the history of her country without trying to emphasise the truthfulness of it, and without even judging the other kingdoms in nature.

The fairy was quick to convey that her knowledge of the human world was much more profound than he could anticipate.

"I have even visited your world a time or two. Though it happened years before, I still have some memories of those brief visits," she said.

Simon was curious to learn more about her visits to his world. He was excited by the mere prospect that it might be her flapping wings he had heard years back, but the fairy didn't want to disclose any details of those journeys.

"Your world is beautiful, but I would prefer my own as that is the most natural part for me to love, live, and understand." The fairy was quite careful in her use of the words as she had no intention of ridiculing or alarming her guest.

14

Zeibi was trying to present her own world, which was quite contrary to his part of the world. Her world was uncomplicated, where the vices were constantly confronted and sought solutions for, where the virtues were appreciated and well-guarded. They were all free and equal, but that freedom entailed responsibility and that fact was well understood and sought in earnest by all members of their society. The whole society was built on some simple principles, which demanded an honest reverence by all of them. Live and let live, mutual respect and the collective well-being of society as a whole were the main pillars the whole kingdom stood on. Nobody lied because there was no need to. No one hid anything from others as openness was adopted as a policy, which benefited everyone. Simon was listening in amazement, wondering if he would still be alive if he had practiced such honesty in his own world. The fairy continued with her narrative, unaware of his pondering and comparisons between the two apparently opposite worlds.

Fairyland was not some chaotic and lawless country that would surrender its sovereignty in favour of certain individuals that in return could behave in some uncontrolled manner. There were rules and laws, which everyone had to abide by; the only thing that made them different from the human world was their flexibility. They could be easily broken if needed. Such a provision was not without some consequences. The rules could be broken, but only if one was ready for the repercussions. Therefore, on one hand it could be tempting to defy and break the rule, but the resulting consequences prevented one from doing so. There were some acceptable excuses. So consequences were according to the circumstances and intentions.

"What makes them different from the same rules applied in our world? There too, one faces the consequences of breaking the laws and rules." Simon was at a loss to comprehend.

"The difference lies in implementation and law enforcing agencies, which exist in your world while here it's done more effectively, without any need for an outer force." Simon still could not understand the true significance of her words, but decided not to press her for any further explanation.

Coming back to the matter that affected him personally, she said, "I have had a long meeting with the queen; she seemed to be very much troubled and upset by the news. Your future lies in her majesty's hands. Without a doubt, she is the most prudent, good hearted and understanding being one can ever think of. But even she needs some time to study this unprecedented coming of yours into our otherwise well protected world." The fairy was discussing the dismay of her queen openly.

"What do you think will happen to me?" Simon asked nervously.

"I wouldn't know what she will decide, but my guess is that you will be sent back to where you rightfully belong. I believe that before such a thing happening, it will be properly investigated, as to how you could enter our land. It needs such an inquiry if we are to stop future entries into our land by human beings." Her answer was straight without invoking any false hopes in him. After a long chat, she left him, promising to come back in the morning.

When he expressed his desire to go out and see the fairy

town, her eyes widened in disbelief. "But you won't see anything; you're blind to our world," she told him. "You can see me and my home because I have special permission to make such arrangements for your convenience." There was not much he could do other than to sit idle and wait for the queen to call him for questioning.

The queen was very young and beautiful. She appeared to be kind, but equipped with searching eyes. She seemed unconvinced about his entry from the Giantland. Her sharp questions were hard to answer. She could see that he knew almost nothing of the Giantland's landscape and that he was not equipped with the knowledge necessary to climb the mighty mountains. She could notice he was hiding the truth, but he insisted he was speaking the truth. The rest of his story and his purpose seemed true. She listened to all his answers and then sent him back.

"You will be brought back to hear my decision," the queen informed him politely.

"She might deport you back to your world. You don't have a valid reason to stay here," said Zeibi, the fairy he was staying with.

"That would be a disaster," said Simon in a scared voice.

"Relax, you're not thrown out of Fairyland yet," Zeibi laughed.

"Say, why are you afraid of us?" asked Simon a little disappointed.

"Afraid?" Zeibi looked at him in astonishment. "No, we are not afraid of you."

"Then, why these restrictions? Why these barriers? Why these divisions of visible and invisible?"

"You believe this is all because we are afraid of you?" she asked with a smile.

"What else could it be?" Simon said.

"No, dear stranger, it has nothing to do with fear, at least not that type of fear you imply."

She went on explaining. Whatever caused the separation of the two worlds, they could see now that it was the best solution. All the kingdoms in nature had benefited from it and were flourishing without any conflict. Before those divisions, the kingdoms were exploiting each other to reap fruits that didn't belong to them. They were forced into unnecessary confrontations, depriving them of the precious time that was needed for advancement on the evolutionary arc. Simon felt the need to defend his kind, but Zeibi assured him that he didn't have to. She was well aware of the details of history and knew that the separation wasn't entirely the fault of human beings.

"But, aren't we the only losers?" cried Simon. "You and others from invisible worlds can freely move in or out of our worlds, but we're barred from entering into yours."

"No, you're wrong," she corrected him. "Sure, we seem to have advantages over you. We can function in both solid physical worlds and invisible ones. But believe me, we have to live by the rules as well," she paused to watch his emotional face. "However, I must confess that on subconscious levels, the contact was never broken, so our kingdoms intermingle and cooperate on planes you don't have any idea of. Likewise, the contact is retained on the highest possible levels." Without going into detail, she continued explaining. She stressed that all individuals of the different kingdoms belonged to the same great family. They had varying characteristics, and developed different tools in order to make progress in their given tasks.

Simon confessed that he did not know much about the causes of the separation that prohibited all types of contact between the visible and invisible. He was a simple man who couldn't question the wisdom of those who had devised such a solution. He only wanted to find some understanding heart, which would allow him to stay in that country in order to seek his destination and destiny. The only interest he had in their country was to get more information and then to pass on. Whether the kingdoms flourished, or decayed was not his major concern.

"You see, I'm a simple person who has never caused any harm to anyone. And yet I suffer from the follies of those of my kind, which were committed ages ago."

Zeibi could see that Simon was too preoccupied and was refusing to confront the truth. But she had done her best -- at least for the day.

A few days passed, and Simon was waiting impatiently for his call from the queen. He was confined to Zeibi's home for two main reasons. First, it was useless to go out since he would be blind to their world and second, his presence in the kingdom was not disclosed to the general public. It was considered unwise to inform people of his arrival because it would have invoked curiosity and even fear among the citizens. The queen was aware that it was wrong to withhold information of that magnitude, but after deep pondering, she deemed it a necessary thing if she was to avoid panic. No one was to discover that a human being had entered into the country if Simon was to be deported. Less reason there was to inform the general population if Simon was to be extradited.

"How much chance do I have, of getting permission to stay in your country?" he asked Zeibi repeatedly.

"That little!" She teased him and laughed, when Simon moved back and forth nervously.

"Come, don't be a child," she made fun of him.

"I know it sounds ridiculous, but I'm helpless. I need to search for that valley. That's that."

If he were to sit and wait for the decision all alone, he

would have gone mad if he had not died of anguish and fears first. His long days and nights were filled with an unending excitement of having the most beautiful person by his side, who wasn't only pretty, sympathetic and inquisitive but had an innocent golden heart. She was capable of making him forget about his fearful state of mind. They sat and talked for hours about different things. She was very curious about human beings. All of her knowledge about the world of humans was old and bookish. Even if she had visited his world a few times, her contact with human beings was nonexistent. She wanted to update her knowledge. Her questions demanded elaborations and details. He tried to be honest and hid nothing, even if it seemed to embarrass. Her dark blue eyes glittered with excitement. They talked and talked and never had enough of each other. Simon was happy that Zeibi was there to keep him company.

He became pale when he got the call from the queen. He shivered like a dry leaf.

"What type of man are you?" Zeibi laughed hysterically when she saw his poor condition. He felt ashamed, but knew no means through which he could control and hide his feelings from her. "What's worse, to be deported, or to become food for some giant?" She teased, before taking him to the queen. Simon knew well that she was reminding him of the fact that he was to be sent back in the direction he came from. Though it was a joke, it sent shock waves through his body, knowing perfectly well that he could not survive in the hostile Giantland.

The queen received them in a cordial manner. He tried to bow, but Zeibi stopped him. They kept silent, waiting for the queen to speak. The queen looked at Simon intensely before she started speaking. She explained how the human kingdom, always had been close to her heart, how she admired the bravery and empathy inherent in humans, and their unique quality of sacrifice was something they all needed to learn. She went on for some time. Finally, she came to the point.

"I've considered your case with great sympathy and interest. I can see that you are a good, nice being, who is not any danger or threat to our country. I doubt your wisdom, when you have come so far, searching for something that is just a myth. I do believe that your purpose is not to stay, but continue onwards to your set destination." The queen kept silent for a few seconds. She surveyed his pale face and continued.

"I'm sorry to inform you that despite all the good things I've said, my decision is to follow the rules, and send you back to your world. I can understand what this decision must be doing to your heart, but believe me, that was the only thing I could do in the given circumstances."

"Your majesty!" he cried.

"I've come this far by dying a hundred times. No pain has ever been worse than I'm feeling right now," he pleaded. "Is it possible for you to deport me to the direction of the valley?"

"Yes, we could offer you that favour, only if we knew where that valley lies."

"You don't have any connection to our world, so you have to leave it. Such is the law. By dawn, you shall be transported away from here, not to the Gaintland but directly to the human world. That's all I had to convey to you."

Simon opened his mouth to plead once again, but his glance met Zeibi's, who looked both sad and concerned for his sake. He felt ashamed and embarrassed for exposing such a wonderful creature like her to any kind of anguish. He immediately decided to withhold his further requests and pleadings. With bowed head, he spoke with a trembling voice and assured the queen that he would accept her decision and cause no more distress to her. He looked once again at Zeibi and smiled sadly.

"You are the most wonderful person I have ever met in my life. Thanks for all kindness you have so graciously bestowed on me. I'll always remember you with great warmth." Zeibi was sitting and listening to his words but avoided his gaze.

"Milady!" Zeibi spoke softly in a respectful manner, and asked permission to speak, and said when she got the sign to go ahead.

"According to law, you've the power to allow a stranger to stay in our country if he or she married someone."

"Yes," said the queen in an astounded voice, "but who will marry him?"

"I shall if he wants to," said Zeibi boldly.

The queen kept silent for a few seconds. She did not look happy. When she spoke again, she tried to persuade Zeibi not to make any hasty decision, which she was to regret later. She reminded her of long past historical examples of such inter-kingdom marriages, which were mostly unsuccessful, leaving one or both of the partners to suffer and lead an unhappy life. She advised Zeibi to be prudent if it was a crush, an anti-crush potion could be arranged for her. If she was doing that out of sympathy, it wasn't worth it as wedlock demanded love and not pity to become the foundation of such a bond. But it seemed Zeibi had made her mind and wasn't moving an inch from her decision. The queen saw there was nothing more, she could add to change her resolution. With a troubled sigh, she agreed to reverse her deportation decision and granted them permission to marry, and thus Simon could stay in the Fairyland.

15

Simon was very happy and thankful to Zeibi. First, she had saved his life and now she had saved him from being thrown out of her country. But despite that thankfulness, he made it clear to Zeibi that his stay in Fairyland was of a temporary nature, and he would move on, when he had enough information of his destination. She was quick to declare as well that her interest in him was more of a helping nature than a romantic attraction. Both of them agreed to remain close friends, even if their ways separated from each other's.

"I won't stay here even a day after I have found the way to the valley," warned Simon.

"Yes, I know that, you stubborn man," Zeibi answered with a big smile. "But you would be a prisoner of mine if there wasn't any such valley," and laughed.

He was summoned once again to the queen. "What now?" Simon was afraid.

"You know you're blind; someone has to operate you," Zeibi told him jokingly. He didn't like the word operation, and feared what they were about to do with him. Zeibi told him that he had nothing to fear, and besides that, she was to be by his side, holding his hand, if necessary.

"What if this operation does not work?" Simon spoke out of fear.

"Then we must send you back to your own world, I don't want to be married to a blind man," she said seriously, looking deep into his eyes, and laughed when he became all pale. At times, Simon loved her sense of humour, but at other times, he hated it. Without saying anything further, he waited for the time they were supposed to visit the queen.

This time queen wasn't alone. A male fairy sat by her side. They both smiled at him, and queen signed them to sit in front.

"You know why you're here?" The male fairy asked in a low soft voice.

"Yes," was his answer.

"This blindness of yours is a result of a decision made centuries ago and is inherent in all members of your physical kingdom," said the male fairy. Simon understood that the reference was to the great separation of the worlds. "After that division, the invisible beings were allowed to keep all their senses and qualities while the physical beings were deprived these gifts. One of these gifts was the third eye. This third eye could not be taken out of a human, so it was decided to close that eye till the time your kingdom was again ready to use it." He went on, explaining that not all his fellow beings were blind like him. However, there existed people in all times who had earned the right through sacrifice to use that closed eye, and as a consequence had the complete sight.

"You have not earned the right to get your sight back in a traditional manner. Nevertheless, you have this right as a member of our society. This process is normally a gradual process, so as to eliminate the dangers of things going wrong. But we do not have that much time. So we need to adopt speediest methods." The male fairy told him.

"How long will it take? Simon asked,

"It depends on many factors. There is no set rule, which could determine the speed of the work."

"When will you start your process of awakening my third eye?" Simon asked.

"I believe we have to start right away," The male fairy said.

Looking at Zeibi, he added. "I hope your husband will not make much of a fuss about living separated from you." Zeibi just smiled.

Simon was to accompany the male fairy until his third eye was functioning perfectly. It could take days, months, or even years; no one could say for sure how long the process was to take. The only guarantee the male fairy could give was that his third eye would not be permanently damaged by his treatments. He felt nervous to leave the familiar company of Zeibi, but had no choice other than to depart immediately. He took leave of her and went with the male fairy. Mr. Tontis asked him to hold his hand and close the eyes. He did as he was told and felt as if he were swaying in the air. A few seconds later, he was asked to open his eyes again. The atmosphere and landscape reminded him of Elvesland.

"Where are we?" he asked Mr. Tontis, who told him that they were in the bordering area, at the place where Fairyland and Elvesland met. Most of the trees were no longer green, but had all shades and colours, reminding everyone that it was autumn. Nature was bracing itself to face new realities, the trees, foremost among everything which grew, were in the process of getting rid of their leaves, in order to get ready for the hard winter.

Mr. Tontis was a gentle and kind fairy, who was not very talkative or asked many questions about him or his world. He didn't live in that place, but had a beautiful, comfortable hut where he used to spend a few months each year. Without losing time, he started working with Simon, by making different tests. Before each test, he would give him some soothing cold drink, rub his forehead softly, and make him sit motionlessly for several minutes.

"Can you see my third eye?" Simon asked.

"We all can. And thus we know that you're blind," was the

answer of Mr. Tontis. After the tests, started the treatment. He applied very strange and special fruits and drinks at intervals. His sleeping room was arranged with flowers, which gave very penetrating smells. He was given a few stones and crystals to carry at all times. Mr. Tontis gave him soothing massages on the forehead twice a day. He could feel his head growing full of flowing energy. Sometimes, he felt so great a flow that he got afraid. Noticing his great tension, Mr. Tontis would immediately stop his activity and leave the room, asking him to calm down and relax.

The whole process went on, and with each passing day, he was becoming accustomed to those new energies. Still, there was no apparent progress. Simon could feel signs of discomfort and worry in Mr. Tontis's eyes.

"Is there any chance of my remaining blind?" Simon asked Tontis, who didn't try to hide the fact that it was possible.

If a person stood a chance of gaining the visionary eye back, it was a very complicated thing, requiring a long range of experiments and observations, Tontis told Simon. "Your case is even more complicated than we imagined as it seems that you have been straining your third eye in recent times, which has caused some damage." Tontis was a bit perplexed as to how and why Simon had succeeded in doing something he was not even aware of. But he was not a pessimist and was confident of opening the third eye, even if it took a longer time than he had previously hoped for.

From time to time, he went through new tests and careful observations by Mr. Tontis. Sometimes he could see certain things; sometimes he did not. Mr. Tontis believed that he was making very slow but encouraging progress. Metaphorically speaking, he could not be considered wholly blind anymore. His occasional sight was a clear indication of a success and that his eye was not damaged as Tontis had earlier feared. But according to Mr. Tontis, they had little time left before it was winter.

"I can't go on with the treatment without certain juices, fruits and herbs," he looked concerned. "Soon, it'll snow and it would be almost impossible to have access to all those necessary ingredients. We'll be stuck here until the end of winter."

One day, Mr. Tontis was out searching for some fruits and herbs, and Simon decided to have a stroll. He looked at the flowers and trees and felt happy because he knew them well from the Elvesland, and had grown love for them in his heart. He kept walking until he came across an elf who was busy plucking some berries. He put them in a basket and moved to the next bush. He seemed to be happy, and was singing some folklore. All of a sudden, he turned and caught sight of Simon. For a few seconds he looked confused and afraid, but then smiling, he came forward and exchanged a few greetings with him and went his way.

When he told Mr. Tontis about that encounter, he looked surprised and asked many questions. How tall the elf was? What did he wear? How exactly did he greet him? He listened carefully and then asked him to lie down and relax. After all the checkups, Mr. Tontis shook his head.

"Your story indicates that your third eye is now functioning. But I see it is still closed." He told Simon that he must have seen the elf with his third eye. There was no other explanation for the phenomenon. Because if the elf was moving in his physical body, he would only disappear the moment he had noticed that he was being observed.

"He must have seen your third eye and knew that you are not blind." Tontis was sure of his theory, and he was absolutely right in his analysis, as at times Simon could now see the invisible things, while at other times he could not. Each time Mr. Tontis made the tests Simon failed.

One day Mr. Tontis informed Simon that he was to be away for the rest of the day for some personal reasons. He instructed him what to eat and drink when to rest, and so on. "Never ever go north, because then you'll be out of our territory with the surety of not being able to come back." Mr. Tontis left.

He was bored and started looking for some books in the bookshelf. Most of the books were written in strange languages, so he was about to turn away from the bookshelf when he saw one strange wooden box, lying in a corner of the room. He went forward and opened it.

There were a few very old books in that wooden box. One of the books was about Elvesland. He got interested and started reading it. There were some charts and maps. The book was hand written; many words had faded completely the others were difficult to read. This book was no fiction. It described in detail the length and breadth of the kingdom, which other kingdoms it bordered, and how one could approach it from different directions. There were even hints of needed preparations and instructions as to how to behave and make friends with them. Simon could swear that the writer of the book surely knew his topic.

Suddenly, he heard something moving in the hut. He watched Mr. Tontis enter the room and looked surprised to find him back that quickly. Simon asked Tontis if he had come back early or if he had dropped the idea of going on his errand.

Mr. Tontis didn't answer and kept looking at him. "Sorry that I am reading this book, without your permission. Hope you didn't mind."

"No, I didn't," he said with a big strange smile. "You can't

imagine how pleased I am seeing my work accomplished."
He came forward and patted Simon on his shoulder.
"Greetings! Now you're a man of full vision." If there were
any doubts before, they were gone now. Mr. Tontis had
never left the hut and was there all the time, making
himself invisible. When Simon found the invisible wooden
box, and started reading the invisible book, he knew that
his work with Simon was done. Now he was looking at him
with deep smiling eyes, very content.

"By looking at the shine and sharpness of your eye,
nobody can tell that it had ever been blind," Mr. Tontis
said and smiled. He seemed to be proud of himself and his
work. Simon's happiness knew no bounds. His days of
isolation were over. He was to join with Zeibi shortly, who
would be even happier than he himself. He was about to
see that which he had so desperately wanted from the
time he came to the Fairyland. The people and their
habitations were to open themselves in his sight.

"This is an interesting book," Simon commented.

"Yes," answered Mr. Tontis. "All such books were written
before the separation, and served no purpose anymore,
and were withdrawn consequently." He said that though
correct, such books were not updated and lacked many
details, which were later but vital additions.

Simon wanted to discuss the Elvesland with Tontis
because he had very many unanswered questions about
that mysterious land, but he restrained himself, as he was
fearful of betraying his secret of being there. He was full of
excitement and couldn't wait to tell Zeibi about his
breakthrough regarding his sight. She was very happy for
his sake and welcomed him home, when he finally arrived.
He was transported by Tontis, who looked content and
proud in his first-ever achievement of restoring some blind
person's sight.

"Did you see the city while you were returning home? Isn't it wonderful?" Zeibi asked with enthusiasm. No, he had not seen the city yet as he could not have enjoyed the pleasure without her company, she was told by Simon. She felt touched and promised him an unforgettable experience.

16

The moment of the final encounter with the Fairyland had finally arrived, making his heart throb faster and faster, out of indescribable exhilaration, in anticipation of viewing some magical scenes, of seeing something, which had remained hidden even though he had been living in that reality, ever since he came there. Zeibi was there to witness his stunning experience, and he was happy for that. Surely, he was the first human to have come this far, but even other guests from the invisible kingdoms occasionally came on brief visits to the Fairyland and were enchanted by its rare beauty. "Shall I open my eye?" asked Simon impatiently.

Simon was astonished to look at the Qaf in broad daylight as it opened itself to his sight. Indeed, it was the most wonderful world that lay before him to watch and enjoy. It was a more magical place that he had ever imagined existed in our universe. It was a way outside our everyday world, beyond our ordinary senses and knowledge. This fabulous world looked as if it was made of millions of colours, the colours that were interwoven into each other in the most natural and harmonic fashion, complimenting and contrasting in an amazing way. The incredible beauty is the result of that perfect blending of the colours and the strange but attractive materials that the world was made of. The strangest feature of the scene was that these colours were not dull or hindered the view from viewing the other details. It seemed as if each stone of that the world was placed in the proper place, each and every thing was proportional and in perfect harmony with other objects. Nothing was over- stretched, nothing was excessive, and nothing was deficient in that affluent world. Simon looked at the landscape and found incredible, beautiful trees and flowers spread in every direction, uplifting the spirit of the viewer. He went closer to watch the details and felt a welcoming perfume embrace him. He touched one glowing red flower and felt like he had come in contact with the softest material in the world, even softer than silk.

"Welcome to our wonderful world," Simon heard the flower say and almost jumped, making Zeibi laugh.

"What was that?" he inquired, still baffled.

"The trees, plants and flowers in our world can communicate not only with each other but even with us," Zeibi told him with a smile.

"Why has no tree or plant ever talked to me before?" Simon still thought it to be some trick.

"Have you ever seen the trees, plants and flowers like you do now?"

"No, what's the difference this time? Why can I see their glory, which remained hidden before?"

"It's because your third eye enhances your other senses as well. You consciousness levels were raised to a level hitherto unknown to you."

"Can I speak to them as well?"

"Sure, just give it a try." Zeibi looked amused by his careful approach to the flower that had just spoken to him.

"Did you really speak to me earlier; how did you know that I'm a stranger over here?" Simon asked.

"Well, it's not some deep secret. The astonishment with which you look at everything reflects that you're new in this world."

"I hope you don't mind my moving on, perhaps we could talk some other time," Simon apologized.

"No problem, I'm not going anywhere soon, see you around," said the glowing red flower and smiled, it was obvious that the flower lacked eyes and mouth and yet Simon could swear that he saw the smile. Simon moved around very excited, taking notice of every tiny detail and felt as if he were in the heavens. He looked at the tall trees, their tops almost touching the sky and felt astonished to find so much variation. It appeared as if they all sprang forth from gold dust, which glimmered like diamonds without even sunshine or other light touching it.

"Is it pure gold?" he asked in disbelief.

"No, nothing can grow out of the metal you call gold. The soil in Qaf is naturally this color," Zeibi explained.

"What about the shine?" Simon wasn't convinced.

"Remind me later, I'll explain about the secrets behind shines and fragrances. Keep enjoying your encounter with our world, which is of course also your world now." Zeibi was amused at his child-like excitement. When he calmed down a bit, Zeibi told him that he had all the time in the world to get acquainted with Qaf and its environment, so there was no need for him to stress. She reminded him that his newly evolved faculty to see in ether was permanent, and for that reason he could count on discovering many amazing things in the days to come.

"Right now you are looking at the Qaf from the ground, which offers a different experience than the one you will get when I take you to the heights for a view. You will see the beauties of our world in a different light when you watch it at nighttime. Just enjoy every moment and try to absorb, save all your questions for some other time and I promise to give you the best answers I can."

"Why don't I see many birds in Qaf?" Simon asked, and Zeibi smiled. "Didn't I just advise you to simply enjoy watching?"

"You're right, I'm ever so impatient," Simon confessed with a shy smile.

"Go around and see the wonders with your own eyes, come back when you believe that you have enough for the day. I'll take you out once again later on. You need to rest before you can enjoy breathtaking scenes."

"Would you answer my questions when we come home?"

"I would have preferred it if you asked them after seeing everything but let me see what I decide, when we reach home."

Simon walked briskly in all possible directions and felt extremely happy to watch the amazing things. Despite the fact that the soil beneath his feet felt different and even gave a soothing odor, he had a feeling of being near to earth, and thus felt secure. He looked at the bushes, which could be found abundantly in Qaf, and of which he had been eating and sustaining himself in the days and weeks when he first entered the Fairyland. These bushes looked different than before; he saw their fruits glowing with energy and beautiful colors vibrating. Simon could clearly see energy patterns in these fruits, and immediately knew what they would contribute to the consumers. There were wonderful lakes around, so calm and so clear that he could see each and every life form. The transparent water soothed his nerves almost to ecstasy. He was enjoying every single moment in the fabulous world of fairies. He wanted to go on with his awesome observations, but Zeibi asked him to be careful and not overburden his already strained senses.

"We go home now, so that you may rest for a while before we return and you can watch Qaf from new angles," Zeibi suggested and strangely he didn't object to the idea.

"What a world!" Simon exclaimed after they came home.

"Yes, our world is fantastic and we love it more than

anything." Zeibi answered proudly.

"Tell me a little about these talking plants, trees and flowers." Simon couldn't wait anymore.

"What do you wish to know?" Zeibi asked with a smile.

"Everything! I want to understand the phenomenon."

"The vegetation in our world is different from yours, as you have already noticed. These plants and trees thrive, pulsate and provide like nowhere else in the entire universe. They are generous and open, keeping no secrets from their surroundings. Their attributes are known to all of us, and even if there is some obscurity, one can always approach them and inquire."

"It's amazing that they can talk," Simon confessed.

"Would you be surprised that even your trees and plants do the same, though your ears are deaf to their tiny voices?" Zeibi said with a smile.

"No way. You've got to be kidding me." Simon was quick to respond, but Zeibi ignored his comment and went back to her explanation.

"The flora of our world is highly developed and home to those kind spirits, who have chosen to be close to our hearts and thus develop a closer relationship with us. They flourish in the harmony of our society and munificently exhibit their achievements to us."

"What kind of achievements do you mean?" Simon looked puzzled by her choice of that peculiar word.

"In different kingdoms, the measure of development varies and I'm sure you must be aware of this fact. There is no individualization in the vegetable kingdom, but there are different classifications and divisions, which show their points of achievements through the colors, shines and fragrances. Just by looking at these three qualities, one can tell the status of a certain plant or a tree."

"Are these the only criteria?" Simon asked.

"Of course not, there are other measures like the taste of fruits, healing powers and many other features that we will not discuss at the moment," Zeibi told him.

"The most peculiar thing about these trees and plants is neither their wonderful colors nor their heavenly fragrances or their ability to communicate."

"What are they good at then?" Simon looked curious.

"The flora is in some mysterious way connected to us so intensely that it gets affected by our state of mind and in return affects us positively. When we are harmonised, the plants and flowers thrive like nothing else, giving the best they contain within, the colors, the brightness, their wonderful smells and their other qualities. It's our joy that gives them the energy they need and it's our dance and music that fills them with harmony and power. Our world takes care of these evolved spirits and in return they are bountiful."

"What happens if you stop being in harmony or some unfortunate event takes away your pleasures?" Simon asked without thinking and saw the worried face of his wife and felt remorse.

"I hope such times will never come to our world, but if that happens one day, these plants, trees and flowers will certainly wither and die. They simply can't survive without receiving their nutrition of love, harmony and power." Zeibi spoke slowly as if she were afraid of speaking out aloud of such disastrous possibility.

"Can an individual's mood disturb the balance of this kingdom?" Simon asked.

"Luckily no, it's a collective impact we make on them, our individual moods have limited influences on the greenery around them alone. Even such happenings are rare as most of these trees and plants are good listeners and excellent counselors, fairies troubled by one or the other factors do go and take advice from these green ones and thus recover," Zeibi explained in detail.

"That's great, so there are hardly any major threats involved."

"Theoretically, yes. But we are anguished by the knowledge that our world and its harmony hang on our collective states of mind. We try hard to live balanced lives and control our temperaments, as they can make or break our wonderful world."

"How do you remedy any imbalances?" Simon asked.

"Simply by meeting the challenges at their root levels, never letting these grow to some monstrous levels," Zeibi replied and then continued. "As long as we can go on restricting these problems to individuals, we don't have to worry about our collective well-being."

"I'm astonished to hear that even your world is not perfect," Simon confessed, still doubtful of what she had just revealed.

"There is nothing like perfection in any world, we all have to realize that the worlds are made by us and we have responsibilities to sustain them. Luckily, our species is aware of the vulnerability and is actively striving to safeguard our world," Zeibi said with a broad smile, her fears were no more lurking in her beautiful blue eyes.

"You promised to tell me about the reason why there aren't any birds in this part of Qaf?" Simon asked remembering.

"The birds belong to our kingdom and therefore are part and parcel of our evolution, where we fairies are at our best. The birds' presence in your world is more as a symbolic representation than any other practical value. They are there to witness and learn some lessons that can teach them to appreciate the beauties of Qaf."

"That explanation is good, but it doesn't answer my

question."

"I know that," said Zeibi smilingly. "The ordinary birds are deliberately deprived of entering and living in protected parts of Qaf, so that they may not know what awaits them in the unforeseeable future. It's for the best of birds."

When Simon asked her to elaborate, she told that she couldn't tell him more as it involved the secrets of her own evolution.

"Here in the midst of Qaf, the fairies are the only birds that are allowed. Many birds can penetrate the atmosphere but would remain blind to the place beneath."

"Is it to avoid accidents in the air?" Simon tried.

"There are no such dangers involved," Zeibi said and smiled at his attempt to ask the same question differently.

"Not quite yet, you have to wait a few more moments, if you want to have the maximum effect." He heard Zeibi's melodious voice. He could notice that she was enjoying his childlike excitement.

She had deliberately chosen the time near dusk, as it could be the most appropriate moment for any first-time viewer to see the magnificent unfolding scene.

When he finally opened his eye, the picture was beyond any words or descriptions; it wasn't like anything he had previously seen or even heard of. He looked around in amazement, unable to concentrate on any single scene, propelled to move on with his bewildered gaze. The sun had set and darkness was rapidly covering the landscape, but there was still enough light for him to witness the most incredible panoramic view. His whole being felt the sensation that ran through his veins.

They were standing on some great height, from where he could observe the entire city without even the slightest effort. Far away, he could see an unending chain of mighty mountains, with their sky-touching snow-covered tops and knew without a doubt that those were the mountains bordering the Giantland, the direction he had approached the Fairyland.

The sky was full of fairies who were swaying, flying around with great ease. The clothes they wore were of very beautiful colours and fabrics. No one seemed to be in a rush, making the whole atmosphere harmonic and relaxed. Every now and then, a fairy would only opt for a stroll instead of flying. The whole scene was filled with carefree laughter and melodious sounds.

The mighty mountains were changing their colours and instead of their original black colour, were turning into orange red. This transformation was an amazing happening. He felt like turning and inquiring of Zeibi about that particular occurrence, but so absorbed was he with the strange surroundings that he didn't bother. Orange red mountains were getting more and more dark, and it didn't take long before they were glowing as though set ablaze.

"What's that?!" Simon could not help his exclamation.

"That's the sign that night has set in. These are our lamps in the absence of the sun. It's light, enough for outer atmosphere," Zeibi tried to explain the phenomenon.

He looked at the sky and saw twinkling stars shining far above and felt their magical beams falling on the Fairyland like raindrops. He could swear that it was really happening in that fashion and not only in some metaphorical sense. He looked down at the city, which lay spread before his eyes and felt confused. The city had disappeared from his sight and instead he could watch uncountable stars beneath his feet.

"These are our city lights!" he heard Zeibi explain before he could burst into another exclamation. The city lights were glittering and making everything visible, which otherwise would have gone beyond the cover of darkness.

"So you don't have any darkness in Fairyland?" asked Simon in astonishment.

"Yes we do, but only when we want it," Zeibi was feeling proud to see his enchantment. Simon was enthralled, and went staring around him, overwhelmed by the unprecedented experience. Perhaps he could go on for the rest of the night, but suddenly he felt weary and dizzy, and surely, he would have fallen on the ground, had not Zeibi rushed to his side.

"I believe that's enough for tonight. You have plenty of time to learn about my country, so why hurry?" Bringing Simon back home appeared to be a tougher task than she could anticipate.

Simon wouldn't sleep; he wanted to go on discussing the awesome event of his watching her town. Zeibi could understand his pleasure, but tried to cool him down, assuring him that the excitement was of a temporary nature, which would disappear within a brief period of time. Few days more and he would get so used to all those things which excited him at the moment.

"No, one simply can't get used to the magic like that," Simon was insistent. Zeibi just smiled, without any further argument. If he was enjoying his experience, then who was she to destroy it by disillusioning him, she thought and kept listening, without encouraging him. "Why don't we go out and watch the fairy town?" begged Simon repeatedly.

"What's the rush? You know that this experience is heavy for your body and senses. Why do you want to overburden yourself?" Simon could feel the excitement lingering on, and thereby keeping his mind all alert and far away from sleep. He was unable to relax and enjoy the images that kept entering his head.

"Come, I know a remedy to your problem." Zeibi invited

him to sit erect and he did as he was told. She disappeared into the house and appeared after a few minutes, holding a bottle with some liquid in it.

"What's this?" Simon asked. She told him that it was some oil that could help him relax and release the tension his body was not letting go. He was asked not to ask any further questions or say something, but to close his eyes and unwind his mind. She took the thick, pinkish oil, poured it on the palm of her soft, beautiful hand, and slowly rubbed it into his hair. An incredible odour spread in the room when she was anointing his head. A soothing, penetrating, wind-like sensation was replacing the excitement in his body, making him sleepy. He had liked the comforting change and wanted to ask something of Zeibi, but instead he was driven deeper and deeper into sleep, until he lost all sense of time and was fast asleep.

What would have made Fairyland, worth its name, had it not been for all those remarkable and unique characteristics, if it had not its magical surroundings, its awesome beauties, and above all its peaceful existence? Fairyland was without any possible doubt a place from the realms of dreams, with all its colours, odours and wonderful vibrations, which in its own turn bestowed tranquillity throughout the whole region. The initial shock was soon replaced by a constant appraisal of this kingdom's perfection, of all its novelties and its fully functioning systems. There existed nothing but exactitude in all matters. Solutions had been found for all thinkable problems, touching all fields of life. Precision and truthfulness were the key words of their serene society.

There was hardly anything in that place that could remind him of his own world, which he had left behind not so long ago. The air, sky, and even the sun and the stars looked different here. They were brighter, more soothing, and even closer than they seemed in the human part. The trees bore sweeter and larger fruits and so did the soil. When it came to the city, there wasn't any comparison, as it looked like no other habitations he had ever visited before. The streets of Fairyland looked dissimilar in the daytime than they did after the sunset. In broad daylight, when the sun shone brighter but without giving excessive heat, the streets remained cool and pleasant. They were made of some strange stones, which gave the impression that one walked on a soft, fine carpet. These stony pathways absorbed the heat in the daytime, only to reflect it back in the night, and that explained the phenomenon Simon had witnessed, while watching the Fairyland for the very first time. The shining stars on earth were nothing else than the reflective light coming from the pathway stones.

These stony pathways were very broad and luxurious, spreading for miles and miles in all directions. Sometimes they appeared to be some straight lines laid there for no particular reason, as the fairies seldom used them. But the formations were not just straight but adopted all geometric shapes, turning here and there, if for no other motivations than for aesthetic reasons. The same could be said of the fruit bearing trees on both sides of the huge roads and streets. Those trees were strange; he could swear that he had not seen them before, even if they occasionally reminded him of something from his own world. One could believe that rubies, emeralds, and other precious stones were hanging from their delicate branches. What really surprised him most was the fact that the great town was not built in the ordinary manner as he had been used to from his human world.

17

The fairies built their homes far above the land. The places of their dwelling were lofty, airy, and large. It was almost impossible for him to know what material they were built of as he had not seen such a thing before. Though the stuff seemed to be natural, it had so many colours that shimmered with a different intensity that he suspected it to be some artificial material. There were all types of houses, large and small, decorative and simple, whirling ones and static ones. The characteristic that was common in all those beautiful, breathtaking buildings was an apparently impossible construction technique. They all lacked foundations and any direct contact with the land, forcing Simon to wonder how they could remain hanging in the air, without any support or connection. To watch something hanging between the earth and the sky was a scene of such a great magnitude that he found himself speechless. He had not been in many of these houses, and therefore, could not describe the interiors of these wonderful houses. Looking at Zeibi's house and a few others, he had recently visited; he could tell that the fairies lived in Spartan style, just having the things; they absolutely needed for a comfortable life. When he asked Zeibi about the strangeness of the hanging houses, she smiled, but saw no weirdness in it.

"Logic is not some absolute and universal entity, demanding the same results and rules in all conditions and circumstances," she said trying to make him understand. "I can recognise your bewilderment as I myself had experienced the same disorientation when I visited your world the first time and saw your habitations." Zeibi was trying hard to solve the mystery of the hanging houses by explaining the laws of nature and how they could be broken by knowledge. She was telling about some pull of the earth, which forced everything to fall back on earth if not supported by some opposite force. That opposite force was found in the skies in a latent shape. All they had to do, in order to sustain their houses suspended in the air, was to release the required pull of the heavens above, which they did without any difficulty.

"What would happen, if one of these pulls was disproportionate?" asked Simon looking down at the earth far below.

Zeibi smiled seeing his anguish and assured him that there wasn't any such danger as the pull of both ends were regularly checked and adjusted by the fairy world.

"Even if it was to happen one day, it would not cause us any harm since we all can fly. On the other hand, it would be a serious problem for you." Zeibi was teasing him by looking down and making him aware of the fact that he was far from his natural grounds. She laughed when he looked helplessly at her.

Fairyland was not as deprived of greenery as was his very first impression. The forests of that wonderful country were equally thick, colourful, and full of varying flowers, trees and all kinds of birds. There was the most striking and peculiar fragrance in the air, soothing the nerves and intoxicating the senses. One felt uplifted and content because mother nature seemed to be pleased and generous in her openhandedness, and was expressing her inner harmony without restraint. The whole kingdom was living and breathing in the soft, kind embrace of nature and appreciated each minute of it, fully aware of the unique possibility it offered to them. They did so by returning the lovely gesture in the same gentle way. No one would ever harm any other life form, on the contrary a helping hand was offered to a needy co-creature, whenever needed. No one appeared to be unhappy or in pain, or at least not in his worldly sense and meaning.

The whole of Fairyland looked like a controlled dream from which one never had to wake up. There were fairies of all kinds and sizes. There were males, females and children. But the strangest thing of all was that they all looked young. He had not met a single elderly until then. Some of them walked like humans, but most of them preferred to fly and could be seen swaying in the air. Their big wings looked strong and superb, capable of even resisting the highest pressures and making their way in the stormy winds. But what really staggered him most was the discovery that a few of them were without any wings.

No one took any notice of him; they simply smiled and nodded as if he was one of them. He never felt odd or a stranger in the Fairyland.

"Why can't anyone see that I'm a human being?" Simon asked from Zeibi.

"Sure, they know," she answered. Simon became puzzled. She smiled and explained. "Few of us fairies don't have any wings as you may have noticed."

"How come?" Simon asked.

"They are the offspring of bygone generations, the products of the marriages which took place, centuries ago, between fairies and beings without wings."

That explained away his confusion. "How do they fly then?" he inquired.

"What do you mean? Don't you know that we can all fly with or without wings?"

When he answered negatively, she explained that their wings were more of an aesthetic than a practical value.

They had outgrown the need of those wings and could easily fly without them. Their wingless flying was more rapid and comfortable, and not at all as tiring as it had been in the past. "Flying to us is a most natural thing. It is a natural and unconscious act like breathing," she tried to explain. He was unable to believe her, but she looked serious. "Our children don't learn crawling, but flying first."

"You mean even I can learn to fly?" Simon asked.

"Of course, even you can learn to fly. But it would be neither easy nor a natural act for you as it is to us," was her answer.

Time went by in Fairyland. Simon was so happy with his life that he almost forgot why he was there. His wife Zeibi was the best thing that had happened to him. She was beautiful, wise, and witty with so much knowledge about everything that he was surprised if she didn't know about something. Physical work was none existent there, so they had constant leisure time. All their needs were taken care of.

"What a luxury!" he would think in the beginning, even arguing at times that it was not the right thing to do as it was sure to take away the driving force in the long run. He refused to accept the argumentation and the objection that in no way was he capable of thinking independently. What he believed to be his own thoughts were in fact the thoughts taught to him by his society, and that was the only truth valid in his part of the world. Now he had gotten accustomed to all the comforts of life, like all the other members of the Fairyland. Unlike elves, fairies were quite lazy and luxury loving creatures. Instead of doing physical work, they used the power of the mind and dominated the unformed shapes of life. The elemental beings did the entire necessary jobs and they did so without any questioning or reluctance on their part. All the fairies had to do was to think and wish, in a certain manner, and the armies of unthinking slaves belonging to the kingdom far below, started working to accomplish their commands and the jobs were done like magic.

The fairies hated the word magic, and called it mental supremacy or mental domination of the elements. Nevertheless, it was magic. They were the master magicians, who had complete knowledge of the blind forces inherent in the elements. To invoke them and to exploit them they had perfect tools of colours, sounds and lights. Smells of flowers, herbs and other minerals were equally used to control those neutral but useful forces. This so close contact with the natural forces brought other benefits, as well. They were all perfectly healthy and unaware of major diseases, thereby eliminating the risks of sudden and unexpected deaths. They were vegetarians, living happily on the substance and nutrition offered to them by Mother Nature. They could not even understand the necessity of consuming each other, when the task could be achieved through harmless ways. Simon had tried in the beginning to defend his meat eating habits, but finding disgust on Zeibi's face had forced himself to avoid the subject. Strangely, he had not missed his meat eating and felt perfectly at ease with the delicious food he was offered.

The long, healthy lives had somehow not disturbed the balance in their population. The numbers of their population were almost stagnant. There were no restrictions placed on the number of children one could produce, but very few children were conceived in Fairyland. So the number of dying ones and those who were born almost matched. The children in Fairyland were always few, making the community of young ones a rare commodity. So they were dearly loved, cherished and taken care of. The children were not only the responsibility of the parents, but they were equally a collective responsibility. These children were easy to take care of as they were taught the sciences of elemental control at a very early stage. And it was here the collective approach was needed most because to play with these elements was more dangerous than to play with fire.

Simon was very happy to be in Fairyland. Here was all that he could ever wish or dream of. Life was a dance on the roses. Everybody was kind to him. They didn't care if he came from some other kingdom or some other planet. As long as he looked like he did, having his eye of vision open, he was most welcome to live and be part of them, enjoying the fruits of their wonderful kingdom. In their town, the weather had no influence. Summer, winter and, autumn came at their appointed times, but their arrivals were more of a formality, a humble visit, without the extremes of cold or heat. Without any doubt, the spring was the only reigning force in that magnificent place.

Simon often sat in the garden with his wife looking at the stars. "I've always loved these vaults of heaven," he would say with a sigh.

"These stars have been my companions in the long, lonely hours of the night, when I needed some comfort or understanding."

"They are the lamps placed there to invoke our fantasies, to give us assurances of continuity of life, and they serve as a reminder of the presence of other life forms, which have risen so high from our world," Zeibi said in a good mood.

"What do you mean by that? How could they reflect those things?" Simon was puzzled.

"Don't you know that our planet is just a tiny part of that gigantic whole, which we call our galaxy and that the unimaginably vast galaxy is just a tiny fraction of the universe," Zeibi inquired a bit surprised.

Simon had no shame in confessing that for him, those stars were nothing more than a deep mystery, about which he didn't know anything other than that they lay at a far distance, giving humanity a guiding light in the dark hours.

"Please tell me about them, so that I may rise above the ignorance that I so helplessly find myself in," Simon requested.

Zeibi was more than eager to tell him what the fairies knew or believed about the stars. "The planet earth is nothing more than a very tiny ball, hanging in space," she started.

"You mean like your hanging buildings?" asked Simon without much surprise.

"Exactly! You are learning quickly," Zeibi said with a broad smile and then continued. "These stars, which seem to be far away and look like tiny balls to your naked eye, are not that little as they appear to be. In reality, they are so big that you can't even imagine their size. They are so far away that it would take millions of years to reach, even to the fast travellers like us." Simon was listening with awe and disbelief, without suspecting her of exaggerating her narrative.

"These stars are our future destinations, for which we prepare ourselves now and here," Zeibi told him enthusiastically. She was comparing those stars with a staircase she had prepared for his going in and out from her home, adding that those stars were the places they all had to reach before striving for even further heights.

"Where does it end?" asked Simon.

"That's the beauty; there is no end, no ultimate goal. One could go on and on, without reaching anywhere, which could be the end of all endeavour."

"Why do you think it's beautiful? I'm horrified by this endless struggling." Simon didn't hide his dismay at her description. Zeibi laughed seeing him getting depressed by the notion of endless strife.

"Don't get upset!" she comforted him. "I'm talking about a process and not of one lifetime. So there is no point in getting panicky."

According to her, those stars were made of some shining stuff from which emanated cold, serene light, which was guiding, healing, but contained the seeds of hope and ardour, as well. The speed of that light was the fastest thing anybody could know in all the worlds.

"Is that really so?" Simon asked surprised.

"That truth holds only partially," was the answer he got, which puzzled him more. "There is something else, which can move with even faster speed, but unfortunately, we can't use it as yet in any world. Though at the very highest levels of existence, that force is being used as a mode of transportation and that is the energy of thought" she explained, but Simon failed to understand.

"Do you know where we go, after we are dead?" She asked.

"No, I don't know," Simon answered.

"We believe we go to that star," she pointed in one direction.

"That's Orion," Simon told her.

"Maybe so, but that's Farlin to us, which means paradise," Zeibi said, staring at Orion with a strange smile at her face. "Both of my parents are there, and one day even I'll join them." Zeibi said happily, making Simon anguished as he hated to discuss the topic of death.

"How does it look in your paradise?" At last, he asked, taking interest in her subject.

She was happily describing the place she believed the deceased fairies went, after their earthly tenure. He was listening to her lengthy description with great interest and laughed heartily when she came to an end.

"What more can a paradise offer, which you don't have here?" Simon said looking deep in her beautiful eyes. "Believe me, we are already in heaven."

She was very amused and kept laughing, "You see, you are even learning our humour. Would you tell me honestly how and from which direction you came to our land?"

"Through Giantland" he answered confidently.

"That was a great answer," she laughed again. "Not even a fool could believe you,"

"Why not?" Simon asked.

"Even if you did make it through the land of giants, you needed the skill and necessary equipment to cross the mighty mountains, not to speak of your complete ignorance of those incredible and cruel hosts in that hostile part of the world."

He had to give up. He could not go on lying. He told her the parts of the travel story he had omitted before, and the transportation help he got from some jinni, his entrance in Elvesland and all the rest. A triumphant smile was on Zeibis face while she listened with interest and concentration.

"I knew that you were not telling the truth," she said. "But could never have guessed that you came through Elvesland. You are the first being who could enter from that side," she went on telling him that she knew exactly where he must have landed because it could be the only place where a genie could drop him without being detected. The Enchanted Plains was the name of the place. A buffer zone existing between Elvesland and wasteland. It was a big green field, where there was neither food nor water to be found, and which worked like a trap with no apparent escape route.

"It's really a wonder that you came out alive," she said. The only way to cross it and reach the green hills was to do it in the darkness of night. In order to do that one was forced to run all the time. It could only be his intuition, which had helped him come out of the trap. The green hills or labyrinth, as she called the hills, were, in fact, the first outpost of the elves.

"I must say that you had luck with you all the time. Otherwise, no one could survive that long in Elvesland," Zeibi told him. Simon had been lucky to survive, but more amazing was to learn how he got the contact and finally the permission to enter into Fairyland.

"They must have liked you; as they agreed to let you go."

Simon asked her what the problem really was between the two kingdoms. She sighed before saying anything. According to her, there was a big black stone in Fairyland. This round stone was believed to be not of the earth, but from the sky, as a gift from some other world. This stone could store the light of the sun and reflect it in the darkness. For centuries, it was the only source of light for them in the darkness of night. Years ago, this stone was stolen. Some fairies acted unwisely and started accusing the elves for the deed. The things got worse when the elf population of Fairyland was outraged. The anger was translated into disloyalty to Fairyland. There were accusations and counter accusations by both sides. Things calmed down after a while, but relations between two friendly kingdoms were damaged.

"Did you finally find the black stone?" Simon asked.

"No, it was never found," Zeibi told him.

"I didn't know that you had a population of elves here."

"Oh yes," she said smiling. "They have their members in all kingdoms. That's how they got the nickname of "eyes and ears of nature.""

They went on talking about elves, about their love for nature, their humour, their drinking habits, their wonderful music, and their lovely dances. Zeibi was very much impressed with those tiny creatures.

"They have very many qualities and are gifted creatures, but what scares me most is their temperament. They talk loud, they are easily angered, and they are unpredictable at times," Zeibi concluded. "I love them anyhow, sweat little creatures."

"I can't say I love them, but they are some characters," said Simon and laughed. Getting serious, he turned to his wife and said. "Just by looking at your face, I could find the feelings of dismay and annoyance at the very mention of the word genii and the help I got from them in transportation. Tell me honestly, do you people really hate them that much? Can't you forget the happenings of the past and just move on?" Simon asked frankly.

Zeibi kept silent for a long time, her face getting darker and her eyes full of dread. Either the question was unexpected, requiring some pondering or she had no desire to discuss it, in both cases he had to wait for her decision to talk about the matter or not. He noticed her tense face getting normal, but the sadness remained lingering on.

"Talking about genii is never an easy task for us," she confessed and went on. "The subject is so very loaded, associated with pain, suffering, and anguish, so we prefer to avoid it completely. No, we don't hate anyone, but at the same time we can't forget about the darkest period of our existence, during which we had been enslaved, humiliated, and bereft of all the gifts bestowed upon us. For us, that life was not worth living."

She was terribly disturbed and poignant, making him feel sorry to bring up the subject. It seemed as if he had awakened demons from the past, and reopened the wounds their long history had failed to heal. He wanted to apologise for bringing up such a distressful matter, but had no chance to do that. Zeibi continued, "Time is the greatest healer, we are told, but even that mighty force has failed to remove the heavy burden of bitter memories from our hearts. Getting rid of genii subjugation was not an easy task, which required untiring and resolute efforts of members of our kingdom, for centuries." Zeibi stopped and looked overwhelmed by bitter memories.

"It is strange that it affects you that much as if you yourself have been suffering from these awful events, though I have heard that it all happened long, long ago," Simon said, a bit surprised.

"Oh. Only if you could penetrate into the heart of a fairy, could you know that past, present, and future, are but the fragments of the same one entity we call time. I can never get rid of the pain and suffering of my bygone generations as it lives in me, as a constant reminder so that I may never have the need to experience it again," Zeibi said with a sigh. "If the pain from the bygone times is a silent memo from the past that commands us always to be on guard, then the pleasures I enjoy right now are the fruits that the coming generations shall cultivate."

Simon was nodding as if he understood, but he didn't want to interrupt her and therefore, kept silent, not asking about the things he didn't comprehend.

Zeibi was telling him about the kingdom of genii, which had turned evil in the wake of the immense power they had acquired by the great efforts of their forefathers, which never had the intentions of enslaving and dominating the other kingdoms. The huge power of genii was irresistible, and thereby opening the gates of oppression and superiority complexes in the genii world. She agreed that not all members of that community were necessarily evil, but did believe that the evil was still very strong and potent in that kingdom, which could cause pain and harm to others. "Recognising this fact makes us more careful and vigilant against that threat the genii pose," Zeibi concluded.

"I have heard some strong warnings have been issued to the genii not to venture in your direction," Simon said.

"I really hope that they'll heed these warnings," was her short answer.

"Sometimes I wonder, what has stopped genii from seeking your world again as I don't see any defences in here, no armies to protect you from the onslaught, if it was to come one day," Simon spoke his mind.

"Basically, we are peace-loving beings, who seek no hostility, nor do we expect any animosity from other kingdoms, but nevertheless we are prepared to meet any major threat posed by others," Zeibi answered.

"Would you please elaborate?" Simon didn't understand what she meant.

"When it comes to defending our country, we have discovered that the task could be accomplished without using outer force. Knowledge is the only thing which can free us from fighting our foes. For centuries, we have gathered information about all possible threats, which could menace our existence. Our best defences are not the acquiring of power and outer force, which ultimately corrupts and turns one to evil, but the absolute understanding of our enemies. We study the inherent weaknesses in our possible enemies, and in times of emergencies, all we have to do is to create those circumstances, which can drag them into perdition and utter destruction," Zeibi explained, underlining that that was not the first-hand choice of her world.

"Can you give me an example, so that I may understand what you mean?" begged Simon.

"Yes, of course. Look at the genii world; if they were to threaten us again, all we need to do is to quench the inflowing heat supplies. That would be our weapon if we were to make them flee from our kingdom. Nevertheless, if we chose to vanquish them, we could open the gates of freezing hell, and we would have defended our world without coming into direct confrontation." Zeibi explained her kingdom's defence strategies in such a simple way that even he could understand and see the ingenuity of it.

18

Simon was in Fairyland for some years, and was well assimilated, adopting the ways and traditions of that country, leading a comfortable, uncomplicated life. He felt happy and content, almost forgetting why he was there in the first place. Like other fairies, he became lazy and spoiled, doing nothing but enjoying the fruits of nature offered to him and in abundance. He was so used to the comforts and getting everything effortlessly that he hardly could imagine a life without those secured supplies of indefinite resources. He was the father of a beautiful daughter, Alice. She was a duplicate copy of her mother: blue eyes, golden hair and a very fair complexion. The only thing that Alice took from him was his stubbornness. Simon loved her and spent long hours playing with her as he lacked any other occupation. Her tiny wings suited her, and he was happy that she had them.

They all talked, walked and laughed together and lived happily. Before going to sleep, little Alice would insist on listening to some story. She loved the tales of the human world, her other homeland, which she hoped and wished to visit one day. She was so fascinated by the human tales that she could go on listening, asking for more and more, never getting tired of them. She seemed to be excited about her double heritage, and wasn't shy to show it to others, who would smilingly affirm that she was different from many of them.

One day Simon told her a bedtime story and kissed her goodnight, but she wouldn't let him go from there. It was obvious that she was not yet sleepy. Simon smiled and told her that he could tell her some other story. She thought for a moment, but didn't find the proposition, so attractive.

"Why don't we talk instead?" Alice asked.

"That's a great idea, what would you like to talk about?"

"Tell me something about you, when you were a child," Alice asked with a glimmer in her beautiful eyes. Simon became uncomfortable, but tried to hide it by smiling.

"My life has not been very glamorous, so it won't be exciting to you," he attempted to persuade her to abandon the idea.

"You can tell me about you, your family and all that you remember from the period you were little. Tell me about my grandfather and grandma, about your siblings and friends," Alice said with excitement. Simon couldn't help feeling pain and anguish engulfing him. He wanted to spare his beloved daughter the details that tormented him, but she kept insisting. Simon looked deep into her pretty eyes and kissed her forehead before he confessed that his childhood was not something he wished to remember. He told her the plain truth that he never met his father and didn't even know if he was dead or alive when he was just a kid.

"What, why couldn't you just ask your mother about that, she certainly would have known?"

"No, I never dared to ask, perhaps I should have done so," Simon confessed that her conclusion was wiser than his, when he was a kid.

"Okay, tell me about grandma, then," Alice asked.

"Your grandma was a brave lady, who took care of her family until the last minute of her life," Simon told her and felt terribly sad remembering her miserable life and her efforts to sustain her family despite her ill health.

He sat beside Alice and told her all about her grandmother, describing the way she looked, her features, her character and her brave fight against her disease. He noticed that Alice wasn't getting sad as he had feared. She listened attentively and with a smile on her shining face. Simon felt relieved to see that his lovely daughter was arrayed with the positive energy of Qaf and wasn't burdened by his emotional burdens.

"I'm happy that you aren't sad for your grandmother," Simon stroked her hand.

"Why should I be, I'm proud to have such a brave lady as my grandmother," Alice told him and continued.

"What does she do nowadays, I'll visit her when I grow up one day." Simon knew that Alice had misunderstood his story; he wanted to tell her that her grandmother wasn't alive but couldn't do that, recalling that she was so young and didn't know much about human life and its bitter realities. He was about to proceed further, but couldn't leave her with a false hope of meeting one day with his mother.

"My mother doesn't live anymore; she has gone to the hidden world, like your maternal grandparents," Simon told her at last. Alice looked at him with disappointed innocence.

"Why have all my grandparents moved to the other world?" She wondered without sounding angry.

Simon took her soft, tiny hand and kissed it, assuring her that her grandparents loved her, regardless of wherever they lived. Alice remained quiet for some time, and Simon guessed that he could say goodnight and leave, but she grabbed his hand tightly as he stood up to go.

"Tell me about your siblings and friends."

Simon had been avoiding the question for some time. He

sighed and told her about David, the only relative he had after the passing away his mother.

"How wonderful! I have an uncle living in the human world, tell me everything about him," Alice got excited.

"Perhaps some other time. You go to sleep now and have wonderful dreams." Simon kissed her and left without turning back and waving as he used to do. He didn't want Alice to see his wet eyes.

Just by glancing at the face of her husband, Zeibi could tell that he was not in best of spirits. By now, she had got accustomed to Simon's mood swings that tormented him occasionally. She was aware that this human vice was not to disappear just because Simon lived in her world. She also knew that as long as her husband kept pulling himself out from that negative state of mind, it was nothing to worry about. She stretched her arms and invited him closer with a soothing smile. He looked sad and in need of comfort, she knew.

"What bothers you today?" she asked in her usual soft tone. Simon told her about his conversation with Alice and how it had made him sad.

"Why should that talk make you sad? I, myself always feel elevated and pumped up with energy, when I remember my parents." Zeibi tried to tone down his sadness.

"I can't help feeling sad that life had not treated my mother well." Simon still looked miserable.

"Wherever your mother is, I'm sure she is better off, and you don't need to worry about her." Zeibi sounded optimistic. Simon's silence betrayed that he was still unhappy. She waited patiently for his words that would reflect his inner turmoil, but he remained silent.

"Spit it out; tell me what bothers you besides your deceased mother?" Zeibi pressed him, and he confided in her that he was mostly unhappy for remembering that he had not kept his promise to his dying mother. He regretted he had not kept looking for his brother after he was robbed by some young men. He had a bad conscience for giving up his quest so easily. She listened patiently and tried to convince him that nothing he did was wrong, so no finger of blame could be pointed at him.

"I know, but I can't get it out of my mind. It seems there wasn't any closure; it would be different only if I had a chance to meet David, even for the last time." Simon wasn't letting her uplift him.

"Maybe you should go and talk to some tree and get some extra strength," Zeibi suggested.

"No, I won't bother those refined spirits with stupid problems of mine. I always feel sorry, seeing them look weary after having a session with them," Simon told her, and she smiled in agreement. She was aware that Simon's depressed states of mind were too negative burdens for the trees to manage in a normal fashion.

"You know that we all need to fight back negativities, your need is even bigger as you are prone to negativities a thousandfold more than us," Zeibi tried to give him courage to fight back.

"Don't worry, I'll be fine soon," Simon said, trying to sound confident, but couldn't cheat Zeibi, who wished him to be normal again.

"I know David is your brother and that you love him, but now you have your family, who needs your joy and lust for life." Zeibi was not giving up easily.

"How wonderful it would have been if David could have accompanied me to this wonderful world!" Simon said as if talking to himself.

"Forget about such a possibility, just because you succeeded entering and getting permission to stay doesn't mean that your brother would have been able to do the same." Zeibi looked amused by his thoughts.

"He is not as bad as you believe." Simon looked cross.

"I'm not judging him either, but just reminding you that our world remains closed for others, including your brother," explained Zeibi.

"You are right, and I'm sorry for thinking out loud. All I wish is that David lived a somewhat comfortable life. If only I could get the knowledge that he is doing fine, I would stop worrying about him," Simon said in a sad voice.

"Are you sure it'll help?" she asked doubtfully.

"Of course. It'll fill my heart with joy, and I would better concentrate on my own life, but unfortunately I have to live with uncertainty." Simon remained gloomy.

"Perhaps I can help here, but then you have to promise never to get sad about your brother." Zeibi said and looked at his face with a glow of hope. Simon was impatient and wanted to know what exactly she meant by her words.

"I can talk to the Queen, who may ask the fairy with the crystal ball to discover the whereabouts of David. Who knows, maybe she will succeed in finding your brother and tell us how he fares," Zeibi told him.

Simon became very happy just at the mere possibility.

"How does the magic of the crystal ball work?" Simon couldn't control his inborn curiosity, making Zeibi smile.

"As I told you many times, there is no magic involved in our world, it's all based on the logic and laws that govern nature," she reminded him politely. Simon tried to counter-argue, but refrained.

"It won't be easy for me to explain how the crystal ball functions as you are not initiated into many secrets as yet. However, I'll try to describe the phenomenon in a somewhat easy manner," Zeibi contemplated before she continued.

"The crystal ball is nothing but knowledge about the rays and frequencies that sweep freely in all possible worlds. These rays can be used as ears and eyes of the one that has the crystal ball and even knows how to use it." Zeibi tried to make him understand. She did her best to explain, but she gave up after he failed to grasp it.

"Regardless of how you put it, it's magic," Simon insisted, and she just smiled.

Simon was aware that it would take some time before he could get an answer regarding David. By now he had learnt that Qaf functioned without the usual stress and strain, things moved according to their natural tempo and sequence, and there was nothing he could do to alter it, so he waited patiently. Finally, one day he was told by Zeibi that the fairy in question had succeeded in finding his brother David.

"The good news is that David lives a family life now. He has a wife and kids and seems to have grown out of his wild days. He lives in your old home, though the house nowadays looks in far better condition than when you knew it," Zeibi told him with a smile.

"That's great, tell me more, tell me all of it," cried Simon happily.

"What more can I add?" Zeibi asked surprised, she had believed that her husband would be content with the important information. Simon told her that he was very pleased to learn that David had made it and lived a somewhat normal life, but she easily could see that he had expected more.

If Zeibi had hoped that Simon would be content with the knowledge that David fared well, she couldn't have been more wrong. Even though he pretended to be fine, his gloom was strong enough to disturb the harmonic balance of her home. She didn't waste time, but confronted him, asking what he wanted this time.

"I just want to meet David, if only for one last time." Simon confessed the reason of his despair.

"You know very well, this wish can't be fulfilled," Zeibi told him.

"Talk with the Queen, I promise never to come with some unreasonable request again," Simon pleaded. She just looked at him with her big eyes, as if she herself felt lost. Simon could watch dark shadows in her eyes, a clear sign that he was burdening her spirit.

"I'm sure the Queen will remind me once again that I was foolish to marry a human, but I'll give it a try and seek her permission." Zeibi told him this without her normal smile and went out, perhaps to seek some counsel from some tree. Simon felt sorry for her and even hated himself for causing distress to his beloved wife and yet he felt helpless to control his desires.

When Zeibi informed him that she had succeeded in convincing the Queen and he had permission to leave for the human world, and he could return on a few conditions. He was supposed to return within one human month's time and was not to disclose anything about Qaf and its secrets to anyone. If he did that, he would burn all the bridges leading back to Qaf. She explained how all that would take place, how he was to be dropped at a set place and would be picked up from the same spot after one month's time.

"What will happen if I am slow to return?" Simon inquired.

"Then you would never get another chance to get back to us," Zeibi said seriously, avoiding his eyes, and he knew she didn't approve of his going back to the human world.

"Don't worry, I'll come back far earlier so as not to risk any accident," Simon promised.

"I'll be extremely happy if you can make it back, but to me

you are already lost," Zeibi said as if she didn't care, and he felt his heart ache.

19

A fairy transported him to a desolate place in the neighbourhood of his town and wished him well in whatever errand he intended to do there. It was obvious that the fairy didn't know anything about why he came there. It was still a few hours before dawn, but he didn't feel like wasting the precious time waiting for the morning. He started walking towards the town and felt both happy and anguished at the same time. He was joyous to meet David and yet couldn't forget the indifferent face of Zeibi as she waved him goodbye. He was confident that she loved him, but was cross for his stubborn insistence on visiting the human world despite inherent dangers involved. He was sure that Zeibi's anger would disappear as soon as he returned to Qaf.

He walked in pitch dark, but didn't fear anything. He smiled, remembering the day he left town for the first time and was filled with millions of fears. He knew that he was a different person now, much wiser and more experienced than before. He thought that his walk towards the town would take many hours, but there he stood in front of the ancestral home at dawn. The house did look newer though it had the same structure. It was obvious that the house had not been demolished and rebuilt, but was just renovated at some time. He thought it would be impolite to wake up David and his family that early, so he went around and looked at the surroundings and noticed that quite a few changes had taken place during the time he was away. There were many new houses in the neighborhood, and even the streets looked much cleaner than before.

Simon came back to the house after daybreak and knocked at the door, no one opened. He tried again and knocked the door a bit harder and longer. He heard someone approaching the door and his heart throbbed faster. Someone opened the door and looked at him with inquisitive eyes without saying anything.

"Is it David's house?" Simon asked in an unsure manner.

"Yes, and who are you, what do you want from him?" the woman asked a bit harshly.

"Is he home?" Simon asked, ignoring her questions. She stared at him with angry eyes while holding the door half ajar with her right hand. Simon looked at her tired face and gray hair and wondered who she could be, when he heard a male voice, inquiring from the woman who was at the door.

"Come and check it for yourself, someone's looking for you," said the woman before moving away from the gate.

Simon waited with excitement and a big smile on his face, which froze when he looked at the person who appeared at the door. It came as a great shock to Simon when he became convinced that the person standing in front of him was none else than David. Simon couldn't believe his eyes, when he looked at the middle-aged man.

"Yes, what can I do for you?" Simon heard the voice of David, who looked confused, as well.

Simon couldn't stop jumping on David and embracing him. "It's wonderful to see you again! Today is the happiest day of my life!" Simon was beside himself, making David uneasy. David freed himself and pushed him gently to the side before carefully looking at him. His pupils became large, and his lips trembled, before he could utter.

"Are you Simon's son?"

"No, silly, I'm Simon, your brother, don't you recognize your own brother?" Simon laughed hysterically. David kept silent as if he refused to trust the words of Simon.

"Where have you been? I searched for you everywhere, and then gave up when I couldn't find any more clues." David just stood there perplexed, unable to say anything.

"What, would you not invite your brother in the house?" Simon asked, patting David on his shoulders.

David signed him to come in while he still was in shock. Simon looked at the disarranged living room area and smiled as this home still looked unlike the way their mother had it before getting seriously ill. David introduced the woman who had opened the door for him as his wife, Simon couldn't understand what had become of David and his wife, why they looked elderly and worn out. He remembered Nora, his mother who also looked far older than her real age. David asked if Simon had eaten his breakfast and asked his wife Margret to bring something to eat when he told them that he had not. It was mostly Simon that kept babbling while David remained of few words.

"So, you are Simon?" David asked suspiciously.

"Who else, why this doubt?" Simon said with a smile. He sat there and reminded David of times when their mother was still alive. He recalled the tough times that followed after the mother died. He mentioned every little detail, which no one but the two brothers knew. David listened with open mouth and then suddenly said, "I don't have a shred of doubt that you are my brother Simon and yet..." David couldn't complete his sentence.

"What? Just say it."

"What happened? Where have you been? You look almost as I saw you years back." David finally asked that which had been bothering him.

"Oh that, I don't know," Simon said with a broad smile. "I live in a faraway land, perhaps one grows older a bit slower over there." He offered some explanation. He could see that David wasn't convinced, but was ready to move on.

"Why did you leave me? I was worried to death." Simon started anew.

"I was young, wild and irresponsible, too selfish to think about others." David looked remorseful.

"I knew all this and yet you could have remained close to me," Simon said with a smile.

"You know I was in a rough crowd, and I thought it was best for me to run away."

"You could have left some clues, a message so that I could have come and helped you," Simon said.

"I was angry with you. I considered you a hindrance in living the life of my own choice. Your refusal to sell this house made me furious." David looked ashamed when he mentioned all these things.

"Well, as you put it yourself, you were young, inexperienced and wild, so no harm was done. The same house can provide shelter for you and your family now. Do you have any children?" Simon pretended not to know.

"Yes, we have three kids, all grown up and flown off the nest," David said with a smile. "In our old age, only I and my wife live here. Without much to do, we quarrel most of the time," David said and looked at his wife, who giggled in agreement. It was time for Simon to get disoriented, making him wonder how many years had passed since he left his home. As far as he could calculate, only a few years had passed since he shifted to Qaf, then how come David had grown old and even his children had had time to build lives of their own. He didn't want to ask directly.

"When did you come back?" Simon asked.

"It seems centuries have passed since then, but I did return four years after I had fled the town. I had hoped to find you here, but was told that you left the house to me."

David told him all about his adventures and the troubles he faced during the years when he was away. He answered all of Simon's questions and thus provided him with the information he sought. Simon easily could calculate that what he thought as just a few years' time was actually a period of forty five to fifty years. So even if he just looked in his twenties, both he and David were in their sixties. This realization filled him with awe and bewilderment, and he could understand the shock of David, when he first saw him as young as he left him half a century ago. From time to time, David looked at Simon stealthily as if he still didn't want to believe his eyes. His narration was amazing, and Simon couldn't stop admiring his younger brother's rise from the pit.

"What made you turn back and come home?" Simon asked.

"You were responsible for that change of mind," David confessed, staring at the floor.

"Me, how?" Simon asked, surprised.

"When you came searching for me, I was still hiding in that town, the story of your being robbed by those bandits made me furious and I found them and beat them for what they did to you." David looked ashamed. "It was then that I realized that I had caused you nothing but pain and anguish while you always took care of me like a good brother."

"Those idiots had no right to rob you for some debts I collected by chance," David told him and avoided looking at him.

David said that he came to know about the incident few days later and tried to find him, but he had already left. He presumed that after losing all his money, Simon had goneback home.

"So you decided to come after me?" Simon asked.

"No, I stayed there for another couple of months and left the place when one of the young men was killed by another over some money issue," David said.

"Were you involved?" Simon asked.

"You mean in killing?" David looked at him in horror and said, "Heavens no, I was stupid but, not a killer."

"Why did you leave then?" Simon was curious.

"Didn't I tell you, my conscience was already troubling me, and I wanted to return to some peaceful existence and knew that I could find that where I rightfully belonged," David explained.

"When did you marry?" Simon asked.

"Long ago, but my marriage was not successful, we didn't suit each other. Many times I had wanted to go my way and leave the wife and kids behind."

"What hindered you?" Simon asked.

"I didn't want to repeat the mistake of our father. I wished my children to have a functioning home," David said and looked proud. When Simon asked how he could be so sure that their father had abandoned them, he just smiled and said, "Even though Mother never mentioned her tragedy, it was all written in her eyes." David looked confident in his conclusion.

Both brothers sat and discussed the days that had passed long ago and looked happy for having the possibility to do so. David was happier for getting a chance to show his remorse to Simon, he was talking without making a pause as there was much to narrate. He had grown unsure of things and didn't know how long they could be together and for that reason he felt stressed. Suddenly he stopped talking and looked deep into Simon's eyes and said.

"How very stupid of me, I keep talking instead of listening to your story. How did you fare all these years? Where have you been, what you did and what adventures you have experienced?" David asked and Simon smiled, seeing that his kid brother had indeed developed and was less egocentric.

"You can see that I have been lucky as well and did manage beautifully," Simon said and sounded proud.

They kept talking, telling each other stories of their lives. David looked impressed to hear all the happenings in Simon's life and couldn't help admiring his brother in his heart. Many times he tried to verbalize his thoughts but each time he failed to bring forth the words.

"So, deep down you were even tougher than me," David finally confessed.

"Aren't we all tougher when life exposes us to bitter realities?" Simon said, trying to tone down the praise.

"Not all would survive, I can bet. You weren't a weakling as you gave the impression. All my life I hated you for being a chick, but it is obvious that the wrong was with me. I'm happy to know the truth, even if it comes too late." David was brave to confess. Simon deliberately omitted the narration about his quest for the unknown worlds and his settling down in the Fairyland, the reason of his not aging. He knew that he was bound by his oath and would just bring misfortune on himself by even mentioning the word. Many times he was close to mentioning Zeibi and Alice, but succeeded in restraining himself from doing so. He felt unhappy for not being able to boast about his family and rich life, but there was little he could do to change the situation. For two days and nights, the brothers just talked and talked until they both felt exhausted. David's three daughters and their families came and visited Simon. They were equally shocked to learn that he was their uncle, the elder brother of their father and yet looked younger than them. To each niece Simon gave some gold he had brought from the Fairyland and felt happy to watch their surprised faces. They all believed that the gold looked of unusually high quality.

Simon had thought that one month's stay was too short and had protested and tried to make it at least for three months, but after a week he thought he had enough of his visit and wished to return to his wife and daughter. After having intensive talks with David, he realized that they had a few things in common. They simply had grown towards different directions, and there was no common thing than their childhood and a portion of their youth, which they had already discussed so thoroughly that it had no charm left in it. Simon looked anguished by the mere thought of spending another three weeks in the human world. He could have never have believed that he was no longer connected with his former world, and had become an integral part of Qaf, where Zeibi and Alice were the reasons of his existence. He knew that he had already achieved his aim and there was no point in lingering at David's anymore. He was struck with the idea of visiting Michael and Richard, but his face dropped, remembering that the possibility of those friends being still alive was meager, if not completely non-existent. The only one he could still hope to see alive was Paul if some battle had not already consumed him. He was not ready to go and check that, well aware of the circumstances in which he had once escaped that place of captivity. Regardless of what he did with his remaining three weeks, he had decided to take his leave of David and his family.

David looked astonished when Simon told him that he was leaving the next day. He was unable to understand why that sudden decision was made.

"Is it me or did my wife say something? You know it is as much your home as it is mine," David said.

"I came to see you and your family. I'm happy that you are all doing well, I must go back to my life now, and I can do that happily and with knowledge that warms my heart. This house belongs to you; I'll never have a claim on it." Simon told David with a smile before he searched his pockets and brought a tiny clothed bag out and handed it to David.

"What's that?"

"A humble present from your brother," Simon said and watched the glow on David's face, which opened the bag and looked inside. He took the object, placed it on the palm of his hand and looked surprised.

"WOW, what a beauty!" David exclaimed loudly. "Where did you find this precious stone? Why are you giving it to me?" David's voice shook with excitement.

"It's for you; I'm sure for the rest of your life you can live comfortably if you chose to sell it." Simon told him.

David sat there holding and staring at the diamond as if he didn't believe his eyes. Simon could see that David was struggling hard to say something.

"There is something I have to confess," said David at last without even looking at his brother.

"Just say it; you don't have to think twice." Simon tried to encourage him.

"You remember mother's missing ring, which you searched and searched for without ever finding it?" David spoke still avoiding an eye contact and continued when Simon remained silent. "It never went missing, I had stolen it." Simon could feel the shaking of David's voice.

"It's all irrelevant now, why torture yourself." Simon patted David with a smile. "We all make mistakes and grow by learning the lessons." Simon went on but then asked.

"What made you remember the ring?"

"It's the diamond." David pointed to the stone in his hand and looked sad. "It brings the memories back and the apparent difference lying between two of us. I never gave you anything but trouble and pain and you remain generous even to this day."

"Don't be hard on yourself; the most important thing is that you grew out of that character of yours." Simon said with a broad smile.

"You don't seem to be surprised at all, did you know about it all the time?" David asked, and Simon smiled back.

"Yes, I know about it for some time," was the short answer he got from Simon.

"How did you come to know?" David looked perplexed, and Simon felt forced to tell him about the trader to whom David had sold the ring and who had even told about his whereabouts.

David sat with bowed head, unable to hide his shame.

"I'm sure you hated me then."

"Do you think I would come looking for you and get robbed if I hated you?" Simon asked with a smile. David kept pondering before he got up, came near and embraced him tightly.

"For years I have lived with a bad conscience, but you by coming make me feel even worse. Can you ever forgive me for the past?" David looked shaky.

"I forgave you a long time ago. You are my brother and will remain so for all time to come." Simon comforted David.

"When would you come and visit next time?" David asked.

"I can't tell, I live far away and there lay a lot of difficulties in coming and visiting you." Simon answered tactfully. Simon asked David not to be surprised if he wasn't around when he woke up in the morning.

20

When Simon came to the desolate place where he was supposed to be picked up by the fairy that had transported him to the human world, he was weary, well aware that he was three weeks earlier. It was a bright day, and a barren land lay in front of him as far as he could see. There was hardly any vegetation that could soothe the sight or provide him a shelter. All of a sudden he realized that he had made a terrible mistake to come there so long in advance without bringing enough water and food. He could walk back for a few hours and find water, but the food was a real problem as he had no money or other valuables left with him with which he could buy the stuff. The scorching sun made it clear that he had a very tough time ahead. Why the fairies had chosen to leave and pick him up from such an unfriendly place, he couldn't understand.

Simon was about to turn back to the town when he saw a fairy flying high in the sky. He waved at her enthusiastically, but the fairy didn't react, perhaps she couldn't see him from such heights. He didn't stop waving until he saw the fairy coming down, descending towards him. She came closer and still looked surprised, but then relaxed when Simon greeted her in Qaf manner.

"Are you a fairy?" she asked.

"Not really, but I do live in Qaf," Simon told her.

"How very interesting!" she exclaimed and looked amazed.

"Why is that so interesting?" Simon asked.

"You are a human and live in Qaf and I, a fairy, prefer to

live in the human world, and you don't think it's funny?"

"Your own world is so fantastic, why have you chosen to live in our world?" Simon inquired.

"Tell me first, why do they allow you to settle down in Qaf when they never do such a thing normally?" The fairy was curious.

"I'm married to a fairy," Simon told her, and she smiled, still unable to grasp the reason.

"What do you in the human world, why are you allowed to return or perhaps you have been deported here?"

When Simon told her about his conditional permission to visit the human world, she said with a smile.

"So you are on your way back to Qaf?"

"Not yet, I'm three weeks ahead." Simon told her, making her look at him in surprise. She was quick to make him understand that three weeks in that barren land was something he could never survive, even if he had food and water. "Go back to the nearest town and stay there until it's time to go home.

"Why did the fairy choose such a place to drop and pick me up from?" Simon asked.

"Don't you know, didn't anyone tell you?" the fairy asked.

"No, what do you refer to?"

"The transporting fairies aren't some super beings that can carry heavy weights like these." The fairy said, pointing at Simon and laughed before continuing. "They manage to do that by taking 'Feather Routes.'"

"What's a feather route?" Simon asked, not understanding.

"These are the Skyways, where the heavy weights disappear and thus make all kinds of transportation between Qaf and other worlds possible," the fairy explained.

"If it's that easy, why couldn't my wife do that herself?"

Simon wasn't convinced.

"Most probably your wife is not a trained transporter and needed a professional to do the job." The fairy gave a possible reason.

"No, she is quite an expert herself; she can easily take me to wherever I want to move in Qaf," Simon bragged, making the fairy laughed.

"Is she really that strong?" She pulled his leg, but became serious quickly, telling him that within Qaf, it was no problem as the entire atmosphere was like a 'Feather Route'.

"You promised, but never told me why you live in our world?" Simon reminded her.

"It's also love that enchains me here," she said with a smile.

"Have you fallen for some human?"

"No, it's a Genie," she replied.

"Are you happy here? Don't you miss your wonderful world?" Simon asked.

"Why would I stay here if I were unhappy?" the fairy asked logically.

"I suggest you to go back to the nearest town if you want to meet your family in Qaf or send a distress call to your wife."

"How can I send it?"

"Have you any object that belongs to her?" she asked.

"No, I don't," Simon said, but then looked in his pocket remembering something. He took out the comb Zeibi had put in his pocket and which had lain there untouched. The fairy looked carefully and smiled seeing a single strand of hair.

"Burn it and she will know that you need her to contact you."

"I don't have a fire."

"Do you still need a fire, when you have blazing sunshine," she laughed and placed the hair on the ground, where it started burning. Simon couldn't tell if the fairy had set it on fire or if the heat of the ground did that, the only thing he could say for sure was that it got burnt in a brief moment, in just a flash.

The fairy smiled before she started ascending towards the skies, leaving him there to sit and wait for help from Zeibi and the kingdom of Qaf.

Simon's coming back to Qaf made Zeibi very happy. She saw that visiting the human world had left a good impact on her husband, who looked tranquil and content. He felt thankful for getting a chance to live a harmonious life along with a loving wife and a lovely child. There wasn't a thing in the world he desired more. All he wished was that it went on that way unendingly. The only cloud of worry that used to give Simon an occasional sense of gloom, which came abruptly and took hold of him for hours and sometimes even for days, was gone. At those moments, he hardly participated in any discussion or activity. Zeibi and Alice tried to drag him out of that terrible state of mind; he remembered and smiled at his previous behavior. In a strange manner, his guilty conscience regarding David completely disappeared, and he could see that despite all his brother had managed to make a comeback and now lived a somewhat comfortable life.

If Zeibi had believed that Simon's return from the human world had given him the necessary insight and taken away all manifestations of his dejection forever, she couldn't be more wrong. Hardly any time had passed when she realized that he was back to his commuting between the moods. She tried hard to know what bothered him this time, but he wouldn't tell her. Zeibi and Alice tried to cheer him up; sometimes they succeeded while at other times, they failed. His mind kept straying to some faraway place, some fenland, where he sank deeper and deeper, without any solid support, which could help him to stay afloat. The world he lived in and loved was the most harmonic and inspiring place he could think of, with the most devoted and understanding, beautiful wife, and a most wonderful, charming and loving daughter. What more could one demand and expect from life? But Simon was a peculiar person who could find reasons for unhappiness, even when life was kind and gracious. Perhaps it was because he had come from an imperfect world, where one could not afford to be content. He had failed to recognize that he had already been in that heaven which he had so desperately been looking for.

The attraction of the unseen worlds kept calling his name, inviting him to pursue his quest, teasing him for being a coward, whispering the poisonous taunts, pronouncing seductive words, all those things to make him restless, and to drag him back to being on the move once again. He tried to ignore these callings by shutting the doors leading to his eardrums, but soon acknowledged that he had failed to stop the deadly inner sounds. He made up his mind and stood without flinching. His place was with his family, Zeibi and wonderful Alice. He had come home and wanted to search no more for anything else. What more could he expect from life?

Zeibi knew about his decision to stay with them forever and was happy for that, but somewhere deep in her heart, she was still worried. The thought of losing her beloved husband anguished her, making her terribly sad for a moment. But the next moment, by looking at Alice her whole face would light up.

"He wouldn't have the heart to leave Alice behind," and such thoughts gave her hope and calmed her down.

Zeibi had started accepting her husband's mood swings as a natural part of her life and didn't mind it as long as they were less frequent and didn't infect the atmosphere of her home. Simon was aware of the negative impact of his gloom on his surroundings and cooperated by going out for long walks in the woods or going talking to the plants and trees. He had learned a lot about botanical life, their qualities and the purpose of their existence, and all that knowledge made him love them. His long strolls did help him change his state of mind, and he came back home in a somewhat balanced, joyous mood.

Simon knew that the Queen was sick, but just shrugged his shoulders, as though it was some kind of minor sickness rather than a strange phenomenon in otherwise healthy Qaf. He was aware that fairies could just drink some potions and get well within no time. He was alarmed noticing that the Queen didn't recover as he had expected.

"What's going on here, why does nobody give her the medicine she needs to recover?" Simon inquired one day.

"She isn't that kind of sick." Zeibi told him without wishing to explain in greater detail.

"What do you mean, what kind of sickness are we talking about here?"

"The Queen is waning, taking her inevitable course before she departs to Farlin." Zeibi told him reluctantly and watched the pale face of her husband.

"You mean she is dying?"

"It seems that way, I guess!" Zeibi responded.

"She is dying, and no one tries to save her life?" Simon was hysterical.

"You are aware that our world functions differently from yours. We live our lives as healthily as possible and we don't resist death when it comes to claim us. Life and death are not two separate entities for us." Zeibi looked as calm as ever.

"We human beings never give up without a fight," Simon declared, trying to impress her.

"Maybe so, tell me one single example when you could beat death?" she asked smilingly. "Isn't our way more prudent? At least there is no suffering in this world, not even when it all comes to an end."

Simon didn't answer but kept thinking. He looked miserable. He had gotten another reason to worry, but Zeibi didn't try to soothe him as he was expecting.

"How long will her sickness last?" he asked finally.

"What do I know, perhaps days, if not weeks and months," Zeibi told him, shrugging her shoulders.

"You talk in such a detached manner as if you don't love her." Simon said looking at her fresh face.

"I know how you reason, but I'll not try to defend myself or our behavior. However, one thing I wish to stress and that is that even our love is wiser." Zeibi didn't look cross at his accusation.

"Would you mind elaborating?" Simon asked.

"Perhaps some other time; right now is not the proper moment to discuss such things," she said and looked determined.

One day, it was announced that the queen of Fairyland had expired. The brief news declared that the death of the queen occurred without any complication. She had passed on to her afterlife destination peacefully, they were informed. No one was more devastated than Simon. He was astonished to see that everything went on as if nothing of importance had taken place, no mourning, no sad faces and no exchanges of condolences did he notice. The fairies had expected the death of their Queen for some time and had already selected the new Queen. Zeibi tried to downplay the importance of the event by inviting him for some interesting excursion, but he turned down her offer, saying how could they celebrate the death of the Queen, one of the most revered persons of Qaf. Simon sat and sighed again and again.

"How could she die? She was so young!" He kept exclaiming.

"No, she wasn't," Zeibi tried to confront and persuade him. "Queen had lived a normal, full fairy life circle. She was at least eighty-eight years of age, if not ninety."

Simon kept repeating, "what a waste to die that young!"

Zeibi looked at him and wanted to confront him, but instead decided not to argue and remained silent. Simon kept lamenting the death of Queen until he realized that he had taken the occurrence too hard, almost to the level of absurdity. After this self-realisation, he started becoming normal again.

"How old are you Zeibi?" Simon asked.

"I'm thirty-one, fairy years," she answered.

"So you are a few years younger than me," he said. She kept smiling without saying a word.

"Shall you also die one day?" he asked in a gloomy voice.

"Yes, but I still have more than half a century to enjoy, before I'll worry about death," Zeibi tried to make the atmosphere lighter by adding a laugh. She noticed that Simon was hardly there. He was busy fighting his own demons which had him in their iron grip. He was all by himself, ignoring his wife and child.

This time the depression attack was different. He had been dragged into a quagmire from which there seemed to be no return. He was going deeper and deeper, but the worst part was that he was not even struggling against being sucked into that marshland. There seemed to be no end or bottom to that hopeless situation. He kept dropping further and further away from her. Zeibi could not sit idle and see her husband fall into some unknown abyss; she had to do something to change that horrifying state of affairs. He showed such symptoms that she became awfully worried and dreaded that something terrible was to befall Simon. She called for Tontis, who immediately came and attended Simon.

Tontis' diagnosis was that Simon suffered from deep-rooted fears and conflicts, which had no remedy on earth, except if Simon faced and solved them himself in one way or another. Zeibi was well aware of what bothered her husband. He was obsessed with fears of death and wanted desperately to overcome them by finding the spring of life. She knew that Simon never abandoned his desire for immortality but had just stopped talking about it. She was not worried though, fully convinced that there was no such valley with life giving water.

"A new conflict is the last thing he needs right now. So try to have patience and understanding, even if he sounds unreasonable," was his recommendation. "Deep down, he's a human, who needs some activity to keep him busy," said Tontis and left.

After giving him the treatment suggested by Tontis, she could see little betterment in his condition. Several weeks passed, and he became quite stable. He was a completely changed man, deprived of all interest in anything. He stopped laughing; he talked seldom, looked very serious and was often absent-minded.

"What was your favourite activity in your own world?" Zeibi asked him one day.

"I loved reading books," Simon told her without much keenness.

"I have a friend who keeps the records and has uncountable books at her disposal. Maybe you should visit her."

"Maybe I should," Simon answered half-heartedly.

A few days passed, and Simon showed no interest in the subject.

"Have you talked to your friend?" Simon asked Zeibi one day.

"Ask who? About what?" She inquired, forgetting about her offer.

"That record keeper friend," Simon reminded her.

Zeibi was happy to notice that he had taken the initiative, and immediately contacted the friend and requested her help. Zeibi's friend accepted her request, allowing Simon to come and spend as much time as he wanted at her place but made it plain to Zeibi that most of the books were not to be taken home.

"Don't worry! I'll explain the rules and regulations to Simon." She thanked her friend for her kind gesture, and gave the good news to Simon.

Simon became very busy. Most of his day was spent in that great hall, where there were millions of books and records. The archives were the largest not only in the Fairyland but also in all the worlds, according to the record holder and bookkeeper fairy.

"If you don't find a thing recorded here, you'll not find it anywhere else," she proudly told him. One could see that he was less interested in books, and was looking for something in the records.

"What're you looking for?" the record keeper asked curiously.

He was hesitant. "I'm asking because maybe I can assist you. You see, that's my job."

Simon told her that he was looking for the legendary valley, which according to his information had its clues in their country. She listened to all the characteristics and attributes of the valley and then went away for a long time. When she came back, she shook her head in negation and told him that there wasn't any such valley recorded in their archives. There could be only two explanations, either this valley was just a myth or that it came under some different name or characteristic. Before leaving, he requested the bookkeeper not to mention to his wife about his search for the record. "My lips are sealed," she said, smiling.

21

He didn't give up and kept going to the hall and going through the records, subject-by-subject, page-by-page. He found nothing. There wasn't a trace of any such valley however much he searched. Suddenly something hit his mind, and he became nervous and excited all at the same time. He rushed to the record keeper and begged her to provide him with the map of Fairyland.

She looked at him startled and went smiling to bring one. He sat looking at the map for quite a long time, but seemed somewhat puzzled. At last, he decided to seek help. He went straight to the record keeper and asked if she had time to help explain the map. She was willing to do him the favour.

Spreading the map before her, he started saying, "As we can see, here is Giantland, and here is Elvesland, this direction is this great lake. The map doesn't say if it lies in Fairyland, Elvesland or some wasteland," Simon explained. "Now I've been studying this map for some time. Why is nothing mentioned on this side of the map? What lies here?" Simon was pointing to the fourth direction of the map.

He could see her getting pale. She kept silent, staring downwards as if thinking deeply.

"It's called a void and we don't like talking about it," she gave a short dry answer.

"Do you have any information or record about this area

you called 'void'?" he asked.

"No." Again she gave a short answer.
"Maybe, the valley I'm looking for is situated here," he asked in an excited tone.
"Maybe!" was her indifferent answer.

In the evening, he took up the matter with Zeibi. She was taken aback when he asked her about the void. She was not very interested to talk about it either. When she realised that he would not stop asking, she gave up.

The void was a dark, gloomy, mysterious, and undiscovered area bordering their country. For thousands of years the fairies were told to never go that way, death, destruction and dread would wait and annihilate the breaker of the rule. The fairies believed that it was the hell for bad spirits, which lay in that direction. Just the mention of that name could give them nightmares.

"But why do you ask?" she asked suspiciously.

He was excited. "I believe all these stories are discouraging people from seeking the truth, but I believe the legendary valley lies in that direction."

Zeibi could not believe her ears. She stood paralysed, frozen with horror. After coming out of her initial shock, she tried to convince him that his theory could not be true and that nothing good could ever come out from that direction.

Throughout the ages, there were many who had laughed at the warnings and had defied the prohibition to go that way. Many of them had lost their way and ended up there, but none ever returned.

"Even the animals and birds don't dare go in that direction." She tried to convince him. She begged and cried, but Simon went on telling her that there was nothing to fear. He would go that way, reach the spring, drink some life water, and bring some for her and Alice and then they all could live happily ever after.

"Simon, do believe me when I say that I'm happy with things as they are. I don't wish to have it any other way. I don't want to live forever," she desperately tried to convince him; she tried to explain that they did have long, healthy and carefree lives in Fairyland.

"You call eighty, ninety years a long life? I want to live an eternal life with you." He was cheating himself, when he kept saying that he didn't seek the life's water for his own sake. He was lying.

"Simon, our 80 years are equal to 800 years of your world. Don't you think that is enough?"

Simon was obsessed by his idea, and nobody could say or do anything to deter him from his renewed pursuit. Zeibi knew that fact and had given up all hope. Her blue eyes cried oceans, but that was no help in deterring him from leaving. Her heart was filled with pain and anguish. He was using her and Alice for purposes of his own. With a heavy heart, she decided not to resist his will. If he was happy to go his way, then she had to accept that as their fate. She had decided to surrender with dignity.

She arranged his transportation to the area bordering the void as he still had not learned the art of flying. As he was saying good-bye to Zeibi and Alice, for a brief moment his determination looked shaky. His emotions took over and in a great confusion, he re-evaluated whether he was making the right decision. The very next minute he was kissing and embracing his wife and daughter, promising to return shortly. Zeibi did not question him and smiled as if he was making some ordinary journey. But her face was not betraying her inner turmoil, where she felt a chill and fright suffocating her and her heart was bleeding. She knew that was the last time she was looking at the man she loved so deeply. She was a brave fairy, who had learned how to endure pain with dignity.

The fairy who had taken the task of transporting him was an old friend of Zeibi. Before returning back to her town, she confirmed that he was still determined to make his journey. He was absolutely sure, so she said farewell to him and returned without looking back.

He walked and walked, guessing that he was now out of Fairyland. He couldn't be absolutely sure because there were no signs or clear demarcation separating the two sides from each other. The land wasn't at all dark and gloomy as he had learned from the descriptions, though it appeared to be barren and without much animal life. At a distance, he could see grey-coloured mountains. Deep in his heart were still doubts about his search. He kept suppressing those fears and doubts as they served no purpose anymore. It was too late for anything else except a strong conviction, a firm tenacity and steadfastness. Excelsior! He demanded of himself, as a command, an appreciation and a soft push forward. He was moving fast because he had to come out of that wasteland if he was to find any water or food. "Just imagine, that they all are right," Simon thought with fear entering his heart "and instead of a legendary valley I'm moving to some terrible hell." He rejected these thoughts and tried to divert his attention to something positive. By positive thoughts, he had not meant his family. The crying face of Alice, her sobs and the touch of her little arms around his legs at the time of departing started bothering him. The silent tear-stained, pale face of Zeibi he could never forget.

He hadn't seen her that sad before. All these thoughts were crushing him, with such an intensity that he broke down, and his determination to proceed diminished. "Hell, I'm going back! Ally, I'm coming back to you. Zeibi don't be sad, I love you!" Simon was crying, when he turned back, without much further thinking. He had taken a few steps only, when he heard a great roar. His heart filled with terror when he saw a large beast in the distance, which was making those terrible sounds and was about to rush towards him. He ran as fast as he could, not even turning to see if the beast was still behind him. He kept running until he could move no more. Before stopping, he turned to look back to see if the monstrous beast was there or not. He was running fast, or the beast was too slow, in both cases he was happy to have gotten rid of him. Simon could not think of going back that way again.

"I'll not think of my family right now," was his pledge of the day. For days, he kept walking, living on those dry foods, which he had brought with him. He had some potion with him, only a few drops of which could appease his thirst for hours. He could survive on those for weeks. All day long, he moved forward at a fast speed and at night, he rested. Nothing strange had happened during all that time. He hadn't met anyone or seen anything of significance. Except that he had suffered several homesickness attacks and after each time decided to return. Every time he wanted to return, he was deterred by some ferocious animal, forcing him back to his tracks. Was that just a coincidence, or was it the confirmation of the myth that there really was no way back to Fairyland?

By the ninth day, he reached the foothills and rested for the rest of the day and night, before taking up his journey any further. There were deep ditches around the high mountain, making it almost impossible to reach up to them. He walked for miles until he found a narrow path leading to the grey mountain. He stood there hesitating, not knowing what to do. There was no other apparent way to proceed. Just looking to the depth of the ditch made him dizzy, and he feared that he would not make it. "What to do?" he thought. "How great it would be if one could accomplish certain deeds just by thinking?" Simon smiled even in those fearful moments.

The path was too narrow, and there was no chance that he could convince himself to go across. So he found a middle way on the stomach. He started crawling without looking down the bottomless pit. Not caring about the pain, he toiled and toiled and at last reached the other side. The hard rocky path had injured his knees and elbows, and he was bleeding. He was glad to have made it.

He kept going forward, uphill to the summits, downhill to the lesser tops, just to go uphill again. His movement was painstaking, laborious and made breathing difficult. However, he showed no signs of fatigue, and kept moving in an energetic manner. When that chain of mountains came to an end, he entered a valley. It was the first time he saw signs of life, food, and water. He ate fresh fruits and wild berries and drank water. The cool, clean water was very sweet; he went on drinking, even after his thirst was appeased. The valley was not very big. He decided to move on the next day. Then, he was forced to stay because it rained heavily without any interruption all day long. His body needed that rest, so he slept and slept, without feeling any hunger or thirst.

At daybreak, he came out of his hole-like cave, ate some fruits and drank water and was about to start his moving forward, when the whole valley started shaking. He was sure that it must have been some earthquake, but rejected the idea shortly afterwards. The jolting and shaking of the earth was too prolonged and rhythmic. There were quiet intervals followed by a loud sound, followed by the shaking of the earth. He became jumpy, fearing that some calamity was about to befall him. What was that sound? And why did the earth keep shaking violently? Before he could figure it out, he noticed a giant approaching him. His heart came to his throat. The giant seemed quite far away, and he believed that he had a fair chance to run away. Simon collected all his force and ran for his life. He had no clue that giants lived there. He dared not turn to see if he could outrun the giant or not. He ran for his life and fell a few times due to the shaking of the earth, but he never gave up, always getting back to his feet and rushing in a mad race. With great difficulty, Simon succeeded in coming back to the cave where he had spent the night before. Though he felt safer inside the cave, his heart trembled with fear. He noticed that the shaking of the earth had stopped, indicating that either the Giant had not taken notice of him or was too slow to catch him. It was obvious that he had been lucky.

He stayed there all day long and dared not venture out, where the danger lurked. He knew that he had to wait till the next morning as he considered it unwise to travel during the night, when the visibility was zero and dangers were too many. He slept badly during the night as he kept worrying about the Giant, who was still out somewhere. He believed that he had a good chance of escaping the Giant if he left the cave at dawn and pressed ahead fast. Simon peeped out before he dared set his foot out of the cave. It was still dark, and he couldn't determine if it was safe or not, he had to take his chances if he wished to run away from there. With a pounding heart, he came out and started walking in a careful, vigilant manner, looking around like a scared animal. Hardly had he gone a hundred meters, when he noticed that all his ways of escape were blocked, he stood surrounded by something strange. In panic, he rushed to the side, which still remained open but it was too late, the circle was all closed and he stood there like a prisoner. The realization that he was captured froze the blood in his veins. The giant took hold of him in his index finger, and the thumb, lifted him up and placed in the palm of his right hand before he closed it. It grew dark, and he sank in the clutch of the giant. The whole valley trembled with the laughter of the giant. Simon knew it was the end of his struggle. He didn't expect any miracle that could save him from a sure death as he stood paralyzed and captured. His brain had stopped functioning and instead there was just horror that filled his entire being.

"I knew it was human. My sense of smell would not betray me." Simon heard the giant say when he opened his hand a bit.

Simon was sweaty, his heart pounding with dread while he waited for the giant to put him in his mouth. Suddenly the giant opened the palm of his hand completely. Like a fast animal, he tried to run away, but gave up by noticing the height at which he stood.

"It has been some time now since I last met one of your kind," said the giant in a voice like thunder. "Or rather, one of any kind," the giant laughed again, making Simon shiver with fear while the giant's laughter echoed around him like winds accompanying a storm.

"What do you intend to do to me?" Simon asked.

"What a silly question, what do you expect?" the giant laughed. "It has been centuries since I ate a delicacy like this."

"O, mighty creature, spare me, what will you get by eating me? I can't fill even a tiny portion of your big belly. I promise to help you find some animal that is big enough." Simon tried, and the giant laughed once again.

"You human beings never change, do you think that you can easily outwit us, right?" the giant looked amused and seemed not to be in a hurry to eat him. Simon was terrified, and yet could see that the giant sought some conversation before he consumed him.

"How would you like to be eaten? I prefer raw while many claim that you humans taste best when you're roasted." Simon trembled at the thought.

"Have mercy, you great being, I promise to pay you back someday." Simon tried once again to plead, convinced that the giant was not a very compassionate fellow.

"Enough about having a conversation with you, I need to eat you, if only to recollect the good taste," the Giant said before picking Simon up with his thumb and a finger and placing him in his mouth. Simon looked at the sharp teeth of the giant and almost fainted when he placed him in his mouth. Simon closed his eyes and trembled, all aware of his terror-stricken state of mind. He waited for the crushing, tearing teeth to close on him, but nothing happened. He opened his eyes and saw nothing, as the mouth of the giant was closed, and there was no light in there. He felt the tongue of the giant touching all around and knew that the giant was not in a hurry and wanted to prolong his own pleasure and was not in any way trying to prolong Simon's agony. He wished it to be all over as quickly as possible.

The terrifying moments finally came to an end; the giant opened his mouth and spit him out on the palm of his hand. Simon saw astonishment in the eyes of the giant, who kept watching him intensely.

"Who are you?" the giant asked a bit shocked.

"I told you I'm a human being, who intends no harm to anyone."

"I thought so too, but here I stand all confused. Tell me why you come from the direction of Qaf, instead of coming from the side of the human world?" the giant looked unhappy.

"I live in Qaf," Simon explained, but the giant still looked uncertain.

"Are you a fairy?" the giant asked once again.

"No, but I'm married to a fairy and have even a child." Simon still trembled with fear.

"That explains the bitter taste in my mouth," the giant looked devastated. "You're lucky, our treaty with the fairies prohibits me from eating you up. Go away, before I crush you to powder, since nothing bans me from doing that." The giant said and looked so furious that Simon shivered with fear again. The temporary sense of relief was all gone from his heart. He couldn't tell what stopped the giant from taking his anger out at him as that clenched hand of his opened itself again and he was gently placed on the ground.

"Thanks, great being, I'll always remember this kindness." Simon was joyous.

"Don't thank me, but the agreement between Devia and Qaf."

"You could still kill me as you said."

"I lied, I simply couldn't harm you according to the covenant." The giant confessed.

"How could you see that I have some connection to the Qaf?" Simon asked, feeling fearless now.

"Not only do you give off the wrong kind of smell, which I ignored, believing that over time, you humans may have even changed your fragrance a bit, but placing you in the mouth clearly sent a signal that you even tasted differently. The bitter taste was a warning that you were forbidden food for me." The giant sighed.

"How do you survive without fauna around?"

"By adapting myself to the vegetation."

A vegetarian giant, the thought was soothing, calming and freeing.

"Who are you and what do you do here? Why do you choose to live here instead of living in Devia?" Simon asked.

The giant shook his head in disbelief, "you humans never stop amusing me. It's for me to ask these questions. Not the other way around." The giant was one of the stern guards of the valley of the legend. How was he to convince him to let him go? Simon explained his journey starting from his birthplace. "It's not that I've no time, but come to the point," said the Giant, not interested in his long story.

"Are you heading to the valley?" the giant asked.

"Yes," was Simon's reluctant answer.

"Ok," said the giant and tried to turn and go from there.

Simon could not believe his ears. He stood in disbelief. Was that all? Was the guard letting him go that easily? Without any resistance, without any effort to stop his march? "Are you not the guard?" asked Simon.

"Yes I am," the giant replied.

"And still you let me go to the valley?" he asked once again, making sure there wasn't any misunderstanding between them.

"Yes, why should I not let you go," answered the giant in a low voice.

Simon was allowed to proceed. No, he was heading wrong; he was told by the giant and got the correct directions. He walked for another few days, hiking, trekking, up and down in the mountains. He met many guards of varying shapes and sizes. Certain forms he recognised and some he didn't. Strangely, no-one tried to stop his march. Some watched him with interest and others looked with indifference. They all had piercing eyes and stern faces. The giant was the only guard, with whom he had spoken. He felt suspicious, why was he allowed to pass without even the least effort on the part of the guards. There was something wrong, something missing. Only he didn't know what.

22

The legendary valley lay beneath his feet. Never in his life had he felt as blissful and yet something kept him worried. His triumphant scream must have been heard for miles around as it echoed, reverberating his joyful laughter in all directions. He started jumping, dancing and singing loudly. He felt like expressing his feelings of achievement, success, and victory over the hurdles of the way. He demonstrated that will power could achieve all given tasks. His apparently impossible quest was nearing its end, a happy ending was at hand, he believed.

"Life water, here I come," he shouted again. Why should he restrain his feelings, when no one was there to witness his frenzy? Though very excited, he decided to remain where he was and rest properly before going down to the valley.

The likes of this valley he had not seen before. He had been to Elvesland and Fairyland and loved the incredible beauty swirling all around him, but both places combined could not match this place. Nature was in full bloom here. Hundreds of millions of colours could be seen spread around, in trees, flowers, animals, birds; in short, everything was so marvellous, so pretty, and so magnificent that he didn't believe his eyes. Yet these colours intermingled in such a fantastic, harmonic way he had not thought possible before.

Each moment, the movement of animals and birds changed the colour patterns and one felt as if peaceful vibrations were not just touching, but were even entering into the body like a refreshing breeze. There were so many such birds and animals of varying sizes and shapes. The legend was not only true, but far more beautiful than anybody ever could describe it. It was morning when he made his entry into the marvelous valley. He was certain that it took place some hours before and yet in the valley, there were no signs that could tell him of the approximate time. The sky was clear, and the light kept streaming in and yet he couldn't find a trace of a shining sun. All day long, he went strolling from one direction to the other without getting weary. The shade of the sky remained dark blue, making him forget that he had been there for so many hours, and yet there were no signs of any dusk. He felt fresh and energetic, without the need of rest or sleep. The wonderful valley was spread in all directions.

He kept walking and saw the waterfalls reflecting all the colours of the rainbow. He noticed the springs, gushing forth from the stones. He saw the vines full of grapes, and flowers embracing each other. Each sight made him happy. There were streams with glittering diamonds lying in their clear water bottoms. Emeralds, rubies and other precious stones were spread here and there, without being taken by anyone. He cared less for such stones and precious metals, and was looking for some unique stone to take for Zeibi and Alice as a souvenir. Mountains like animals and other horrifying beasts kept coming his way. He feared them not, and they passed without posing any threat. If all that was true, then the myth of life water was to be true too, he thought logically. He was there at last and was in no hurry to find the life water.

He kept walking, looking for strange things and enjoying each moment fully. He marvelled at all the species that he knew from his world, as well as those that he had never seen. He had considered that Fairyland was a paradise, but the real paradise lay beneath his feet at that very minute. The fruits of that place tasted like no other fruits he had eaten before. Simon saw a male fairy and greeted him in the fairy language. The fairy smiled, came near and asked if he was the newcomer. Simon told him that he had hardly been there for some hours.

"Are you a human being or a fairy?" the fairy asked.

"Why do you ask, can't you tell?" Simon was in a good mood.

The fairy apologised for being rude and asking unnecessary questions, but confessed that his indecision and incapacity to place him in one or the other kingdom depended on Simon's double identity. "Your third eye indicates that you are from Fairy kingdom, but at the same time there is a clear indication that you have never been flying."

Simon couldn't help but feel impressed by the fairy. "You're absolutely right; I'm a human being living in Fairyland." Simon considered the fairy, who seemed more confused than before.

"Has the separation of kingdoms come to an end! Has so much time elapsed in the world of time and space!"

Simon could feel that the perplexity of the fairy was genuine. They stood talking there for a while, talking about different things. Mostly it was the fairy who kept asking him questions regarding his world. He must have been away from his country for an incredibly long time and was eager to know the developments, which had taken place in his absence. The fairy was inquisitive and talkative, and had his golden opportunity to freshen up his memory and update his obsolete knowledge.

"You don't have to worry about your wonderful world any longer. No genii or any other world can ever enslave them again," Simon said with a smile. He was proud to show that he was aware of Fairy history. The fairy looked shocked by the news that his world had been subject to some occupation. He went on begging Simon to tell him all he knew about Fairyland. Simon told him all he knew and then asked permission to move on his way.

"I don't want to be rude, but I have to press ahead, searching for the spring of life water," Simon was apologetic.

"I can lead you to that spot," the fairy offered.

"Is it far from here?" asked Simon.

"Nothing is far here. Everything is within reach, just stretch your hand and you'll have it," the fairy said with a smile.

One has been never far from anything, especially from the spring of life, he was politely told. If Simon wanted and wished, the fairy could lead him there right away. They walked for a few minutes and came to one rocky place.

"There it is, " the fairy pointed with a smile on his face. Simon looked, and felt his heart jumping out of his body with joy. The spring looked like any other spring, except the place it was gushing forth from was very strange looking. There were stones and crystals he had never seen before, lying everywhere. The bluish water fell into a pond, which seemed very deep. So clear was the water that he could see down to its bottom, where lay the gems, crystals and other strange objects.

"Go, fill your cup and enjoy the fruit of your hard striving," invited the fairy smiling. Simon took out the empty bottle he carried with him, filled it and instead of drinking from it closed it. The fairy looked astonished, but said nothing. Simon made a cup of his hand palms, filled it with water and looked at the fairy. Seeing his questioning face he explained, pointing to bottle, "It's intended for the family." The fairy burst into laughter. Simon stood there amazed at that hysterical laughter. Suspecting something was wrong, he waited for an explanation.

"We all make the same mistake," the fairy laughed in amusement.

"We the poor newcomers believe we can take it for the loved ones?" Simon could say with certainty that the fairy was feeling pity for him. "Can't we take it with us?" he asked in surprise.

"Heavens no!" the fairy exclaimed.

Simon stood there like a statue, his hands falling, and water dropping out of the cup of his hands. He stood in deep depression. He was standing in front of the spring of life and could easily drink it and live forever and ever. His destination, his seeking had come to an end, but there he stood with a renewed dilemma. Was he to enjoy the sweet reward of his search? The fruit of his hardships was there for him to just grab it.

"So why the hesitation?"

Three times, he raised his hands and filled them with water and all three times, he dropped them. The fairy watched him with a big smile on his face. He could well understand his state of indecision.

All the newcomers were forced to weigh and choose that the gift of immortality was not without the price. What was the worth of eternal life, if his family wasn't a part of it? What was he supposed to do with that life, when everyone he loved kept perishing. He felt anger and rage and threw the bottle away in indignation.

"The immortality of this water is of no value if I can't share it with those I love," Simon screamed at the pond and spring. He was in pain, outraged, and frustrated. He sank down to his knees and cried bitterly, without caring that he was being watched.

After weeping for hours, he felt sad, but better. The fairy stood watching him with big eyes. He came near and comforted him, assuring him that his choice was wise. He was never to regret his decision. On the contrary, he had every reason to be happy and proud for having withstood the temptation.

"If you drank from the spring of life water, you would be living forever as promised by the legend, but not as you've foreseen in your imagination," said the fairy in a sad voice. What was never mentioned in the legend were the details in connection with this immortality. Those who drank from the spring could only live forever if they drank that water again and again. Those who drank the water could never leave the valley, making them practically prisoners. That explained the disappearance of fairies which came that way. Stern guardians guarded the valley, but their job was not to stop those who approached the valley, but to guard and stop those who had had a taste of the life water. In the valley, they had creatures belonging to almost all kingdoms, who lived forever and ever, never getting sick and never suffering death, but what happened to their lonely souls and minds full of old beautiful memories of their loved ones? No one wanted to even think of that.

Simon stayed a few days in the valley, and met many of its residents and listened to their stories. Many of these residents were from different kingdoms, and had been there for varying periods of time, though none had been able to keep the record of time flow. The entry into the valley by the newcomers had subsided from immemorial times, and that explained the curiosity of the valley's inhabitants in any kind of information. The most miserable of them all were the human beings who were sitting in a most resigned and depressed manner, hardly participating in the discussion. Their sensitivity and remorse were deadly in the valley, where that liberating force was absent.

Simon tried to console those of his own, but couldn't help feeling sorry for their wretched states of mind. "There is nothing more torturous than the memories of those dear ones we left behind in the long passed days," one of the human beings stated, without even looking at Simon.

He could see they all regretted their decisions to drink from the spring of life water. Had they known what they knew now, they would have never sought the valley and would not have come to that tragic end. "But you can use magic to come out of this prison," he told the elves. "And you could just fly away," was his advice to the fairies.

No, they could not do so, he was told. No magic worked in the valley, and the magnetic pull of the area, made it impossible to fly. They all were to live forever, but only as unhappy prisoners of a meaningless, dull life.

"Are you sure these stern, heartless types will not make a fuss when I'll try to leave?" Simon asked.

No one could answer for sure, but since he didn't drink from the spring water, he didn't fall in the category of their captives.

Simon left the valley, retracing his footsteps. The guards, who looked confused, astonished, and even irritated, confronted him. There was nothing they could do to stop him. Strictly speaking, he didn't fall under their jurisdiction. Just by looking at him, they could see that he was a mortal who had all rights to proceed to the mortal world. Perhaps it was the first time someone had earned that right by rejecting the great temptation.

It was only several weeks later that he re-entered into the Fairyland. He was making history. He was the first being ever to come back alive from the mysterious void. A happening, which not only stunned the fairies, but also even made them rejoice and jubilant. Not only Zeibi and little Alice, but all their friends were joyous when they came to know that he had returned. Zeibi cried with happiness and loved him deeper than ever when she heard that it was Simon's love for her that had given him the strength to refuse eternity. All three had a beautiful, comfortable long life and lived happily ever after. Or maybe still live, because they can live for a thousand earthly years.

THE END